"We've had a letter from Steve!" Curlin said in a sorrowful tone.

McRae looked up fearfully.

"Oh! Is it that girl again?" she said, as she took the letter.

"I—don't—know—" he answered lamely. "He's married, McRae!"

"Married?" she said, giving Curlin a startled glance.

Then she read the letter, and considered it carefully before she looked up. . . .

Suddenly McRae, with a look in her eyes such as an angel might have worn, swooped and kissed him on the forehead, a kiss like the breath of a whisper, and it brought a glory light into Curlin's face.

Tyndale House books by Grace Livingston Hill.
Check with your area bookstore for these best-sellers.

Grace Livingston Hill

BY WAY OF THE SILVERTHORNS

LIVING BOOKS ®
Tyndale House Publishers, Inc.
Wheaton, Illinois

This Tyndale House book
by Grace Livingston Hill
contains the complete text
of the original hardcover edition.
NOT ONE WORD
HAS BEEN OMITTED.

Printing History
J. B. Lippincott edition published 1941
Bantam edition published 1970
Tyndale House edition/1991

Living Books is a registered trademark of Tyndale
House Publishers, Inc.

Library of Congress Catalog Card Number 91-65771
ISBN 0-8423-0341-3

98 97 96 95 94 93 92 91
 8   7   6   5   4   3   2   1

McRAE SILVERTHORN arrived at the bride's home in the middle of the afternoon on the day before the wedding and was met at the door by the maid, Thelma.

"No, Miss Sydney isn't here just now," she said calmly. "Her mother took her off up to the farm early this morning to make her take a good rest. It couldn't be had here no matter how hard she tried. The telephone and the doorbell and all just made it impossible. Anyway, Miss Rae, she said you were the only one who would come before six, and I was to explain to you. She was sure you'd understand."

"Why yes, of course," said Rae with a pleasant smile. "I'm glad she had so much sense. I'll just get a good nap myself and then I'll have time to read awhile. I was sorry to have to come so early but Sydney knows there was no other train that would get me here in time for the dinner. Where are you going to put me, Thelma? Not my old room, surely, when you are having so many guests? You know it doesn't matter where I go this time."

"Yes, your old room, Miss Rae. Miss Sydney said she wouldn't be happy to have you anywhere else. And there's plenty of room without that. They've got it all fixed. Miss Sydney said she wanted you just where you always had been when you visited her. She wanted to be able to run in on you at the last minute if she needed to ask you something. And Mrs. Hollis said, 'Yes, of course!'"

"Well, that's nice. I'll go right up, then. I'm rather tired. You see, I had a bit of shopping to do for mother before I came up here. Mother's staying in town at Aunt Harriet's, on the north side, you know, and she wanted some doodads sent up there for tomorrow."

"Well then, we'll go up, and I'll send Sanders up with your bags. I can come and unpack for you in a minute or two when I finish something I was doing in the dining room."

"No, Thelma, I don't want you to. I've nothing in the world to do but unpack, and I really want to do it myself. I want to be sure my dress for tonight came through all right without crushing."

"Well, all right, if you say so, but if your dress needs any pressing you just ring and I'll be up pretty soon and get it."

"Oh, it won't need pressing, I'm sure. I packed it very carefully myself. Now you run along, Thelma. I know the way to my room without your help. And I know you've got plenty to do without running after me."

Thelma thanked her and departed, and Rae let herself into the big airy room next to the bride's own room, where she had spent so many pleasant week-ends and holidays for years back almost into her childhood.

For a little while she busied herself unpacking and hanging her things in accustomed places. Not so many things this time as she usually brought, for the maid of honor's outfit was already here, hanging in the closet of the sewing room like a great confection, shrouded in a protecting cover, ready to put on tomorrow night for the wedding.

Sydney Hollis had been her most intimate friend since Rae had stayed one winter in the city with her aunt and started high school. Sydney had been her classmate. Then they went to college together and were roommates. If only Sydney were not going so far away! California seemed the other side of the world.

Why couldn't Sydney have fallen in love with some of the boys here at home? How grand it would have been! There was Curlin Grant, and his handsome brother Steve; or her own beloved brother. They were splendid boys, and more than once she had suspected all of them of being half in love with Sydney. Why couldn't she have cared for one of them? Or Paul Redfern, or Reeves Leighton? But she hadn't, so what was the use of thinking that all over again?

She took out the pretty new dinner dress and admired it and hung it up on one of the lovely pink satin hangers with which the closet abounded. She patted it, and smoothed out the frills and shook out a fold in the skirt, and then just stood and admired it. It was new and a great surprise, a present from her brother Lincoln. For since her expensive college course was completed there hadn't been quite so many new dresses in Rae Silverthorn's wardrobe as there used to be when she was in college and needed them for so many functions. And she hadn't expected them either. She had planned to wear her last year's evening dress for the dinner tonight, and not go to any expense at all for this wedding. Nobody in the city had seen it, for she had been saving the lovely mulberry velvet for some formal occasion that hadn't materialized all winter, so it was almost as good as new and quite in style. Only of course it was a trifle late in the season for velvet. But "Well, what difference?" she had said to her mother with her cheerful little smile. "The top part will just look like one of those luscious velvet dinner jackets that everybody is wearing, the skirt will be under the table anyway, and who will see it afterwards when I'm just standing around in a crowd talking?"

"But, my dear! Aren't you rehearsing in the church after dinner? You'll have to walk up the aisle in the procession!"

"Well, I'll be only one of the procession, and you know that dress is becoming all right! Who's to notice what I have on? And when the wedding comes off I'll be so grandly dressed nobody will remember what I had on at rehearsal. I'm certainly glad Sydney insisted on furnishing all the dresses for her bridesmaids."

"But you're the maid of honor, dear. Your dresses should be all right on both occasions. We don't want your friends to think we couldn't see that you are dressed suitably."

"Now, mother!" Rae had said. "This thing is decided, I tell you. I simply won't have a cent spent on me for this wedding. I'm saving up for a lot of things when the present set are worn out. So there! Don't you try to cross me, mother, for it won't do a bit of good. Besides, I've talked it all over with Sydney, and she thinks I'm right, and says the mulberry velvet will be lovely!"

Rae saw the whole scene in her mind's eye as she stood there patting the new dark blue taffeta. She saw that troubled look in her mother's face, the premonition of giving in to her arguments and then her brother Link's face as he looked up.

"Hi! What's all this economy talk, I'd like to know? Don't you women know that there are times to economize and times when it's all wrong, as the woman said who paid ten cents carfare to run down to a cheaper market and buy three pounds of meat at a cent less a pound than she could have got it next door. Say, Mc-Rae, I've got a job, didn't you know it? Hadn't you heard that yet? *I'm* going to buy you a new dress. Wait till you see! Sure I know how to buy a dress. Size fourteen, isn't it? I heard you say so the other night. Now, don't let's hear another word about this. I'll attend to that dress. I guess I'm not going to let my sister go to a party in a lousy dress when everybody knows I've got a wealthy job. Now, stop all this chatter. I want to read the paper!"

They had laughed gaily and Link had returned to the paper. Nothing more had been said about the dress and Rae thought Link had been just fooling, and everybody was satisfied. She hadn't thought about it again herself either, for she was quite satisfied to wear the velvet dress.

And then the very next day the delivery man from one of the most exclusive stores in the city had delivered a great white box for Miss McRae Silverthorn, and there had been the dress, the lovely dark blue taffeta, with a long sweeping skirt, cut in the very latest lines, with a darling fluffy little ruching edged with a minute line of real lace. It was just perfect! And to think of a young man selecting it! Dear old Link! He must have paid a whole month's salary for it!

Wear it? Of course she would. It was wonderful of Link, and she loved the dress doubly because he had bought it for her. He oughtn't to have done it of course, but she mustn't discount it even by reproaching him for spending so much money.

And her mother was as pleased as Link was, and so was her father.

Rae had tried on the lovely garment and it had been voted a perfect fit.

"Look who bought it!" swelled Link with satisfaction. They couldn't make him tell who had helped him.

"Nobody!" he said. "I just told the gal I wanted the latest thing in dinner gowns for my sister who was just out of college, and had blue eyes and a pink complexion all her own, no lipstick, and she wore size fourteen, and I wanted a pretty nice one for a swell affair, and that's what she brought me! I don't see why women make so much fuss about shopping! It didn't take me fifteen minutes to get that dress!"

They had laughed a good deal about it, and Rae had cried in secret over the dear funny way her brother talked about it. He had always been that way about her, doing nice funny things on the sly in his queer boy way. She loved the way he looked at her with that comical twinkle in his eyes, just the way father looked at mother sometimes, only a lot more condescending.

So Rae Silverthorn stood and looked at her lovely new dress with a smile on her lips and tears in her eyes, and loved her dear family.

Then suddenly there came a tap at the door. That would be Thelma of course, come to insist that she would press her dress. But her dress didn't need pressing.

"Come in," she said with a smile, still holding the closet door with one hand. Thelma would like to see her dress. Thelma would admire it and love it.

But the girl who entered was not Thelma. It was Minnie Lazarelle, a quasi third or fourth cousin of Sydney's whom Sydney had never liked. They had never been very intimate, but occasionally she had been at the Hollis home when Rae had been there, and back in their younger days she had gone to high school with them for a few weeks before her family moved to another state. She was always an annoyance wherever she turned up and somehow she seemed to have uncanny ways of turning up. Even when everybody thought the Lazarelles had moved to a distant city, Minnie would arrive whenever there was anything unusual going on and say she had come to stay for the week-end. And somehow there was never an adequate reason for sending her away.

But Sydney had rejoiced several days ago at the fact that Minnie had moved to the far west and would not be at her wedding. "For of course we shall not invite her. There would be no reason to invite her, you know, even if she were in this part of the country, for we have never been intimate at all, and I'm only inviting my dearest most intimate friends. The relationship between us is so very slight, only by marriage, and a 'step' at that. Yet I'm positive if Minnie were in this neighborhood she would be certain to appear. She always has."

So it was with a startled face that Rae greeted the newcomer.

"Oh! Is that you, Minnie! Why I thought they said you were in the west."

"Yes, I was," drawled the girl coming in and closing the door behind her, "but you couldn't think that I would stay there and let dear Cousin Sydney get married without me, as close as we've always been, could you? Not I. I would have come home from Europe to be at this function."

"Oh!" said Rae looking blankly at the girl, and noticing for the first time that Minnie was wearing an elaborate though rather shabby kimono of scarlet satin embroidered in fuzzy dragons that were much the worse for wear, and her hair was adorned with metal curlers. "When did you arrive? This morning? Does Sydney know you're here?"

"Oh, no, I just came in about five minutes ago, and I'm such a wreck I came in search of a bath. I've traveled day and night to get here in time. There was an accident on the road ahead of my train and we had all kinds of delays. I'm simply filthy. I came over here to see if anyone was in this room. I can't abide the room that dumb Thelma put me in, the little old nursery at the end of the hall. The bathroom is across the hall, and the tub is so short one can't lie down in it and thoroughly relax. I like this bathroom so much better. You won't mind if I come in and take a scrub, will you?"

"Why—of course—come," said Rae trying to be pleasant. She didn't enjoy the prospect because Minnie wasn't at all neat and was apt to leave smears of face cream and lipstick around in the most unexpected places, but of course she couldn't say no, and really it wasn't in Rae's sunny nature to be cool or disagreeable to anyone, much as she might dislike them. "I was just about to lie down and take a little nap, so help yourself."

"How sweet of you," said Minnie condescendingly. "Nice you got here in time to choose the best room!" Minnie smiled her old catty smile.

"Oh," said Rae laughing, "I didn't choose my room. This is where Thelma brought me. This is where she said Sydney wanted me to be."

"Yes," said Minnie with a toss of her head, "you always were one of her favorites! Well, it's all right of course, even if I am a relative. A relative always expects to take second place! And of course she didn't know I was coming. She'll be awfully surprised when she finds it out. Say, do you happen to know who is to be here tonight?"

Minnie dropped nonchalantly down on the edge of the bed, one shabby slipper clacking against the hardwood floor as she swung her foot idly.

"Why, no, I don't know that I do," said Rae, standing by the bureau and arranging some handkerchiefs and gloves and ribbons in the top drawer. "I suppose just the bridesmaids and ushers, don't you?"

"Well, likely," said Minnie, as if she were conversant with all of the bride's plans. "But I was wondering who they all are. Really I did feel a bit hurt that she didn't ask me, as close as we've always been. Who are the ushers? I suppose they're friends of the groom. I don't know him very well. Syd was awfully secret about it all. She never dropped a hint. I was simply amazed when I found she was marrying a western man. So silly of her when she has such a nice group of friends in the east, and some of the boys were just dandy, don't you think? But who are these people tonight? Do I know them all? I suppose the girls are just the old crowd, aren't they? Carey Carewe, Sue Richards, Lou McHale, Bets Patterson, Fran Ferrin and Pat Nicholson. What she ever saw in them I never understood, but Syd was always that way, whom she liked she liked, no matter who or what they were. But who are the fellows? I'm simply dying to know."

Rae looked thoughtful. She didn't exactly like the role she was being forced to play, telling about arrangements to this girl whom she knew Sydney did not want to take into her confidence. But what could she do?

"Well, I'm not sure about them all," she said slowly. "There'll be Steve and Curlin Grant, I suppose—"

"Steve's all right," conceded Minnie with a kind of contempt in her tone, "but that Curlin I can't abide!"

"What's the matter with Curlin?" asked Rae in an amused tone.

"Why, he has simply no sex appreciation. No sex consciousness, perhaps I should say."

Suddenly Rae laughed an amused little ripple.

"What on earth do you mean by that, Minnie? It sounds rather horrid to me. Remember the Grants are among our best friends."

"Oh, well, I didn't mean anything disparaging exactly," said Minnie with a shrug. "I simply meant that Curlin never senses that a girl is any different from a man. You happen to get Curlin to talk to and he never even looks at you, nor notices what you have on nor anything, just discusses any old topic as if you were a fella."

"Why, I think that's lovely!" said Rae. "I always feel honored to talk to Curlin. He never tries to be frivolous the way some men do. He acts as if you had a brain and as if you were a real person."

"Well I can't be bothered talking politics and what I think of the situation in Europe. If I happen to have to talk to him tonight, ten to one he'll ask me about which side I think is going to win, and if he does I shall simply shriek, I know I shall. Say, Rae, what is that dress I saw hanging in the closet? Is it yours? Why did you close the door so quickly? I want to see it. Say, that's a cute little number. I'm quite taken with that. A bit somber, don't you think, but that's the tendency today. Say, I think I'll wear that tonight. You don't mind, do you? I have an idea a dress like that might please the masculine style. I think I'll try it."

"Sorry!" said Rae Silverthorn, shutting the closet door with a snap. "I shall need it myself."

"Oh, that's all right," laughed Minnie, "I've got plenty of gorgeous things along. You can have your choice!"

"Thank you," said Rae coolly, "I was brought up not to borrow garments. Besides my brother picked this out for me and I wouldn't care to have anybody else wear it."

Rae flung herself down on the bed wearily and yawned wishing with all her heart she hadn't come so early.

Minnie laughed mockingly.

"Try and stop me!" she said gaily. "Now, I'm going in and take a hot bath. I just adore lying in hot water, don't you? And then I'll come out and we'll get dressed together. Take your nap and when you wake up I'll bring an armful of my things and you can have your choice. There's a duck of an orange tulle, only one sleeve is torn out. You'd have to mend it, but it's adorable. Ta-ta till I get my bath!" and Minnie slid into the bathroom and snapped the bolt.

McRae Silverthorn lay on the bed filled with wrathy indignation and for an instant couldn't get her brain to function rightly. Her dress, her lovely dress! To have it defamed by that girl's touch! To have it handled and discussed, and tried on perhaps! She could not bear it! She *would* not! But what could she do? Minnie, when she started out to do a thing, generally succeeded in doing it, all the more when she saw it was distasteful to someone. Rae knew Minnie had always been jealous of her friendship for Sydney.

Suddenly she heard the bolt of the bathroom slide back with a snap and the door was opened a crack.

"How old is your brother?" Minnie asked through the crack.

Rae's mouth twinkled with quick amusement, but she put on a lazy voice as she answered, "How old? Oh, a few years older than I am!"

"And he picked out a dress for you? Well, he must have a girl somewhere who works in a store and he hired her to do it. No man has that good taste!"

Then she slammed the door shut again and shot the bolt.

By this time Rae was on her feet, her eyes blazing angrily.

"I won't stand it!" she said to herself. "I *won't!*"

Then she went into action. Softly she opened the bureau drawers and swept into a bundle the neat piles of garments she had just laid in them so carefully. She stepped to the closet, opening the door most cautiously. She opened her suitcase quietly and laid the garments in swiftly and noiselessly, and then as soon as she heard the water beginning to run in the tub she slipped that taffeta dress off its silken hanger, and onto the hanger in her new suitcase. Then the other dresses, a pastel pink sports frock, a skirt and sweater and white silk blouse, and a little printed silk affair, gay as the spring time. It was the work of but a moment to slip them on the hangers that belonged in the suitcase, to smooth down the skirts, and press the spring that folded them neatly and safely into place! Then her slippers, another pair of shoes. There wouldn't be anything safe if Minnie got started being disagreeable, and she had seen Minnie disagreeable several times in her life. She surveyed the closet carefully, conscious that the moments were going by rapidly. The water had stopped running in the bathroom. Minnie might appear on the scene at any moment now if she suspected in the least what was going on.

Rae took off her kimono and folded it hastily, sweeping her comb and brush in at the last. She snapped the suitcase shut, locking it, and slipped the key into her handbag that lay on the bureau.

Then very noiselessly and swiftly she slid into her dress that she had worn when arriving, put on her hat and jacket, slipped over to the door with her suitcase and set it outside in the hall.

While she had been working she had been thinking, evolving a plan that would be perfectly natural, and yet foil her enemy.

She gave one swift glance about the room to see if she had left anything behind, a regretful glance because she had anticipated a quiet hour or two by herself to read in that pleasant luxury. Then she closed the door silently and gathering up her suitcase went tiptoe down the velvet shod stairs.

A glance through the dining room door showed Thelma arranging dishes on the long table, placing forks and spoons and knives. Could she possibly get out the front door without being seen? Hardly!

Swiftly she walked over to the dining room door and spoke in a subdued tone.

"Thelma," she said, "I've just remembered something I didn't give to mother, and I'm going to run over to Aunt Harriet's and give it to her. I've plenty of time. It won't take an hour. I'll be back as soon as Sydney is. And Thelma," she added on second thought, "did you know Minnie Lazarelle is upstairs? She's taking a bath in my bathroom now, and I slipped out. She doesn't know I've gone!"

"The huzzy!" said Thelma with a vexed look. "Miss Sydney will be that angry! Isn't she the limit! I had the new waitress take her up to the old nursery. Now what'll I do? I better telephone the madam."

"Yes," said Rae with a knowing smile. "Meantime I'm going. Don't worry about me. I'll take any place that's left if that's any easier for you, Thelma."

"Bless your heart, Miss Rae, yer like sunshine on a dark day. But you mustn't carry yer own suitcase. Why don't ye leave it here? I'll put it away safe."

"No, I need it, Thelma, to carry some things, and it isn't the least heavy. Nothing much in it. Now, I'm going!" and Rae slipped out and shut the door quickly, hurrying to the corner to catch the next bus to her aunt's house, her whole being trembling with excitement.

And now she had to think what she should do next.

It was true what she had told Thelma that she had just

remembered something she had meant to give her mother. It was a fine little handkerchief that had been forgotten and she had tucked into her own suitcase. But it wasn't necessary. Well, she would stop on the way and get her mother—what should she get her mother? Some flowers perhaps? And what should she tell of the reason why she had come all the way over to the north side of the city? She would have to think that out as best she could on the way.

2

THE USHERS were getting ready for the dinner. They were housed in the home of Paul Redfern, one of their number, whose family were traveling abroad, and who was keeping bachelor hall with a couple of servants to keep things in order. There was plenty of space and they were having a grand time scattered through three or four palatial rooms, shouting conversation back and forth. They were all friends, three of them having gone to the same college, and the rest had been more or less intimate friends since childhood. For the bridegroom from afar had left the matter of ushers to his bride as the simplest way of solving the problem, since all of his friends were on the west coast.

"Say, fellas, you'd better begin to rustle yourselves into battle array pretty quick! We ought to be starting in half an hour," called Paul, who as host had suddenly become aware of the time.

"You don't say! Is it that late?" said Reeves Leighton, starting up from a sleepy hollow chair into which he had dropped when he came in. "What unearthly hour is this dinner anyway? Man, do you know what time it is?"

"Sure I know," said Paul, "and the dinner's at six-thirty. That's not an unearthly hour. We have rehearsal in the church at eight, and they particularly asked us to be on time, because rehearsals always take forever and a day, and Mrs. Hollis said she wanted Sydney to get to sleep early so she would be all right for tomorrow. Syd hasn't been very well lately, and her mother's worried about her."

"Yes, I guess she's been going a pretty fast pace the last month or two," said Steve Grant. "I see her everywhere I go. It beats me why when a girl gets engaged everybody in the neighborhood has to begin to torment her with parties and things. Say, we're going to miss that gal a lot when she goes away."

"Yes, Steve, you ought to have thought of that before. Why ever did you let a strange bridegroom from afar capture her?"

"I did my best," said Steve jauntily with a handsome grin. "I couldn't help it, could I, if she preferred the stranger from afar to my manly beauty?"

"Sure you could have helped it, Stevie," teased Paul Redfern. "You never fail to get what you want, do you? The trouble was you were indolent. You should have begun sooner, and made hay while the sun shone! If we hadn't counted on you to keep Syd in this part of the country some of the rest of us might have got going in time to save her!"

"Well, at that I hear she's doing rather well for herself," said Curlin Grant with a comical grin. "A million dollars is not to be sneezed at, and everybody knows you can't scare up one of those from any of us poor country guys."

Then the doorbell was heard in the distance, and they all came to attention.

"That's bound to be Link!" said Paul. "He's always

right on the dot for time. Lincoln Silverthorn is a hound for doing everything on the dotted line. But that means, fellas, that we've got to hustle!"

"But where's Luther Waite?" they called out as they scattered in search of their various garments.

"Oh, have you forgotten? 'Luther Waite, he's always late'?" yelled out Steve as he made a dash for the room that had been assigned him. "He'll turn up after we're seated at the table. That's Lute."

"Or maybe as we're marching up the aisle," added Curlin under his breath.

Lincoln Silverthorn came upstairs gloved, overcoated, his hat in his hand to see how near ready they were. He stood in the hall where he could get a fairly good view of each of the four rooms where the young men were hurrying into their garments.

"Hello, Link! Early as usual I see!"

"Late as usual, *I* see," said Link grinning.

"Say, Link, seen anything of Lute Waite?"

"Ho! You wouldn't expect those two to meet up with each other, not beforehand, anyway!" called out Curlin comically.

"No," said Link. "I haven't seen him. In fact I wasn't looking for him. It wouldn't occur to me to expect him so soon."

But while they were laughing at that the doorbell rang again and Luther Waite came pounding up the stairs, his hat in his hand, his hair awry, and a look of distress on his face.

"Hi, there, Lute, you aren't ill or anything are you, appearing on the scene so early?" called Steve wickedly, leaning over the stair railing.

"No, I'm not yet," said Luther panting as he hurried up, "but I don't know but I'm gonna be! Say, Link, you ought ta know, who are the girls in this show? Do you know them all?"

Link smiled at his serious face.

"Why, yes, I guess I can name them all. There's Frannie Ferrin, Lou McHale—you know her, Lutie. Then there's Carey Carewe, Patricia Nicholson, and Betty Patterson and Sue Richards—those I don't know so well—and my sister Rae!"

A look of relief passed over young Waite's face.

"Is that all? Are you *sure?*" he asked anxiously.

"Isn't that enough?" groaned Reeves Leighton. "Just think of all those girls, and we don't know which one we get, yet," said Reeves.

"Calm yourself, brother," said Paul. "They're all a pretty decent lot if you ask me. I should think one might manage a little thing like walking down the aisle with any one of them. It isn't as if it was to last for a lifetime. What's eating you, Waite? You look all worried and jittery."

Waite dropped down on the top step of the stairs and leaned back against the stair railing.

"Well, you see, I've had a shock!" he said with a heavy sigh of relief. "I was waiting for my bus to come along, and the bus came from the other direction, and who should I sight but that goofy cousin of Sydney Hollis', that girl they call 'Min' something, and I thought if she was going to be one of the wedding party I was going to beat it! They'd be sure to put her with me. I am always a sucker for the leftovers that nobody else wants, but this would be the third time in the last year or so that I've served in that capacity, and I'm not up to it again. I just can't take it! You know it's not merely a matter of walking down the aisle with her, Paul my darling, it's the matter of a whole evening more or less, generally more. She's the kind that freezes onto you fast in the course of the amble down the aisle, and boy! I defy you to get away from her again while the convocation lasts! And even *after,* she has ways of hinting that she wants you to take her places the next day and the next week and so on. The first time I met her it took me a week to make her forget me so she couldn't reach me by telephone. And the next time it was all winter I hadta keep dodging her."

Luther Waite had a mop of deep mahogany curls, and gray eyes that had a hint of brown in them. He was rugged, with a lean face and figure and a peppering of freckles across the bridge of a nice nose.

"But look here, Lutie," said Reeves Leighton, "didn't you know that the lady in question had moved far away to the west and isn't in these parts at all? You must have been imagining!"

"Imagining? *Me?* I tell you I *saw* her with my own eyes, and I don't imagine things. I got the very lowest marks always in school for anything that required an imagination, like a composition. I never had any imagination at all! No *sir!* Boy, I *saw* that baby, and she was burrowing in her hand bag for change to pay her bus fare, just like she used to do. No, sir, I wasn't imagining. It was too lifelike. Believe me I dashed across the street and took the first bus I saw going the other way, and I've just got back. I meant to be here an hour ago. I really did. But you know how it was, fellas. I hadta get calm before I could think what to do. And I almost went back to my office and decided to telephone I had been taken with typhoid or smallpox or something and couldn't come at all. But finally I thought I'd come and see if you fellas knew whether she was in the procession. If she was I was gonta beat it again so fast you wouldn't know I had been here."

He broke off and bowed his head in his hands, his whole big frame stooping dejectedly.

Then they all came by and gave him a good pounding on his broad shoulders.

"Get up, Lutie!" they shouted. "Can't you see how you're hindering us all? Get up and put your marcel in order. It's streaming out all over the place. Powder your nose, wipe the tears away from your eyes, and cheer up! We won't let old Min bother the poor little fellow! Not that we're not sympathetic, you know, for we've all had our taste of Cousin Min Lazarelle, but don't be worried any more. Min is far far away, and can't spoil the joy of the evening for you any more!"

They pulled Waite up on his feet and set him down in one of the hall chairs, and then they told him to hurry, that it was time to start to the dinner and they mustn't be late.

He sat for a moment staring at them sadly.

"But I *saw* her!" he reiterated. "I sure did!"

"Okay," they cried, laughing. "We'll protect you! Get up and navigate. We'll ask Mrs. Hollis to put you beside that cute little McHale number, Lou McHale. Now, brush your marcel and come along!"

And so at last they were on their way.

But as they piled into the big Redfern limousine, Link, in the back seat with Reeves Leighton, heard Lute Waite say in an uneasy undertone to Curlin Grant:

"Say, Curly, you don't suppose Syd's mother could have made her invite Minnie Lazarelle to the wedding, do you? Because I *know* I saw her! And if she's here I tell you I won't go near the place. She gets my goat!"

Link leaned forward and said distinctly, so they all could hear:

"You're all haywire, Waite. Just last night Syd was talking to my sister over the phone and she said she was thankful that this was one time her would-be cousin wouldn't walk in unexpectedly. So I'm sure she's not invited. But what's the matter with that baby anyway? I never had any experience with her. I never took particular notice of her. Is she fierce-looking? Has she got a wooden leg or halitosis, or is she just a fool?"

"She's just a clinging vine, my lad," said Reeves Leighton amusedly. "Once stuck with her you can't get rid of her by any rule that ever was tried. Short of throwing pepper in her eyes and running away I can't think of anything that would work. She's one of those girls who has been made to believe that a girl's chief business in life is to acquire a man, and she means to make good and not let a chance run by her."

"I'll say she does!" said Luther sighing deeply.

"Hey! Quit that sighing!" said Link giving the big red head a shaking. "You act as if you were going to a funeral instead of a wedding. Snap out of it or they will all think you were in love with the bride!"

"I *was!*" said Lutie. *"Definitely.* Ever since we used to slide down the cellar door together when we were kids. I never thought this could happen that she would select somebody else in my place and go off to California." Waite got out his handkerchief and pretended to weep, while they all roared with laughter.

"Between losing Syd, and that vision I had of her cousin Min, I'm a wreck!" he announced with a well-simulated sob, mopping his face despairingly.

"There she is, Lutie!" called out Steve suddenly. "That's Min down there by that next corner, isn't it? That woman with the green coat and the small sized wedding cake for a hat? Or isn't it? I'm positive she must be it. You'd better hide, Lutie. Put your head down under the robe, and we'll hide you!"

Waite crowded his big shoulders down, and allowed them to cover his bulk with the robe.

"Hey, there! You're mussing his marcel!" cried out Curlin. "He won't be fit to be seen when he gets there!"

"I don't want to be seen!" wailed Lutie. "I just know Min has come on for the wedding, and if she has she'll get me. There's nothing I can do about it! I'm depending on you, Link, to protect me!"

They rollicked and bantered all the way from the Redfern house to the Hollis place, for all the world as if they were children, and not grown young men with a serious outlook on life.

Arrived at the Hollis home they marched gravely up the steps and waited with becoming dignity and only a few covert grins. When the door was opened, they left their coats and hats in the commodious coat room to the right of the hall door, and then filed into the reception room with the easy familiarity of old friends of the family.

A ripple of laughter from upstairs made it plain that the girls were already on the scene.

"That's Carey Carewe's musical giggle," asserted Luther Waite with relief in his voice. "Now, if I can only get next to her the day will be saved!"

"It's night, not day, fella! You've mixed your signals! Take it calmly, Waite. A few more hours and it will all be over!" advised Paul Redfern gravely.

Upstairs Mrs. Hollis, attired in black lace and smiling composure, about to go down to meet her guests, had just been informed of the presence of Minnie Lazarelle. She retired hastily to the back hall to tap at the nursery door, and summon her to conference.

"Oh, my dear Minnie!" she said in a shocked tone as the door opened readily and the smiling and triumphant face of the uninvited guest appeared, nothing daunted.

"My *dear!*" she reproved in a tone that told Minnie that she certainly was anything but dear just then. "How in the world did this happen? I had no idea that you were in this part of the world, or could possibly come at the present time. And of course it's quite impossible for you to stay here now, we are full up to overflowing."

"Oh, that's quite all right, Aunt Jessica," laughed Minnie gaily. "I don't mind sleeping in the old nursery at all. And of course being a relative it's quite the right thing to put me here. Though I would have enjoyed being over next to Sydney. In fact I did go over there and found that little stick of a college mate of Syd's had preempted the best room, so I decided I'd better room with her. But when I had had my bath and came out into the room I found she had gone, and your officious maid ordered me back here, so I came. But it's all right. I don't mind in the least, Aunt Jessica."

Minnie seldom called the Hollises aunt and cousin unless she had some axe to grind, but she was using the strained relationship for all it was worth now, and smiling blandly into the desperate eyes of the bride's mother.

"Oh, but Minnie, you don't understand!" she said. "We have had a great time getting everybody provided for, and we can't even spare you this room. If you had only sent me word you were coming I would have arranged some place for you to stay till the wedding was over. And we'll try to find a place now for you to go. You see there won't even be room for you at the table. Every place is filled and it will make things very awkward indeed to have an extra one come in. It is quite impossible. Get on your hat and coat, my dear, and we'll call up Mrs. Fremont. She has plenty of room and is always willing to help out. I'm sorry I can't send you over in the car. It has gone to the station for the bridegroom but we'll have a taxi here in a minute or two. Please get ready as soon as possible. I'll send the maid to help you put your things back in your suitcase if you have unpacked, because we haven't much time, you know, and ought to be sitting down to the table very soon."

Minnie Lazarelle's face suddenly took on a deeply injured expression, and then grew gaily hard and determined.

"Well, that certainly is a queer way to look at it," she said. "One would have supposed you would have sent me an invitation to my cousin's wedding. As close as we have always been—"

"Why, Minnie, child, what can you possibly mean?" said Mrs. Hollis in astonishment. "You and Sydney have never been close. In fact you've scarcely seen one another through the years, except once or twice when you were passing through the city and wrote asking if you might stop here. Of course we are not really related at all, except by marriage—and courtesy. You are the stepdaughter of the woman whose first husband was a second cousin of my husband's. Of course we always want to be kind and courteous to everyone, and are usually ready to put ourselves out when another person is in an emergency, but this is an occasion that involves previously invited guests, and it isn't at all possible to have you here. We will see that you are well cared for however. Get your hat on quickly, please. I haven't much time. I should be down in the reception room right now. Did you unpack yet?"

"No!" said Minnie with a toss of her arrogant head. "I hoped you'd give me a better room, and I didn't want to hang up my dresses till I was sure where I was to be. I didn't trust that impudent maid of yours, and I hoped you'd let me room with Sydney."

"Oh, my no! That would be unthinkable! Sydney

must have her room to herself the last night before her wedding!"

"Well, at least you might put me in the room *next* to Sydney's."

"No!" said Mrs. Hollis firmly. "The rooms are all apportioned and the arrangement cannot be changed."

"Well, why can't I room with Rae Silverthorn? I certainly belong as much as she does. She doesn't pretend to be a relative. I never saw what Syd saw in her anyway. She's a little cheap skate, that's what I call her!"

"Minnie! That will be all from you!" said Mrs. Hollis with a gleam of real battle in her eyes. "This is our house and we will run its affairs without your assistance. I have no more time to discuss the matter. Here comes Thelma. Thelma, will you call up the taxi office and ask them to come at once to the service entrance and pick up Miss Lazarelle. *At once,* Thelma! He'll understand. He promised to have a taxi ready for instant service if I should need it. And then, Thelma, come right back here and help Miss Lazarelle to pick up all her things, and take her down to the side door, immediately! It's important to get this matter attended to quietly before they all get here. Yes, Sydney, I'll be down in just a moment."

Mrs. Hollis turned back to the angry young woman who hadn't made a move to get her hat on. Her eyes were flashing and her lips were contemptuous.

"I didn't think you'd be actually rude to me," she said in a tone of suppressed fury. "I thought you prided yourself on always being so genteel and courteous."

"You don't seem to realize that you have transgressed all rules of courtesy in coming here uninvited and unannounced," said Mrs. Hollis. "Come! It is imperative that you go down at once, unless you want me to call my husband to deal with you."

"Well, I don't want to go to some old frump's house.

I wanted to come to this party and have a good time."
Minnie put on an aggrieved look and quivered her
mocking little lips, but Mrs. Hollis, alive to new voices
down in the front hall, turned away without answering,
nearly distracted.

"Take her down to the taxi at once," she said in a low
tone to Thelma who had returned from the telephone
and was gathering up the would-be guest's brushes and
lipstick and powder.

"I'd be willing to stay up in the attic while you eat
your old dinner!" said Minnie with a sullen look. "Then
Thelma could bring me up some scraps that were left
over."

"I am sorry, Minnie, that you are taking that attitude.
I'll try to find time to see you day after tomorrow if you
decide to stay that long, but I really must go at once!"

"I think they've come," motioned Thelma with a lift
of her eyebrows and a movement of her lips, meaning
the bridegroom and his party had arrived.

"I must go!" said the bride's mother in great haste.
"I'm leaving this with you to look after," she murmured
to the maid and departed swiftly, turning the key in the
lock as she closed the door behind her, reassured as she
dimly heard the sound of the taxi arriving at the side
door.

Swiftly she sped down to greet her guests, some of
whom had already entered the large living room, and
were standing about in that awe that precedes weddings
and funerals before the hostess arrives.

"Good evening, Steve, and Curlin! It's so good to see
you again. Reeves, it's so nice you could come down.
We were quite anxious when you said you might be
detained till tomorrow. Oh, and here's Luther! Link, did
your sister come down with you? I haven't seen her yet."

"No, I think she came down on the train. I've been at the office all day, you know."

"Why yes, of course. And— Where is Paul? Hasn't he arrived yet?"

"Present!" said Paul appearing from the hall with a grin on his pleasant lips.

"Then you're all here!" said Mrs. Hollis with relief, wondering if that was the taxi going down the drive or a car arriving with the bridegroom. "Ah! There come the girls!"

There was a soft rustling on the stairs.

Frances Ferrin was the first to enter, saucily with a quick look around.

"Why, they're all here, Syd!" she said in a comical whisper. "Even Lute Waite has come! Who accomplished that?"

Luther Waite arose.

"I've reformed!" he announced gravely, and with one hand on his heart bowed gravely before her.

"Isn't that grand!" said Fran laying her hand on his bowed head in the manner of one conferring an accolade.

Into the midst of the gaiety the groom arrived, looking as handsome and happy as any bridegroom should look, and there were gay greetings of those he already knew and introductions to those he had not met. In the meantime Mrs. Hollis with troubled glance consulted Thelma.

"Hasn't Miss Silverthorn come yet? Are you sure she isn't up in the guest room? Hadn't you better run up and be sure, because it's really time we sat down to dinner. Why did she go away?"

"Why, I don't know, Mrs. Hollis," said Thelma with a troubled look. "She said she had forgotten to give her mother something, but I couldn't help thinking Miss

Lazarelle had something to do with it. She had her suitcase in her hand and as she went out the door she called me and told me that Miss Lazarelle was up in her bathroom taking a bath. And when I got time to run up I found she was there dressing and she asked me what had become of Miss Silverthorn. I told her that she must come out of that room right away. That you had given me directions about it, and she was to go in the nursery till you came—"

"Oh! That girl! I wonder what started her to coming? What time did she arrive? Before Miss Silverthorn?"

"Yes, about half an hour, and I thought she was taking a nap or something. I wondered if you knew she was coming."

"No, Thelma. What did she say when she arrived? Who did she ask for?"

"She asked for Miss Sydney, and when she found she wasn't here she said, 'Well, I'll just go up to a guest room and get a bath and take a rest,' and she was quite nasty about going to the nursery."

"Well, I'm thankful she's out of the way for the evening. But keep a sharp lookout for her. I don't trust her. She's liable to turn up again in the morning. There! Isn't that the doorbell? Perhaps Rae has arrived. We mustn't keep the dinner waiting, because we have to be early at the church. If it's Miss Rae tell her to hurry. Help her if she needs help. It never takes her long to dress, however."

3

BUT RAE SILVERTHORN did not need the assistance of a maid to help her dress for she was already attired.

Thelma met her at the door, and she handed her her suitcase and the hat and wrap she had been wearing.

"Please take them up to my room, will you, Thelma? I can go right in. I'm all ready. Does my hair look all right?"

"Just lovely, Miss Rae," said Thelma happily. "And you needn't to worry about that Minnie girl. She's gone!"

"Gone?" said Rae with startled eyes.

"They sent her away to some friend's house. And Mrs. Hollis says ye're to keep the room you had. My, but you look nice, Miss Rae! That's a pretty frock! Now you can go on in and dinner will be announced at once."

They greeted her with joy as she entered the room where they were all laughing and talking. There was great relief on the faces of the hostess and the bride. Then almost at once they went in to the table.

Lincoln Silverthorn watched his pretty sister with

satisfaction in his eyes. He knew he had been extravagant with regard to that dress, but he was glad he had done it. Of course it had set him back a little in his intentions about that new car which he had all but persuaded himself he was going to buy, but it was worth it. Rae was young and needed pretty things. Of course she wasn't a girl who spent her time running around to parties, but on the few occasions when she did go it was right that she should look her best. It was due their family that she should, and he was proud that he had been able to provide this successful dress for her tonight. He watched her with contented eyes. He was pleased to see that the fellows were all admiring her. They should. She was the grandest kind of a girl. He was her brother and he knew. He didn't know any girl who was at all her equal, unless perhaps it was Carey Carewe, and he wasn't sure about her.

As they ranged themselves about the table looking for their place cards he saw that Carey was almost beside Rae. She seemed to admire Rae, and Rae had said she liked Carey. That was another point in Carey's favor.

Carey had red-gold hair and a dress like the green in a sea wave. Her eyes too were sea green. Then he looked back to his sister. Would her dress have been better some other color? No, for that dark blue brought out the pink tints in Rae's cheeks. Her face stood out in the dark setting like a lovely flower, and she was tall and slender like a willow wand, graceful as a feather in the long slim skirt! Then he snapped his mind back to the practical. Such thoughts as these were sentimental froth. But it was his first venture into the world of fashion, so perhaps he could be pardoned for being pleased that it had been successful.

The table was as lovely as a table Mrs. Hollis had planned was expected to be, and the little gasp of appreciation that went round the room fully repaid her for all her care and thought. A sudden memory of the way she had just expelled that impudent girl so summarily from the house filled her with satisfaction, touched just the least bit with compunction that any girl had to be shut out from this happy time, when she wanted so much to be a part of it. But it was her own fault of course. If she hadn't been so selfish and disagreeable, and almost uncannily cunning in inventing effective ways to make other people uncomfortable, she might have been welcomed wherever she went. But the fact remained that she was most unpopular, a perfect killjoy wherever she chanced to be, and it was therefore a great relief to be rid of this unexpected trouble so easily.

Then she turned her attention to the lovely table, and the bright faces around it. Her own dear girl, Sydney, with her handsome bridegroom seated in the center facing her. She smiled a loving look toward her, resolutely putting away the thought of how soon she was to be separated from them.

The gay company had finished the fruit course and progressed to the delicious soup, when suddenly the doorbell bimmed out in a series of successive and frantic rings, as if the bell had gone mad and couldn't stop.

The guests were laughing and talking and at first didn't notice it, but Mrs. Hollis looked with a startled glance out into the hall. Thelma, who knew the butler was busy serving, hurried from the back hall toward the front door. But the bell went right on insistently ringing with all its might. Suddenly the guests became aware of it and ceased their chatter and laughter, looking up wonderingly, pausing with spoons halfway to their lips. And the bell went right on ringing.

Then the front door opened rather frantically and the bell stopped ringing, though its echoes still lingered hovering in the air, as if the sound had gathered such momentum that it could not quickly be suppressed.

Heavy young footsteps came swiftly toward the dining room in spite of Thelma's attempted interference, and a wild young voice burst in upon the bright scene.

It was Minnie! Her hat awry, her coat wide open and half trailing behind her, real tears making little rivulets down the powder on her cheeks, lipstick all over her delicate handkerchief, her smeary lips quivering wide like a frightened child's.

She stayed not on the order of her going. She came straight to the dining room table and stood there looking at Mrs. Hollis wildly, and as Luther Waite expressed it afterwards, she "turned on the works and began to bawl right off the bat!"

"Oh, Aunt Jessica!" she gasped. "I've had such a frightful experience! I thought I should die before I ever got back here!"

She punctuated her sentences by ducking her face into her handkerchief to dash away the tears.

"There was nobody at home! Can you imagine it? The house was absolutely dark! Not even a light in the hall as people usually arrange it. And there was somebody evidently breaking into the house. Someone with a flashlight going around inside, a little dot of light appearing, wavering across an inner wall, and then appearing somewhere else. It was weird! I couldn't understand it, and I was scared to death but I didn't know what to do. The taxi man said he couldn't wait. He had to get back for another call. So I got out and went up the steps. But just as I was reaching out to push the bell, a hand came out of the darkness and gripped me by the wrist, and tried to draw me into the dark vestibule. The man had a mask over the lower part of his face, and a gun in his hand! I began to scream with all my might, and jerk away from him, and I guess I frightened him, for his hold relaxed a little and I jerked my hand away so hard I fell backwards down the four steps to the sidewalk and rolled over into the shadow, and the man backed into the vestibule and I heard the door slam. By that time the taxi was gone and as soon as I could I got up and began to run. I ran as hard as I could, and I thought I never would get here. I'm so frightened I don't know what to do. Oh, Aunt Jessica, please, please don't send me away again! I'll stay anywhere. I can sit right down here at the corner of the table. I won't take up much room! You'll let me bring up a chair here beside you, won't you?" and she lifted a tearful appealing face toward Lincoln Silverthorn who was sitting at one corner of the table.

Link with a sternly severe face was on his feet at once, drawing out his chair for her.

"Just take my place," he said courteously, stepping back to the edge of the doorway into the wide hall.

"Oh! Thanks awfully!" said Minnie with a quick shift to a giggle. "I was sure there would be one gentleman among you!"

"Oh, *really,* Minnie!" said Mrs. Hollis in what was meant to be a low annoyed tone of reprimand, though it didn't register with Minnie. Her tears were forgotten, and she was seraphically happy now, sitting down serenely in Link's chair and gazing up at him like a queen thanking a lowly subject.

Mrs. Hollis with darkened countenance half rose from her seat, hesitantly, not knowing just what to do with this unparalleled situation. But Mr. Hollis looked at his aspiring relative with disgust.

"Nonsense, Minnie!" he ejaculated as he rose precipitately from his seat, laying a detaining hand on his wife's arm.

"Sit down, Jessica, I'll handle this!" he said in a low

tone, and Mrs. Hollis relaxed into her chair again. Mr. Hollis was a man of quick action and she had utmost faith in his judgment.

He took a couple of quick steps across to where Link stood by the door and spoke to him in a low tone: "Link, could I ask a favor of you? Will you take this young woman over to Mrs. Fremont's and see that she *stays* there? You can see I can't be spared here and no servant could manage her. That story about the house being dark is all nonsense. We telephoned Mrs. Fremont before we sent her, and they are expecting her over there. You are the only one of the crowd I know well enough to trust with this. It ought not to take you long, perhaps five minutes. Do you mind?"

"Of course not," said Link bowing gravely.

"The car is at the side entrance. I'll bring her out," said Mr. Hollis.

Link slid out through the heavy portieres and disappeared from Minnie Lazarelle's sight, and Mr. Hollis stepped to her side, and took a firm grip of her bare arm.

"Come!" he ordered in a low tone, "Come with me!" and Minnie looking up was a little frightened at the stern look on her semi-relative's face, though she had still no intention of stirring. She wore a well-feigned look of surprise on her face, till suddenly the chair upon which she was sitting began to move backward, and the grip on her arm forced her to rise.

"Why, where? What?" she asked in a tone which she tried to make gay.

Over across the table the bridegroom was asking in a low tone, "Who is she? Do I know her?" and Sydney was trying to explain briefly, while the rest of the guests were helpfully covering this forced exit with gay intimate conversation in voices that were a bit too loud and excited, and with eyes that tried to seem oblivious to what was going on. None of them liked the girl who was being led out of the room, but they were too well-bred to let her realize that they were aware of her humiliation. Besides, they all loved their hostess and were glad to ignore what must be a great annoyance to her well-planned festivity.

Minnie Lazarelle was led away from the room so forcibly that she had trouble in keeping her footing, and no leisure to cry out or refuse to go. Skillfully, too, she was guided out of view of the guests, down the back hall to the side entrance from which she had gone a little while before.

Link had the car at the door when they came out, Mr. Hollis setting the pace rapidly, and Minnie dragging back as much as she dared.

Thelma, always helpful, was at the door with the young woman's wrap which she had left on the back of the chair from which she had been lifted, and her suitcase which she had dropped at the front door as she entered. Thelma never had to be told such things.

"Now, Minnie," said Mr. Hollis, "Mr. Silverthorn has very kindly offered to take you back to Mrs. Fremont's. You have made us a great deal of trouble already, and if there is any more I shall certainly have to call in the police. Some of us will be seeing you sometime tomorrow, and in the meantime Mrs. Fremont will look after you. Thanks, Link, and please hurry back as soon as possible. No more nonsense, Minnie!"

Link had his foot on the clutch and the car started on its short journey swiftly.

Minnie, utterly taken by surprise, and rather intrigued by having such a good-looking young escort, was silent for the first few minutes, studying the young man's profile in the shadows of the car. She was planning just how she should open the conversation with him so that she would have his influence on her side, and perhaps force him to take her back to the house where she so greatly desired to be tonight. She had nursed her desires until she was thoroughly convinced that she was slighted by not having had an invitation to this wedding. What she wanted to do was to get it back on the Hollises for the shabby way in which they had treated her, bringing it out into the open that she was not of the wedding party. But the trouble was she did not know this young man. He had not been with the rest of the crowd on the few occasions when she had been with them, and she was not sure just what approach would be best to use. So for the first few seconds she was quiet.

But before she had decided what to say, Link spoke himself.

"Just what did you hope to gain by pulling off a stunt like that, Miss Lazarelle?" he said. "Surely you know that no one admires what you have done. All our crowd love and admire the Hollises, and not one of us likes to see them humiliated. I scarcely see how Sydney can ever bear to look at you again. As for the rest of us, we all feel that you have committed an outrage. Not one of the fellows could ever admire you even though you are all painted up in that heathenish style. You don't know how a decent fellow despises a girl who would carry on the way you have been doing. Why don't you snap out of this and try to behave like a regular human being? I can't see what possible fun you could get out of a stunt like this. You're not drunk, are you?"

In utmost astonishment Minnie listened. She was shaken beyond anything at hearing an estimate of her appearance and character that nobody had ever dared give her before, certainly no interesting young man. Suddenly shame came to her. Shame was almost a stranger to her. She had been doing as she pleased, saying what she pleased, all her life. And she had always reacted in such unexpected ways when anyone dared to call her down that her victims were left speechless with rage.

And so when shame touched her her anger boiled to fury's heat and she opened her mouth to give a choice answer. But instead, shameful angry tears stung her eyes, and dulled the sharpness of the words she would have uttered, and she sat there dumb.

So, this was McRae Silverthorn's adored brother! The man who had selected that nifty dress for his sister. The man whom all the crowd admired! And he was talking to her like this!

As the car drew up at the curb and stopped she ventured a trembling protest:

"I don't see what I've done that was so awful! I had a perfect right in—"

"Oh, yes, you do! You know exactly how you have behaved! You planned to do it. You thought perhaps if you succeeded in getting your way and being at that dinner, and the other festivities, that you would have a good time and some pleasant friends. But you wouldn't! Not a soul of the crowd would have wanted to have anything to do with you. Don't you know that? You wouldn't have been good company either, and you wouldn't have been admired by anyone. You know it isn't necessary for you to be like this. You wouldn't be bad looking if you'd wash all that tawdry paint off, and fix your hair neatly, and stop wearing flimsy finery. You'd have to change your line, but you probably could learn to behave like a lady! Why don't you try it?"

Suddenly Minnie took refuge in tears.

"I've never really had half a chance!" she sobbed. "I never had a nice home like other girls. And I never got invited to nice parties, nor had nice boy friends. I always had to get in anywhere I went by my wits. Nobody wants me."

"I don't doubt it," said Link severely. "Not if you've always acted the way you have been doing tonight. But you mustn't blame it on fate or your environment or anything like that. It's all your own fault and you know it! Now, will you get out? This is the house, and you can see perfectly well that there's no movie-thriller going on inside or out. Get out, please! I haven't much time."

He got out, and went around to the other side of the car. He helped her out, keeping a firm hold of her arm, and so propelled her up the curb, across the sidewalk, and up the walk to the door, not lingering on the way in spite of the drag of Minnie's reluctant feet.

But even as he reached to touch the doorbell Minnie started back sharply.

"Don't!" she said in a low tearful tone. "I can ring my own bell. You go on back. I can let myself in."

"No you don't!" said Link firmly. "I agreed to see you safely inside, and I mean to do it. You aren't going to have any more chances to pull a stunt like that tonight. And by the way, remember what I said. If you try any more monkey shines to worry my friends I personally will see that you get your come-uppance, and I don't mean maybe. Do I have your word of honor or haven't you any honor?"

He looked sternly down at her in the starlight.

"Yes!" she gasped, struggling to fight back the unaccustomed tears.

And just then the door swung open and Mrs. Fremont stood there in the bright light. Link put forward his ward and introduced her, pleasantly enough, but with a look on his nice firm lips that meant business.

"This is Miss Lazarelle, Mrs. Fremont. Mr. Hollis asked me to bring her over to be sure she found the way.

He said to tell you it was very kind of you to take care of her tonight and they will be telling you so themselves later."

"Why, we're delighted," said Mrs. Fremont, possessing herself of the reluctant hand of the unwilling guest, and smiling warmly upon her and the young man, including them both in that smile, as if Link and the girl were friends. That inclusive smile did something soothing to the overwrought nerves of the girl, and Minnie looked up almost gratefully.

"Now," said Mrs. Fremont with welcome in her eyes, "you'll come in, Link, and have dinner with us, won't you? We're just about to sit down and I'm sure it will make Miss Lazarelle feel a lot more at home if you stay."

"That's very kind of you," said Link warmly, "but I'm being waited for, and I can't possibly stay tonight."

Minnie lifted wistful eyes toward the young man as he backed away toward the door. Would a young man like that ever bring her to a place and stay there because he wanted to be with her, she wondered?

And then she suddenly roused to the moment. Something was due him from her, some thanks. Could she drag the words from her bitter lips after the drubbing he had given her?

"Thanks awfully for showing me the way," she murmured, lifting her miserable eyes to his face with a swift glance, hoping he didn't know how deep he had gone into her soul with his scathing words.

"So sorry you can't stay, Link," murmured Mrs. Fremont with a kindly hand on the girl's arm. "We'll try to take good care of this young woman."

If that detaining hand had not been possessively on her arm when the door opened to let Link out, she felt she would have bolted straight out too and vanished into the night. Only, she reflected as she was ushered upstairs to a pleasant guest room to take off her wrap, that it wouldn't be so easy to disappear into the night from a young man like that. He was capable of handling any girl who tried to get away from him, and of course under the present circumstances he wouldn't hesitate to call in the police if it became necessary. Then she winced as she remembered his tone while he was berating her, his keen sarcasm, his strong frank words that left no room for doubt of what he meant. The unbidden tears sprang into evidence again as she turned to the mirror and pretended to arrange her hair and powder her nose. Of course she didn't care what this plain elderly woman thought of her. Or did she, perhaps, after all? If what had just been said to her was true, and she was as unprepossessing as that young man had said, was there a sense in which she ought to care for what *any*one thought?

But what was the word "ought"? Why ought she to be anything unless she wanted to be? Why indeed, except perhaps it was the only way to win the admiration she so much desired.

Her poor selfish blinded mind could not follow her argument further. Mrs. Fremont was waiting for her. The most delicious savory smells were coming up the stairs to tantalize an appetite already whetted by the fragrance of the festive dinner over at the Hollis house. And now the Hollis dinner was definitely out of the picture. So she turned and meekly walked downstairs after her hostess.

If they hadn't sent that Silverthorn man over with her, if they had just sent her over with the chauffeur, or with a taxi man again, she might have played a trick and somehow forced her way back to the Hollis house and the privileges of the evening. But after that dressing down that Link had given her she could never go back and face them—face *him* again, and brazen off some new form of excuse. She shivered as she remembered Link's eyes that had looked at her with scorn. Even in the darkness of the car she had felt it piercing her soul, and she had never felt scorn before. She had always laughed at it. What power did the young man have, that he could do this to her?

So she went down to dinner, and met half a dozen other young people, though whether they were boarders or just friends of Mrs. Fremont she was not able to tell. They were very fond of her, that was evident, and they were having a very good time, and ordinarily she would have entered in loudly and boldly and had a royal time making them all as uncomfortable as she could.

But somehow tonight she couldn't get away from the feeling that Link Silverthorn was there looking at her. She could not feel the release from his eyes. It wasn't in the least likely that he was casting another thought in her direction, but her soul so shrank from the memory of his words that it was just as if he were sitting across from her watching her every move, and condemning her.

If Link had been there he might have been surprised at her quiet attitude. It wasn't at all that she was trying to be what he had suggested. It was just that his words had deflated her lifetime habit of regarding herself as a smart person who always gave back a little better, or rather worse, than she got. She had always prided herself on being able to match wits and humiliate anybody, no matter how dignified or clever or proud they were! And she had always supposed that such triumphs would bring her into the limelight and win her admiration. She had learned tonight that it did not; that the limelight and admiration were not synonymous. She had learned that there were young men who despised a girl who would do a thing such as she had done, and she was utterly dumbfounded. She couldn't even hold her own and speak up proudly to this quiet old woman. She didn't understand it. She felt awkward and out of place. She felt numbed in her mind, shaken, shocked, like one who had been running hard to attain a certain goal and had suddenly stubbed her toe and gone flat, striking her head and stunning every sense. She couldn't even rouse herself when others spoke to her. She felt when she tried to smile that the muscles of her face were stiff, and she wasn't quite sure when she thought she made the motion of a smile, whether it really appeared on her face or was merely a contortion.

Constantly before her eyes was the thought of the young man who had scolded her and scorned her. She had had older people lecture her before, but never a young person like that. Oh, the girls had often said scathing sarcastic things, but she had put that down to the fact that girls were always jealous. She hadn't thought much of that. The boys never scolded her. The nice ones evaded her—and the others she never sought. But a good looking young man, lecturing her in all seriousness like a grandfather! Telling her frankly that no one could like her, and most astonishing of all, telling her she could be different if she chose! It was astounding. That after all was the crux of the matter! That she could be different if she chose.

It was just as if a great couturier had told her her clothes were all wrong, and she should go to his establishment and be outfitted anew!

Minnie had always thought more of clothes than any other subject, unless it was young men, and it was suddenly through clothing that she began to see her way beyond what had happened. She could be different if she wanted to! It all amounted to that. Did she want to?

After dinner the young people adjourned to the piano, and all began to sing. Minnie pleaded a headache, excused herself and went to lie down. She had meant to get over to the church rehearsal and watch the fun, but now all that had faded from her desire. She definitely did not want to appear before any of that crowd. Not after what that handsome Silverthorn man had said. She was experiencing a vision of her real self, perhaps for the first time in her life, and she didn't enjoy it.

She decided she would lie down a few minutes and sort of get over the shock of all that had happened, and perhaps by half past eight or so she would come back to normal and feel like running over to the church to watch them.

But as she lay there and reviewed the afternoon and evening she was more and more averse to appearing before any of the wedding crowd that night. And while she was thinking about it, planning how she could go early to the wedding tomorrow and get away up in the gallery somewhere out of sight behind a pillar where she could just peek out and get a glimpse of the procession and the ceremony, she fell asleep.

4

WHEN LINK came back to the Hollis dining room he slid into his seat at the table so quietly that he was scarcely noticed.

Paul Redfern had caught the look of alertness on Mr. Hollis's face, the quick glance behind him, the relief in his eyes, and knew that the envoy had returned and that the girl was not with him.

So with the courtesy and tact that was a part of his careful training, Paul had a story both absorbing and amusing to tell, and he timed it to the instant as Link approached the doorway, so that the entire table was giving him attention as Link slipped in as silently as a shadow. It was not until the story was finished that one by one the company realized that Link was back among them. It was all effected so neatly that at first they wondered if he really had gone to take that girl away, or had there been some other reason for his leaving for the instant? Minnie herself would have been greatly astonished if she could have known how small a ripple her passage through that dining room had made.

For the moment only one or two of the company

remembered the brief break when Minnie had made them all feel so uncomfortable. Link's sister Rae, of course, was one, sitting there so quietly in the dress that had almost been snatched from her, scarcely able to eat while Link had been gone.

Now as she looked at her brother from across the table she thought he looked disturbed, as if the encounter had been unpleasant for him. Well, how could it help being that? Minnie was that way. She had been fortunate herself to get away from Minnie this afternoon. It hadn't been kind of Mr. Hollis to ask Link to take her away, and yet he knew Link better than any of the other men, and it really was a compliment to his dependability. And poor Mr. Hollis! What else could he do?

The other one who noticed Link was Curlin Grant. Curlin was about the best friend Link had, and he was sitting across from Rae, making talk with Lou McHale. But Rae could see that Curlin was paying more attention to Link than he was to Lou. Curlin was a good true friend, and Curlin was reading his friend's face, just as his sister was doing.

Rae flashed a look at Paul now. Paul had told that story on purpose to cover Link's entrance. Paul was grand! Even if they all did think he was a little high hat with some people, he was a loyal friend. And he had done the courteous tactful thing.

But the unpleasant interlude was passed. Rae had a feeling that Minnie would not again appear on the scene that night. Unless somehow she managed to get into the church. That might happen. But she couldn't do much damage there. They would all be busy rehearsing.

Rae looked down at her lovely dress and felt suddenly very grand and very happy. It was a beautiful frock, and the girls had all told her she looked wonderful. And she couldn't help reading it in every one of the boys' eyes.

Except of course Curlin's. Curlin never noticed dresses. He never noticed girls much anyway. That was what Minnie had said, wasn't it? Disgusting! Well, Curlin was a splendid friend. They had known him ever since he was a small boy. Their houses in the country were next door to each other, and Curlin and Steve both had been as much at home in the Silverthorn house as they were themselves. It was like having three brothers. And they had always taken Rae into their fun, or their work, baseball or football or plowing or building a fence. She had had her part, and was always treated like a good comrade. She had never considered Curlin the way Minnie had been judging him that afternoon. It had been revolting for her to speak of him that way!

She studied Curlin from across the table. His strong face, the leanness of it, and the character expressed in the firm chin, the pleasant lips. He wasn't quite as strikingly handsome as Paul, nor Steve perhaps, not as good looking as Link, but there was something about him that seemed so quiet and dependable.

Suddenly, as if she had been speaking her thoughts to Curlin aloud he looked up and caught her eye, seemed almost to study her for a moment, let his eye take in the pretty lines of her new garb, and then his glance met hers, and she saw for the first time in his face a flame of admiration. It was something well controlled but like a flame it could not hide its quick vital power. Rae smiled back shyly, her face flaming into lovely delicate beauty like a flower, and a sweet embarrassment covered her. She had a new dress on, his eyes said, and he liked it. His glance went quickly around the table and came back to her, and he seemed to be trying to make her understand that she was the prettiest girl in the room!

Silly! This was all imagination, set on fire by Minnie's utterly senseless talk in the afternoon! But yet, several times before the meal was over she found herself seeking Curlin's eyes, as if to find in them that same glad glance again. But nonsense, she must have imagined it she told herself. Although he smiled pleasantly more than once, the smiles were not for her alone. As she sat thinking over the whole situation, Rae's glance went from one to another.

Steve had always been what the boys called "a looker" with his pink cheeks, his gold curly hair and big blue eyes. Steve made a wonderful girl when they dressed him up in girl's clothes for a tableau or a play. And there was Paul Redfern. He was handsome and distinguished looking. She studied him a moment till he glanced her way and smiled. Paul was fine, with a certain dignity about him, a little like Link. Link had dignity too. She looked at him critically, and decided that even though he was her brother she was unbiased in her decision that he was the best looking man in the room.

Then her eyes went over to the groom, and to the best man who was seated so near to herself that she could scarcely tell how he looked. But he was nice enough, too. They had joked Sydney a lot by telling her she had picked out all the good-looking men for her wedding procession regardless of who they were, but she hadn't picked out the best man. The groom had done that. Well, he was all right. Only she wished he wasn't having to walk down the aisle with her. She would so much rather have had one of the boys she knew well. But of course the maid of honor had to walk with the best man.

Then suddenly there was a stir. The dessert was finished, even to the coffee, and someone had discovered that it was time to go to the church. Quickly they were marshaled into cars and on their way.

Then the great stone church loomed up among the

tall trees along the broad lighted avenue and they had arrived.

The church was not brightly lighted yet, just a small light at the front door, a dim one in the windows up near the pulpit end. There were no crowds around. Mr. Hollis had taken care that this rehearsal should be very private and very quiet.

But the lights sprang up as soon as they were inside with the door fastened. Rae drew a breath of real relief when she heard the key turn in the lock. She had had a secret fear lest Minnie might turn up at the church and make trouble again, and perhaps make it necessary for Link to take her away. She didn't want Link's pleasure in the evening spoiled, nor her friends', either.

But there was no sign of Minnie anywhere, and soon the rehearsal was in full swing. The organ was filling the great arches with exquisite music, and the girls in their pretty dinner dresses were making their slow graceful way up the aisle, learning the exact spot where each was to stop and become a fixture for the ceremony. Over and over again they tried it, gradually becoming perfect in the formal picture that the whole affair was to be.

"I didn't think we were going to get rid of our beloved cousin so easily," murmured Sydney to Link. "How did you manage it so briskly and so completely, Link? It was you whom father bribed to dispose of her, wasn't it?"

"Why, yes, I took her over to Mrs. Fremont's," said Link. "It isn't far, you know."

"Yes, but Min is difficult," said Sydney ruefully. "I hardly expected you back tonight. Min has ways."

"Well, I had no trouble," said Link. "I just took her there and introduced her." He grinned.

"Well, I'm sure it was one of two things. Either she found some unattached man there who was most attractive, or else you must have put the fear of death into her."

But Link's only answer was another grin.

At last they were done with the rehearsal, and Mrs. Hollis marshaled them into the cars and took them home, where a pleasant refreshment in the form of tiny sandwiches and hot chocolate awaited them. They had a gay time talking over old days and singing a few old songs, bits of reminiscences of their young days, recalling old times, telling now and then a funny story to the bridegroom, and getting really acquainted with him. And it was all so free and easy and happy that no one even remembered to think of Minnie Lazarelle and wonder why she had not returned. They were having the delightful evening together that they had all anticipated, and even Link forgot the incident of the early evening that had made a few unpleasant moments for himself and their hosts.

It was only after the young men had returned to Paul's house and were merrily arranging themselves for sleep that the incident was mentioned.

"Good old Link!" said Luther Waite, sleepily, pausing beside Link and patting him clumsily on his head as Link was about to pull off his shirt. "You're certainly my good angel, Link. Under ordinary circumstances that act you put over, taking that poor goof away, would have been left to me, and *boy!* I tell you if it had, they would have had to drag the river for my poor body, for I would have run to the ends of the earth before I would have escorted that dame anywhere. I certainly would not have remained to see what became of her in my absence, either, and that's the truth."

"Yes, Link, I'll give you the credit of doing a very nice job in a most discreet manner," said Paul with a smile of commendation.

"Yes," chimed in Reeves Leighton, "how did you do it so neatly and with such expedition? I've seen others fail utterly who were almost as well equipped mentally and physically. Tell us your secret. What mysterious power did you invoke? We might get caught in some such a jam ourselves some day."

"Oh, forget it!" said Link with a yawn. "Let's turn in. I did a big day's work this morning before I drove to town, and I'm not sure but I may have to do another tomorrow morning before I jump into my glad rags and go to the wedding, so have mercy, lads, and let's get some sleep!"

They were up betimes, nevertheless, and Link was off to get his necessary work out of the way so that he could be on hand with the others that afternoon.

The hours seemed to move too swiftly as the day drew to a close, and excitement ran high. There were more and more presents to unwrap and place with the others, and Sydney sat at her little desk in the upper hallway and wildly dashed off notes of thanks. The girls hovered over the presents, admired and sometimes envied, and rejoiced over them all. Then suddenly they scurried to their rooms to get dressed, and the boys dashed back to Paul's to do likewise, and not long after they appeared again as dignified well dressed ushers hovering around the church door, smiling and escorting the ladies to their places, and dropping back again to the door to gaze down the long awning-covered approach to see if the girls were coming yet.

It was Luther Waite who almost caused a panic among them. His station had been the vestibule at the left hand door, under the great curved stairway that led to the left galleries.

"Holy Mackerel, fellas," he said under his breath, furtively peering out from the shadows. "If you see me beating it you'll know that Minerva baby has come. If she turns up you can't expect me to go on with my part. You'll hafta get me a substitute quick! Because if she gets here she'll freeze onto me and take me up the aisle, and smirk at me all the way, and that's one thing I can't take, fellas, I really can't!"

"Oh, shut up, you goop!" laughed Lincoln Silverthorn. "She's not coming, don't you worry! Get back on your job and forget you ever saw her."

"Oh, but I can't forget, Link," said Luther sadly. "She's got my goat, and she *might* come, you know she might!" He was comical in his assumed distress. "And Link," he added in sudden excitement, "I thought I saw her then, I really did. Right behind that man with the goatee. There! Isn't that the gal with those pink doodads on her head?"

"Calm yourself, Lutie!" said Link, lowering his voice. "You take that gray lady and go on about your business. Don't let any more fool gals get your goat. Besides, they don't allow goats in this church, and you've got a job to walk back up the aisle with Sue Richards, so you'd better watch out. Get going, kid, and stop your nonsense!"

A few minutes later Link discovered the girl in question sitting far up in the back of the gallery, out of sight of the wedding party, but in a position where she could see the whole ceremony herself.

He had thought he recognized her slight form scuttling up the gallery stairs just after Luther had marched his gray lady in to her seat on the groom's side of the church. When he could snatch a moment he hid himself for an instant behind the banks of palms up by the altar and searched the gallery until he discovered her pale wistful face. He only gave her a glance, but the impression he got of her was that she was sad and unhappy. Her lips were not vivid as he remembered them, her face was very white, and her eyes were big and tired looking. Also her attire seemed very plain, not at all gay and dashing as she usually was. And this for a wedding! It somehow gave him an uneasy feeling. He was suddenly reminded of the sharp words he had said to her last night and felt that perhaps he was to blame for her unhappiness. She deserved them of course, but it hadn't entered his head that they would make any deep impression on her. A girl who broke every rule of courtesy wherever she was, who had barged into Sydney's wedding unbidden, and come back again after she had been sent away! Could this be just another act she was putting on, with herself for persecuted heroine? Well, he was glad he had said what he had, anyway. It was good she should know for once what one young man thought of her.

She was wearing a black dress with a simple white collar, and a small black hat, not a crazy one. It wasn't like her to dress so simply at an evening affair. Well, he couldn't bother his brains about her. He was only glad she was keeping in the background. So when he went back to the vestibule he whispered to Luther Waite.

"Don't worry, Lutie, the bane of your life is sitting away up in the gallery back by the organ console. And she can't get downstairs till after you've marched out with Sue Richards, so you're safe."

Luther answered with a relieved grin and the wedding came to order as a quartette of gorgeous voices began to sing:

> "Fair bride and groom, greetings to thee,
> Heaven's choicest blessings descend rich and free,
> Long may you live, loyal and true,
> Happy in love ever rich, ever new."

The last notes blended into the good old wedding

march that always has a special thrill for the audience no matter how many weddings they have attended, and a breathlessness went over the church.

Now came the bridesmaids slowly, delicately, in all the colors of the rainbow, leading the procession. And how handsome the groom was, so happy-looking, with his pleasant stranger-best-man beside him! The groom was watching his approaching bride, and his face was as if a great happy light was over it. Did he know what a wonderful girl he was getting? Did he really know her well enough to take her away from them all? Would he treat her as a grand girl like that ought to be treated?

Sydney's maid of honor wondered as these thoughts and questions surged about the electric atmosphere of the church, how he dared to face them all and just look happy that he was getting her. There was assurance in his handsome face. He wasn't afraid that he wouldn't have a happy marriage. He meant to have it. He looked as if it was all in his hands and he had entire confidence in himself. He had on his face the smile that was perhaps the sweetest and most childlike that he had worn for years, or might ever wear again. At least that was the impression Rae Silverthorn got as she looked at him from the vantage point of the aisle, and realized that he was looking straight over her beautiful pink maid of honor dress, back to his lovely white bride behind her. She was glad for Sydney's sake that his eyes were all for her friend, and not at all for the general beautiful effect of everything, colors and flowers and pretty girl faces.

And the girl in black away up in the gallery saw his look, too, and her hungry heart winced. Would any young man, a *nice* young man like that, *ever* look at her that way?

The wedding party drifted into place and ranged

themselves with no seeming effort, and then came Sydney on her father's arm and the solemn service began.

Rae stood there sweetly beside her friend, her gorgeous sheaf of roses and delphiniums lying over her left arm so that there would be plenty of room without shifting them to receive the bride's white roses and valley lilies when the proper time came. Then she settled to listen to the words of admonition, so gravely full of meaning, shadowing forth so many possibilities of life, and almost shuddered at them. Then came the vows. "Do you thus promise?" and Sydney's clear voice so steady and so *glad,* "I do!"

It seemed long while they stood there, but the minutes were over swiftly, and then they were marching down in the procession, Rae with her hand on the arm of the best man. Oh, she was glad this wasn't a permanent thing for all of them. She was glad she didn't have to go off tonight with the best man. He was handsome, yes, and he was a lot of fun at the table last night, but if she had to go away with him forever tonight it would break her heart.

And how about the rest of them? Her mind traveled back along the line of the procession. Frannie with Steve Grant? Well that might be all right, but Lou McHale with Curlin, no, never! Whoever thought they ought to go together? Just because Curlin was so good-natured! And was she quite satisfied with Carey Carewe for her precious brother Link? Her heart shrank back from answering that.

And besides she was marching down the aisle with this strange best man and ought to be smiling up into his face and being fascinating.

Then they were out in the vestibule, hurrying down the enclosure to their cars, with so many curious eyes behind them studying how their dresses were made. My!

She would have liked to be back there for a minute just to watch themselves all go by!

Minnie Lazarelle watched, and took in every detail, and almost groaned aloud, there in the gallery. It was a lovely wedding. The reception room at the Hollis house was all hung with silver wires twisted about with smilax, a white carnation at the end of each wire. It was a lovely place for the bride to stand! And how lovely all their dresses looked together! How the rainbow colors brought out the beauty of the bridal white!

When they were seated about the bride's table again Rae had a passing thought of the poor arrogant girl who had barged in when they were at the table the night before and spoiled things for a few minutes. Remembering her own experience with that girl she half expected to see her coming in again! Oh, that would be so horrid for Sydney to have to remember if it happened again. So horrid for Link, for Link would be sure to offer to take her away if anybody had to do it, and he would be the one of course whom they would ask to help in case she came again, he had been so successful last night.

Then the gaiety about her claimed her attention and she forgot it all and just enjoyed herself.

Then how quickly it was all over, Sydney, going up the stairs in her long white gown and veil, standing at the curve and throwing down her lovely flowers, and throwing them straight at Rae, her best friend, of course.

Rae hadn't intended to try and get them. She felt it wasn't quite modest to seem to be grabbing for the next chance to be married. For herself, Rae Silverthorn had no immediate desire to be married. Some day perhaps, if God willed it, but not now. And yet that bouquet came straight to her, as if with intention, and almost fell into her arms, as if the others reaching for it suddenly saw

Sydney's loving intention and drew their reaching hands back.

When Sydney came back in her going-away garb she seemed almost a stranger; lovely yet, but already gone from them, and Rae felt a sudden desolation settle down upon her. But there was too much hurry to give way to it, for they were all going to the station to see the bridal pair off, and there were confetti and paper rose leaves, and rice, and a few old slippers to think about as they started away. More rose leaves and rice for the station. Oh, this seemed all out of keeping to Rae, after that sweetly solemn sacrament of marriage.

And now at last the train was moving and the last good-by was said, and they must turn back to their old life again with Sydney gone from them into a new life of her own.

5

LINCOLN SILVERTHORN driving down the broad
avenue the next morning on the way to a business
appointment, suddenly saw on the sidewalk just ahead of
him, the slim figure of a girl who looked strangely
familiar, and not very welcome to his eyes which grew
more and more troubled as he came nearer and made
sure his first sight had been right.

She was bending under the weight of a heavy suitcase,
which he also recognized, having carried it two short
nights before. She had also a small overnight bag, and her
slender arms did not seem well adapted or accustomed
to carrying such burdens.

Unconsciously he slowed down, and gave a glance
ahead. Yes, there was a side street where he could turn
off at once and not have to go by her at all. He certainly
did not want to get into her toils again. And yet, his
innate courtesy, and his Christian training could not
quite let him do that. She was a woman, and she was
obviously having a hard time getting that suitcase trans-
ported. There! Now she was stopping, putting it down
on the sidewalk and straightening up as if her back ached,

and her arm was tired. He saw her give a glance at her watch, and then turn and shift the luggage to the other arm. Why in the world didn't she call a taxi? She couldn't be hard up, could she? He had never heard that the Lazarelles were especially wealthy, but surely if she had money enough to come here from a distance where she now lived, she must have enough to pay for a taxi. But obviously she hadn't done it, and here she was out in the street, at least two more blocks from any bus line if she had meant to take a bus, seven blocks from the railroad if she was taking the train. Well, it was not his responsibility. Why should he get tangled up in it, and perhaps have that girl on his hands for the day? She wasn't his cousin, not even distantly, and if the Hollises didn't see fit to look after her why should he worry?

But of course the Hollises would do something about it if they knew she was trudging off by herself that way with heavy luggage. And they had put her in his charge, and he saw her now. Did not common courtesy make it necessary for him to do something about it? What would his mother and father say if it were put up to them? What would the Hollises say if he should tell them he had seen her so and passed her by? What did Christian courtesy demand?

Of course he needn't tell his family, nor the Hollises, and no one would ever know but himself. But—*Christian* courtesy! Of course his Lord would know, and now his own heart was convicting him. Even if he didn't like the girl, he could at least be polite. And after all she was one for whom the Lord had died. Did that demand that he too, who was supposed to have died with Christ, do an unpleasant duty?

Well, he didn't have to be particularly affable, anyway. He could take her to her bus, or train. That wouldn't last long.

Just then the girl put down her luggage, the little bag on top of the big one and drew a deep breath as if she were tired. Of course, from all he knew of her in the past this might be an act that she was putting on for his benefit, to attract his attention. Yet he didn't think she could have seen him. And besides, he had been fairly severe with her the last time he saw her.

Then he drew up sharply at the curb, a little ahead of where she was standing, and leaning out gave her a cold courteous bow. He felt certain there was nothing in the quality of that bow to encourage her further pursuit of him, nothing to make her think he was interested in her.

She looked up and a startled quiver went over her face. She seemed almost frightened.

"Can I help you?" he asked, and tried to make his voice as colorless as possible, not as if he were glad to see her at all, as if it were merely duty that made him ask.

A dreary, dispirited look came into her eyes.

"Oh, no," she said listlessly, "I'm all right. I'll make it. But—" and then she stopped and a sudden wistfulness came over her face, almost an eagerness. "I did want to ask you a question. I've been wishing all day yesterday that I could see you just one minute. I won't take long—" She drew a little nearer to his car. "Would you mind stopping just one minute? It's something you said the other night, and I wanted to know if you really meant it, or were you just mad because you had to bother taking me away?"

He gave her an astonished glance. Was this another act that she was going to try on him? But there was such earnestness in her face, such eagerness in her voice, as if it meant so much to her that he could not bring himself to refuse, or turn her off.

He tried to make his voice sound kindly, though he was all at once intensely annoyed. He had wanted to get his errands done in a hurry and get back home to some work he had planned, and now was she going to upset everything? This was the way Luther Waite said she did, always barging in and insisting on being important.

"What did I say?" he asked. "I'm afraid I was rather rude to you. I was annoyed of course to have my friends so upset."

"Oh, I don't mean that. Of course you didn't like it that you had to bother with me at a time like that. And I guess what you said to me was all true. I've been thinking it over and I've seen myself as I never did before. I guess I ought to be glad you told me. Because I've been trying all my life to have people like me and they never do. I guess I must have been going about it in the wrong way, and you made me see it. But what you said that I want to ask about is this: you said I could be different. Did you really mean that? Do you honestly think I could?"

Link gave her a quick searching look and then said gravely, commandingly,

"Get in!"

"No, I don't want to bother you that way. If you'll just tell me if you meant it or not."

"Why, sure I meant it."

Her face took on a hungry look.

"Oh, if I only knew how!" she said, and her face didn't look at all like Minnie Lazarelle. "I've been trying all my life to be like other people, and I never get *any*where!" There was almost a wail in her voice, a desperate look in her eyes, as she stepped back with a kind of finality in her air, like one who had found out her illness, and now must search till she found a way to attain the cure. She stooped and began to gather up her bags.

"Get in!" said Link firmly, and swinging open the

door slid by the wheel and out on the sidewalk beside her. "Now, get in!" he said again. "You and I have got to thrash this out till you understand. If you really want it. Yes, there's a way!"

He swung her bags into the compartment behind the seats, and went around to the wheel. She looked at him with sudden wonder, almost dread. She wasn't used to grave and gentle service. Young men sometimes gave her what she forced them to give in the way of attentions, but never this grave definite help because they saw she needed it. She crept into the seat hesitantly, not with her old arrogant swing. She had nothing to cover. This young man knew the truth about her. He had told it to her.

"Now, where were you going?" he asked as his hand grasped the wheel. "We might as well save your time."

"It doesn't matter," she said apathetically, "I was just going to the station, but I don't care. If you'll just tell me so I can understand how I could possibly be different."

There was something in her groping voice, in the bitterness of her accent, that gave Link a sudden compassion for her. Was she genuine? If she was, there was something in that cry of hers that called for all the gallantry, all the ability to help that the years had taught Link.

"I think you need the Lord Jesus Christ!" said Link, startlingly, as the car threaded its way through traffic.

The girl was utterly still with downcast eyes for some seconds, a hopeless look growing around her mouth. At last she spoke vaguely:

"Oh, you mean religion!" and her tone grew still more hopeless than it had been. "You mean I should go to church a lot and all that?"

"No!" said Link. "I don't mean religion. Religion is a system of good works serving any kind of a god. I mean you need to know the Lord Jesus Christ, personally and intimately."

"Yeah?" said the girl with a half contemptuous laugh. "A big chance I'd ever stand doing that! You might as well tell me to go and get to be pals with the president, or the king of England!"

"Oh, no!" said Link. "It wouldn't be like that because He loves you."

"Oh yeah? Well you don't know me, that's all. I've never had anything at all to do with Him. I don't know as I've even believed in Him. I've never been interested in going to church, or anything religious. He *couldn't* love me."

"Yes, but He does," said Link reverently, almost tenderly. "He says so Himself in the Bible."

"The Bible!" said the girl half contemptuously. "I've never read that. I never was interested."

"Yes, but that's where you find His messages to you. His love messages!"

"Well, I never read them, but I can't see how that would make me different, anyway."

"You would if you got to reading what He says about it."

"What He says about it? You mean what He says about me being different? But why would He say anything about me? What does He say?"

"He tells you that you must be born again!"

"Born again!" said the girl. "But that's silly! How could I be born again? No, that wouldn't help any. I'm born this way, and I'll have to go on to the end I suppose." She drew a pitiful sigh. "There! I oughtn't to have bothered you. I suppose I've known all along things I oughtn't to do, just like I know now that I ought not to bother you. Only I didn't do them. I thought it was smart to do the unexpected, to make people furious at me, and get away with all sorts of deviltry. And nobody ever told me I could be different. Nobody ever really called me down as you did and told me people wouldn't like me that way, and that there was a way to be different. But even you, when I ask you, only tell me impossible things to do. Be born again! How could I?"

Link drove into the parking space behind the station and stopped his car.

"What time does your train go?" he asked in a crisp businesslike tone.

"Oh, I don't know," she said in a desperate tone. "Somewhere around eleven o'clock, I think. I was going in to ask."

"Where are you going?" he asked.

"Oh, back home, I suppose. There doesn't seem to be anything for me back here any more. I thought I'd come on and have a good time, and perhaps stay and get me a good job, or some friends or something, but now I guess there's nothing for it but to go back. I hate it of course. Somehow I've lost my punch. I don't click any more anywhere. I don't know that I ever did. Only since you talked to me the other night you showed me that I never would, and I've about given up. I think I've reached the end. Perhaps I can die and that will be the end of me. Only I'd make less trouble if I went back to my folks than if I stayed among strangers and put them to all that annoyance. Born again! Why was I ever born at all, I'd like to know? I never asked to be born, and why should I want to be born again?"

Link drew a deep breath, looked at her keenly for a minute, and then swung out of the car.

"Wait here!" he said. "I'll find out about your train and then I'll come back and talk."

He was gone and the girl sat there dispiritedly and thought about it all. This was the first time in a long time that a young man had of his own accord gone out of his way to help her. They just didn't do such things for her unless she shamelessly required it of them in the presence of others so that they were ashamed not to help her. She used to think that if she got young men to go with her places, and do things for her the way they waited upon other girls, that they would enjoy being with her. She wasn't bad looking, she was sure of that. Back in the family history, somewhere she had had a grandmother who was supposed to have been a beauty, and her father used to say she looked like that grandmother. She had always tried to look like other girls, as far as her allowance made it possible. She had tried to look smart and act smart, and often went to extremes of daring in dress and manners, thinking she would thus win popularity.

But suddenly two nights ago Lincoln Silverthorn had made her see that such things were not popular with men, not with the kind of young men that were in her cousin Sydney's crowd anyway, and she felt as if she had reached the limit and there was no use going on any farther.

She ought not to have let Link go in to that station and find out about her train for her. She ought to have insisted on getting out and going in herself. She might have made him feel she had a little shred of self-respect anyway. When he came back she would just get out at once and leave him. She was holding him up in his day's business probably, and it wouldn't do any good anyway. Born again! That sounded like nonsense, and anyway she wasn't religious and couldn't acquire a character like that. She couldn't acquire any kind of a character, except one that all people hated, so what was the use? The thing she ought to do was to get out at once while he was gone, get her suitcases out of the back, and have them on the pavement where she could thank him and swing out of his way as fast as possible. Maybe then he could forget how silly she had been night before last. Not that it really mattered whether he forgot or not. She had made an indelible impression upon him, of a disagreeable girl, and he would never want to think about her again of course. The best thing she could do would be to get out of his way.

Suddenly she grasped the door handle and flung the door open. She was just putting her foot out on the running board, when there he was beside her. She was too late.

"Don't get out," he said. "You've plenty of time. Your train doesn't go for nearly an hour yet. I'll drive over the other side there out of the way of traffic."

"But I'm taking a lot of your time," she said sadly, "and that's not necessary. I don't want to be any more of a nuisance than I have been to you already. It isn't at all important for you to stick around till I get away." There was a sort of a colorless dignity to her voice that made him look at her, and then suddenly as she looked hopelessly up to him his face broke into a smile.

"Snap out of it!" he said pleasantly. "It may not be important for me to put you on the train but it is important that you should know how to be born again. Get back in and we'll drive over under that tree and talk a few minutes."

"I don't see why it's important for me to know about being born again. I didn't do anything about being born the first time, and I don't think I'd understand this other any better. I guess I'll have to stay the way I am always."

"Get in," he said gently, and he pushed her back into the seat and closed the door.

He parked the car over under the big tree across the cinder parking place, and turned around toward her.

"You ought not to bother with me!" she said gloomily. "I know you have lots of important things to do."

"Don't you know that to a believer, a person who is born-again, nothing is so important in life as to show some other soul how to be saved?"

"Be saved?" she repeated with a look of bewilderment. "Be saved from what?"

Link looked at her in surprise.

"Why, be saved from sin. Saved from self!"

"Try and do it!" she said with a bitter little contemptuous laugh. "I was born with this kind of a self, and nobody can change me. Not even you could do it."

"Oh, no!" said Link. "I couldn't do it. It would take the Lord Jesus Christ to do that. No human being could do it."

"Well, I don't understand at all what you mean," she said crossly. "I'm not so much of a sinner. I don't think I ever did anything that was real wrong in my life. I've just tried to get in with other girls and men and have a good time, and I never succeeded in doing that once. What is sin anyway? Why should I have to be saved from sin? I've never robbed anybody, nor told lies, nor murdered."

"The greatest sin, all sin, is not believing in Christ who took all your sins on Himself, and paid the price of them with His blood that you might be free before God from your sin."

"Why should He do that? I never felt I had any sin. God didn't care anything about me."

"Oh, yes, He did. He created you that He might love you and enjoy you. But you were under condemnation of death for sin, ever since Adam's sin in the Garden of Eden. You with everybody else inherited sin, and He cared enough for you to make a way for you to be saved, to be washed from your sin, so that you might be fit to live forever with Him in Heaven and companion with Him."

"Well, I didn't have anything to do with Adam's sin. I wasn't born then. I don't think that was fair."

"Fair or unfair, it is the truth. The sins of the fathers are inherited by their children, whether they like it or not, and the penalty of sin is death. There's only one way to get away from that penalty and that is God's way. The way of believing on His Son who took the death penalty in our place. If you will accept what Jesus did for you when He died in your place, if you will believe that He did that for you, and will take Him as your personal Saviour, that moment you are born again, and His Holy Spirit will come into your heart to stay, and will teach you all the things you need to know. If you will let Him He will make of you a new creature. That is why I told you you did not need to be this way."

The girl sat and stared at him.

"I never heard anybody talk that way before," she said wonderingly. "Do other people believe that?"

"A great many do. You'd be surprised how many!"

"But how do you get to believe a thing like that?"

"It's all in the Bible," said Link gently.

"Well, I never read the Bible. I suppose I've heard some of it read the few times I've ever been to church, which wasn't many. I didn't care for church. It seemed dull to me, and our folks didn't go. I didn't have to go. Sometimes when I was a kid I went to Sunday School for a little while, but I thought it was a bore so I didn't go any more. I guess I wouldn't know enough to be saved as you call it."

"You can learn," said Link earnestly. "Haven't you got a Bible?"

She laughed.

"No, how would I get a Bible? But I can buy a Bible if you think that's important."

"Yes, it's important," said Link quietly. "Suppose you let me send you one, and then I can mark a few verses that will help you to get to know your Lord Jesus who died for you. Will you read them if I mark them for you?"

"Why, of course," said Minnie. "But I think that is taking too much trouble for me. You don't really want to bother this way with me, you know you don't. I oughtn't to let you. You've done enough for me just making me see what a fool I was making of myself. I'll just keep out of everybody's way till I can make something of myself and people won't hate so to have me around."

"But you never can make something *of yourself*, you know. Not without the Lord Jesus Christ. It's impossible because you still have that old sinful nature with which you were born, and it keeps popping up and taking control of you, even when your spirit has been born again. But the whole thing is, when you are born again the Holy Spirit living in you has power over you and He makes you *want* right things where before you always wanted the wrong things."

"But I don't see how all this religious stuff is going to make other people like me," said the girl with a downcast look. "I'm just made this way and I can't help it!"

"Yes, that's your old nature you are talking about, not your born-again nature. If you are born again and get to know and love your Lord, you will find you want to appear well before Him, rather than before anybody else. More and more if you think about Him and read about Him, and live with Him day by day, you will find yourself growing to look like Him, to act like Him, and *He* is 'altogether lovely.' Haven't you ever found yourself copying someone you admired? Trying to please them?"

He looked at her earnestly, his whole thought bent on making her understand this great vital truth, because now he had begun to feel her great need, and that his words would perhaps be the only ones that would reach her sorrowful empty life.

She looked up with a flash of comprehension in her eyes, and suddenly he saw that in themselves when they were not self-conscious and not trying to attract attention, they were really lovely eyes. He was surprised at that, and the thought came to him that probably in the eyes of the Lord who died for her she was very dear and beautiful. She was meant to be beautiful of course, and it had never occurred to him before. He was used to hearing them all cry out against her. The thought was almost staggering, as if he suddenly realized that his Lord was letting him help to bring back a lost loved one to Himself. It was something he must put away and think about afterwards, for he didn't just know why he was taking all this trouble for poor despised Min Lazarelle. It surely must be the Holy Spirit who was working in his heart suggesting to him what to say.

Then she spoke.

"Yes, I know what you mean," she said thoughtfully. "I feel that way about you. I want to appear right before you, because you made me feel how utterly you despised me, and it made me ashamed. I don't believe anybody ever made me ashamed before. They only made me mad. But you made me feel what you thought of me. I wanted to be different so I wouldn't seem that way to you."

A great softness came over Link's face as he answered.

"That's it," he said gently, "that's exactly it. God looks at people and sees them as sinners, and God will not tolerate sin. And though He sometimes has to seem very harsh to us to make us understand that we are sinners, when we do get to the point that we understand then we begin to want to be right before Him. That is when we cry out to Him to help, and take Him for our Saviour. When we do that, we are born again and we begin to want to do what He wants us to do. And constant companionship with Him makes us grow like Him, so that people notice that we have been with Him. It does make a difference to be with the Lord Jesus in every minute of our day."

The girl looked steadily at him with wonder and a new kind of awe in her face.

Then suddenly Link looked down at his watch.

"But say! It's getting late. We ought to be getting over to your train. There isn't much time. Have you your ticket?"

"Yes," said the girl sadly. "I came up here to have a good time and I bought a return ticket so I could get back if everything else failed, but now I see it's no good. I can't get anywhere this way, and I'm going back to try and begin over again."

"Wait!" said Link sharply. "You can't go that way!" as she made a move to open the door and get out. "We must make sure you go in the strength of the Lord. You can't expect anything different out of your life if you try to do it alone. Are you willing to take Christ as your personal Saviour?"

"Oh, I guess so," she said drearily. "I'll try anything once. I've tried everything else and it didn't do any good."

"But it isn't just try," urged Link, "it's *take!* It's really *take* Him, accept Him as your Saviour! Will you do it? It doesn't take but an instant to take Him and change everything for life. Will you do it? Don't say yes if you don't mean it!"

He was still, watching her, seeing the struggle in her face. Then after a long minute she looked up.

"Yes, I will!" she said steadily. "There isn't anything else for me."

"Then we'll tell Him so," said Link in a low voice.

He bowed his head, and there in the quiet of the big cinder parking lot, with the sound of trains coming and going, the voices of porters and passengers, he prayed:

"Dear Heavenly Father, go with this new child of Thine, and keep her safely on her way. Teach her what a Saviour Thou art, and will be to her day by day. Give her a vision of what Thou wilt do in her life. Give her the joy and peace of a born-again believer, and give her some definite work to do for Thee. Don't let her be lonely or sad as she journeys alone. Thou hast said, 'I will be with thee, I will hold thy right hand, and will strengthen thee!' Bless her and make her realize she is Thine own. We ask it in the name of Thy Son the Lord Jesus who died for her. Amen."

She lifted her face with a kind of strange mystical glory light in it, wistful, wondering, and there were tears on her cheeks, raining down, but she did not seem to know it.

They got out of the car hastily. They could hear a distant whistle of the oncoming train. Link got out the suitcases, and hurried her on to the station, his hand under her elbow to help her up the stairs. There was no time nor breath to talk, but they were up on the platform before the train actually pulled in and halted.

"I'll be sending you a Bible," said Link in a business-like tone, "one that will have footnotes that will help you to understand."

She brushed the tears back and flashed a childlike smile at him.

"Will you read it?" he asked. "Read it every day? You'll need it. It is the spiritual food to make you grow like Him."

"Oh yes, I'll read it," promised Minnie with a solemn accent to her voice as if she were registering a vow.

"And you must pray. Pray about everything, always. Tell your Lord just as you would tell a person, what you are feeling and thinking, how you have failed. Ask Him to show you."

"I will!" said the girl gravely.

The train had halted now, and the people had alighted. It was time for her to get on.

"You must give me your new address. I don't believe I've heard it," he said suddenly. "I will send the Bible at once."

She repeated the address, and he scribbled it down rapidly, then helped her up the steps and into the train, rushing to find her a place.

"Good-by," he said, "I hope you'll have a pleasant journey."

"I'll never forget what you've done for me," she said, and she smiled through her tears at him, the farewell of a little untaught, newly saved one! Then Link felt the train begin to move, and with another flashed smile he swung off to the platform, and the train flashed by him and went on its way.

Link went down to his car with a queer breathless feeling as if he had been on heavenly business, and wondered if he had said the right words.

"And that's that!" he said aloud to himself as he got into his car. Was it? Would she ever think of this again? Would he be seeing her in Heaven some day as a result of this most unexpected encounter?

Then before he went about his business of the day he stopped at a book store, and bought her a wonderful Bible done in soft dark blue leather, with gilt edges, large print and a concordance in the back. She might not need such a fine Bible, maybe would seldom read it, but at least she should have the chance of knowing the Word in as attractive a form as he knew how to give it. He hadn't sought this ministry, but since the Lord had given it to him he would do his part in the best way he knew how, and pray that the Holy Spirit would do the real work in Minnie's heart.

So, as he went on his way through the rest of the day he was now and then reminded to pray for Minnie Lazarelle, that she might become an obedient loving child of the Lord Jesus Christ.

6

PATRICIA NICHOLSON was going down to Texas to visit her fiancé's mother, and the group of bridesmaids at the Hollis home had decided to see her off on the noon train. At Mrs. Hollis's request they had stayed at her house overnight. Lou McHale was leaving for a new job she had just secured in a library out in Illinois. Her train went at eleven. So the girls were going to make a party of the two farewells. They sat around the Hollis breakfast table and planned it, and they tried to be cheerful and make her forget that her own girl was not there.

"The rest of you will come back here for lunch, won't you girls?" asked Mrs. Hollis in her tired pleasant voice.

"Oh, thank you, Mrs. Hollis," spoke up Carey. "I appreciate the invitation, but you've done enough for us, and besides I've promised Rae to go home with her for a few days."

"Well, you'll enjoy that I'm sure. But aren't there some of you other girls who would like to come back to lunch? You know you would all be welcome."

"Frannie is coming to me too," said Rae. "She promised last night. And I was hoping Sue and Betty could come too. How about it, girls? You are both foot-loose and fancy free for the week-end aren't you?"

"Why that's grand, Rae!" said Sue Richards delightedly. "Of course we'll come, won't we, Betty?"

"We certainly will," said Betty happily. "It's too much of a come-down from this wedding to go back to a boarding house with nothing to take my thoughts away from the desolation, till Monday morning when my school opens, and I have to be a sour young schoolma'am again. Mrs. Hollis, we feel that you're very kind, and it isn't that we're preferring one place above another you know, but really I think, as Carey says, that you've had enough of us, and we ought to get out at once and let you rest. So, unless there's some way we can help about putting the house to rights after all these festivities, I think we had better go with Rae."

So in a few minutes they all fluttered upstairs, packed their belongings rapidly, and started off to the station in the Hollis car, kissing their hostess tenderly, and begging her to let them know if there was anything they could do for her.

They turned their attention then to the two who were leaving them in a few minutes.

"I suppose this will be the beginning of festivities for Pat!" said Fran Ferrin. "Going to visit *his* relatives is a pretty serious sign, isn't it, Pat?"

There was always something comical about almost any remark Fran made. Her eyes seemed to be almost set in upside down with a sort of permanent twinkle.

"I suppose it is," said Patricia suddenly sobering. "But I give you my word, girls, if I don't like them I'm coming right back and stay an old maid all my life." She said it with a solemn air as if she meant it, but the girls twinkled at her and shouted with laughter.

"Oh, *yeah?*" said Fran.

After the travelers had gone on their way the girls went gaily off to get a bite of lunch, and while they were waiting for their orders to be brought Rae Silverthorn went to the telephone and called up her aunt's home.

"Is mother there, Aunt Fan?"

"No, Rae, she and your father drove home last night. She said she had some things to do early this morning and had to get home. She said she thought you were going to bring some girls, or a girl, home with you."

"Yes," said Rae looking troubled, "but I didn't want her to go home and hustle around getting ready. I told her I would do everything when I got there."

"Well, you know your mother likes to fuss around getting ready for company," soothed the aunt. "And by the way, Rae, your brother called up. He said he wanted to get in touch with you before you left town. He says he is bringing a couple of young men out with him. I think one was Paul Redfern, and the other he called Loo or Lute or something like that. He said if you had any messages or wanted him to do anything you were to call him here at four-thirty or five. He'll stop here on his way."

"Oh!" said Rae. "That will be lovely! Lute is great fun, and it's always nice to have Paul come. We'll get Steve and Curlin in and have a regular party. Aunt Fan, when Link comes, tell him I'm taking Carey and Fran, and Betty and Sue out with me. We're going on the bus in about an hour. No, Aunt Fan, sorry, I won't have time to run up to your house today, but I think I'll be in some day next week. I'll phone and let you know."

The girls were very enthusiastic about the evening when Rae got back to the table, and they ate their creamed oyster stew with great gusto and hurried to get their errands done. They were eager to get to the Silverthorns' and plan a good time for the evening.

There was an appetizing smell in the Silverthorn house when they reached there that almost made them hungry again. Mrs. Silverthorn was icing a great many little round cakes, some with chocolate frosting, and some with white frosting.

The girls followed their noses and swarmed out into the kitchen.

"M-m-m-mmmm!" they chanted in chorus, and gathered around the big marble-topped table where the cakes were parked in neat rows.

"May we have one?"

"May *we* have *one!*" said Mrs. Silverthorn smiling. "How many of you are there? Five? How many bites could you get out of one of my little cakes? Do you think one would go all the way around?" Then she laughed at their dismayed faces. "Help yourselves, girls. Take as many as you want. That's what I made them for!"

So in spite of the memory of creamed oysters, and French pastries in which they had indulged afterwards, they did well with the cakes. All but Rae. She was off to the telephone.

"Oh Mrs. Grant," she was saying, "are the boys there?"

"Why, Curlin is," said Mrs. Grant. "I'm not sure about Steve. Has Steve got back yet? It's Rae Silverthorn. She asked for you both. Come and talk to her."

"Hello, Curlin," said Rae eagerly. "Are you boys busy this evening? We're having an impromptu party and we want you two of course."

"That sounds good," said Curlin joyfully. "Sure, I'll come. I can't answer for Steve. I don't think he's got back from the city yet. Some girl got him in tow and I couldn't wait for him. I had something out here to do. Some work in my garden that was suffering for attention, but I presume Steve'll be home eventually."

"Oh!" said Rae with a light moan in her voice. "Aren't you sure he'll be home, Curl? We won't have the right number of boys unless he does. Who is the girl? Anybody I know? Could I telephone to him?"

There was a sudden pause on the wire, and then Curlin spoke in a tone of withdrawal.

"I don't think you could, McRae! I don't think you would know the girl!"

"Oh!" said Rae in a little tone of blankness, looking in the face the fact that she felt that Curlin didn't want to tell her who this questionable person was. And that was something new for a Grant to do. They had all been such intimates, the Grants and Silverthorns.

"Well, you see, she's one of these highfliers," explained Curlin in a tone that told her a great deal, and made her sure that Curlin thought he hadn't told her anything. "It wouldn't be so easy for Steve to get loose, you know. Steve is hard to pry loose from any girl who promises a good time."

"Oh!" said Rae in a little stricken tone again.

"I wish I'd made him come home with me!" said Curlin savagely. "I guess I could have. And it's dead sure he would want to be out here if he knew you were having a party. I'm sure your party would be a lot better for him than the one I'm afraid he's gone to."

There was another silence and then Rae offered a suggestion.

"Do you suppose he would come for Link, if Link went after him?"

"He might," said Curlin thoughtfully. "Is Link still in town?"

"I think he is," said Rae. "He's stopping by at Aunt

Fan's house to see if there is any message. What time is it? Not quite five? Tell me where Steve is, Curlin, and I'll see if I can catch Link before he leaves."

"Suppose you let me try to get Link," said Curlin. "I can make him understand better where to look for Steve. What's Aunt Fan's number? Boulevard, isn't it?"

"Yes, Boulevard 7535-J. Thank you so much. If Link hasn't been there yet, ask Aunt Fan to have him call you up at once when he comes."

She hung up with a troubled feeling that something might be wrong with Steve. Good old Steve, who was just like another brother. Of course he was full of fun, always up to some monkeyshine, but it had never before occurred to Rae that Steve could be in any danger. Yet Curlin had spoken just that way, as if he were worried about him!

She turned away thoughtfully, and stood by the telephone a moment trying to think it out, and then went back to the girls. But all through the gay afternoon, getting settled in the rooms upstairs, talking over the wedding, all the good times they had been having, and how hard it was going to be to have to count Sydney out from now on, Rae kept thinking about Steve. Oh, nothing must happen to Steve! He was one of themselves and he must not get away into a world where he didn't belong!

But presently the telephone rang and she hurried to answer it. It was Curlin again.

"Well, I got Link," he said, "and he's going to hunt him up. He thinks he knows where he may be, and he'll do his best. Besides Link has Paul and Luther with him, and that will have a lot of influence with Steve. He's crazy about Lute especially."

"Oh, I'm glad! Well, come over early, Curlin. We want you all in time for dinner. Mother has a big ham in the oven, and a great pan of rich baked beans with lots of 'lasses in their compound. The kind you like, you know. And there'll be bound to be some pies of some sort,—maybe à la mode! I don't know all the details yet. I've just got home, but mother's been home all day fixing up for such a possibility as tonight. Nothing fancy, just good old-fashioned things, you know, the way mother makes them."

"The best ever!" said Curlin. "I'll be there, lady, and I thank you kindly for the invitation."

It was more than an hour after that when the telephone rang again and this time it was Link.

"That you, Rae? Well, we're just starting. Be there in half an hour if traffic doesn't get in the way. I'm bringing Paul, Luther, and *Steve!*"

"Oh, did you find Steve?" she said breathlessly. And there was that in her brother's voice as he answered her that gave her pause for more thought.

"Yes, I found him!" he said gravely, "and I'm bringing him. It almost had to be at the point of a gun, but I've got him! Good-by. See you shortly!"

She took a deep breath as she hung up the receiver, and stood thoughtfully a moment, deciding that definitely something had to be done about Steve.

Then she had a flash of gratitude for her brother. How was it that Link always had to go after everybody, always be the goat, and carry burdens? Yet he was usually successful in such errands. But it wasn't fair to Link that his life should always have to be cluttered up with other people's mistakes and wrong doings, and laxities. She still felt a little sore over the fact that it had been Link who had had to take that outrageous Minnie away from the bride's dinner, and see that she would stay away. She wondered how he had done it. She mustn't forget to ask him after they were all gone. But then Link always had a way with him, and all his friends knew it. They had fallen into the habit of putting everything hard off onto Link! And how everybody loved him! Well, she was thankful anyway that Link had succeeded in bringing Steve with him. Frannie was awfully fond of Steve, and he seemed to enjoy her a lot. Perhaps that would help. Then she went back to the girls who were hurrying into festive array.

They were putting handsome permanents into lovely order, donning becoming sports garments, and all talking at once. Each one was planning some new game for the program of the evening.

Sue and Betty had got dressed in a hurry and retired to a corner where they had a lot of little boxes, a cake of paraffin, a box of wooden toothpicks, and a collection of bits of silk and calico and colored paper. From these each guest was to fashion little creatures in significant attire, representing famous personages. Then the rest were to guess their identity.

Even good-fashioned charades were coming in for a place on the program, and lists of adaptable words were selected by the leaders of two groups.

Yet through it all, while she provided pencils and paper and toothpicks and wax and scraps of silk for the workers, and answered questions, and answered the telephone, and ran errands for her mother, Rae Silverthorn was thinking about her old playmate Steve, and feeling a strange worry about him. Gay bright funny Steve. Was there going to be something the matter with Steve, some danger threatening his fine young life?

Rae had never thought much about Steve before, had just taken him for granted, like her brother Link, or like Curlin. They had all been children together. But now suddenly she found herself considering Steve. Thinking how his gold hair waved back from his forehead, one or two recalcitrant locks standing away from the rest and foaming out into stubborn curls. No matter how roughly Steve was dressed, for work or for play, he always looked well-groomed. But there had never been anything of the dandy about Steve. He was just a nice happy-go-lucky, easy-going, grinning boy. That was the way she had always thought of him. And now could it be possible there was some weakness behind all his gaiety, some tendency to be lazy? Was he just seeking a good time out of life?

It troubled Rae as she went about her preparations for the evening and she kept looking anxiously down the road. Surely, since Link had said he was bringing him back nothing could hinder him now! Yet, who was that girl who had put such a grim sound to Curlin's voice when he talked about her? Yes, and a grim sound in her brother's voice when he spoke of having found Steve? And where *had* he found him?

Then the girls wanted to go down to the piano and rehearse a song they planned to use in a charade that evening and as she was the only one who could play it for them without the music she had to go down and preside at the piano.

When Link drove in they all scattered out to give them welcome, and there was Steve swinging out of the front seat beside Link, grinning and waving his hands in the old way, twinkles in his eyes, good-natured and happy and handsome as always. She drew a sigh of relief and smiled.

But afterwards, when Steve came in and began to get around among them, waiting on everybody with his old graceful ease, taking extra chairs out of the girls' hands and carrying them to the dining room, he came to her and took a chair she was carrying, and suddenly she caught a whiff of his breath. Liquor! She had never got that odor on his breath before, and she gave him a quick searching look.

Did he understand? He backed off from her laughing and went out into the kitchen hastily declaring he wanted a drink of water.

Her heart gave a quick lurch and fear came into her eyes. Had Steve been drinking? Oh, was that what Curlin had been afraid of?

Then the gay company swarmed into the dining room, and there was no further time to think. They were sitting down at the long table, and it seemed all at once as if it were just the wedding party over again. For a little while Rae forgot her worries.

Now and again her eyes would glance down and sweep the friendly laughing faces, Steve with the rest, and a quiver of worry would go over her. Not Steve! Surely Steve wouldn't be caught by liquor. He had been brought up so strictly! He had been taught from babyhood, just as they all had! Was Steve easily led? She had never thought about that.

Her uneasiness stayed with her all the evening, while the singing and the games were going on. Now and then she would look at Steve. He seemed to be just as gay as usual. Had he always been like this, easily led? It didn't seem possible that if he had been doing something wrong he could go along with them all, his accustomed friends, and not have a bit of self-consciousness upon him. Yet he was smiling and singing, getting off wise cracks and making them all laugh. Ah! That was Steve's danger perhaps, that he was such good company, he was too popular. Had this just begun? Or had it been going on for some time? From Curlin's tone she felt that it was not a first offence with him, not with that certain girl anyway.

Now and then her glance would meet Curlin's eyes, and there was a sternness there that didn't seem like Curlin's usually genial expression. Curlin was worried.

But they were all having a delightful time. The roars of laughter that floated out the open windows made their neighbors smile and say, "What a good time they seem to be having over at Silverthorn's. I wonder why we never seem to be able to have such good times at our house. They are not worldly people, either. You sometimes think they are rather strait-laced, and have some fanatical ideas, but there's nothing long-faced about them, and the young people who go over there seem to enjoy themselves greatly."

Rae thrilled to the thought that everyone was happy. She glanced at the girls. Sue Richards and Betty Patterson were comparative strangers to the rest of the crowd. Sydney herself had met them rather recently. They were obviously accustomed to fashionable amusements, and yet they seemed to be enjoying themselves as much as the rest.

So she watched the first set of charades go off upstairs to prepare for their act which was next in order, and decided to forget her worries about Steve and just relax and have a good time herself.

Just then the telephone rang, and she slipped out into the back hall to answer it. As she took down the receiver she noticed that her mother was out in the kitchen preparing a midnight refreshment. The door was open and mother was cutting cake, and arranging glasses of fruit lemonade on the small trays. She registered the thought that she must go out and help her as soon as this call was finished. And then her clear voice spoke into the phone:

"Hello!"

There was a moment's confusion of sounds, different

voices, and then a blatant uncultured dominant voice asked:

"Is Steve Grant there? I wantta speak to him right away. Is he there?"

7

IT WAS a girl's voice, but not any girl McRae knew, and instantly she knew what girl it must be. What should she do? Call Steve and perhaps spoil all that Link had done in bringing him home? Break up the charade in which Steve was taking part, and perhaps finish the pleasant party? Precipitate trouble for the Grants?

But of course she had to call Steve. She couldn't just hang up. Besides, how did she know who this girl was and why she wanted Steve? It wasn't her business. Should she perhaps tell Curlin? Or Link? But Link didn't even know she knew about the girl, and Steve would certainly resent it if she drew Curlin into the matter. Anyway it wasn't her business. She had no right to meddle with Steve's phone calls.

All these thoughts went swiftly through her mind in that instant of pause before she answered pleasantly:

"Why—yes, Stephen Grant is here, but he's very much occupied just now. Could I ask him to call you a few minutes later?"

There was almost an electric hush over the wire for an instant while the unknown girl considered this quiet cultured girl's voice answering her, and then her voice boomed coarsely out again:

"Not on your life, you can't! I want him *now!* I've waited long enough for him and I'm not waiting another minute, see? He promised to come back here within two hours, and it's a lot more than that now. I'm not used to being left ta cool my heels an' wait for anybody, and what's more I won't stand for it. You tell him to come to the phone with a hustle or I'm off him for life. He'll be good and sorry if he keeps me waiting any longer! An' I don't mean mebbe!"

McRae took a quick deep breath to steady her voice before she answered, and the girl at the other end of the wire grew impatient!

"Hello! Hello! Where are you? Did you hear what I said?"

"Yes, I heard," said McRae quietly.

"Well then, why'n't you do something about it? Who are you, anyway? A servant? I'll certainly have you reported to the family if you don't get my message to Steve Grant immediately. Who are you?"

McRae drew her breath deep, and struggled with a sense of wry mirth.

"I am Miss Silverthorn," she said quietly, and there was something about the quality of her grave voice that created a sense of startled astonishment at the other end of the wire.

"Oh!" said the other girl, the least bit abashed at first; "Well, I wantta speak ta Steve Grant *at once!*" Her voice grew in arrogance and a kind of defiance with each word she spoke. "I won't stand any more nonsense! You can tell Steve if he don't come to the phone now he'll be good and sorry! There's plenty I can tell that he wouldn't want known. You tell him that!"

McRae didn't answer immediately, and then she fell into her natural cultured manner:

"I beg your pardon, who did you say you are?"

"I didn't say!" said the other girl. "He'll know who I am. But just in case, you might tell him it's Mysie wantsta talk to him!"

"I will see if Mr. Grant is at liberty to come," said McRae sweetly. She laid down the receiver quietly, and stood an instant trying to think what to do.

She could hear that the group who were to act the charade were coming down the stairs. A burst of laughter greeted them. They would likely be comically garbed. Fran Ferrin was in it and Fran had cute ideas.

As she turned away from the telephone and walked slowly toward the big living room where they were all gathered she heard Steve's voice, opening the dialogue. Well, she couldn't stop him in the middle of an act. It would be so awkward.

She went to the door and stood watching. It was a fantastic scene with improvised costumes and Steve was a dream in a long trailing evening gown composed of crimson curtains borrowed from mother's upstairs sitting room. He had managed a bare arm and back effect, and his head wore a contrivance composed of Sue Richards' yellow silk scarf, the fringe of which hung on his shoulders like a page boy's hair. He was standing there with a compact in his hand, holding up a tiny mirror and powdering his nose most affectedly. The audience was howling with mirth. She had left the door open to the back hall, and she wondered if the girl who called herself Mysie could hear. But she couldn't interrupt till the action was over.

There was quite a little dialogue between Steve and several others of the group, and then they trooped upstairs, while the audience debated loudly what the syllable could be. McRae wished she dared let this go till the word was finished. She tried to attract Curlin's attention, but he was talking to Carey Carewe, and she could not get his eye. Perhaps anyway that wasn't the right thing to do. Curlin would be terribly worried and perhaps overbearing with Steve, and Steve would be furious that she had told Curlin about the girl of course.

Desperately she turned and hurried up the stairs to find Steve, and suddenly met him halfway up, in the long black robe of a clergyman, the robe being her old black rubber rain cape. He was looking very solemn, and carrying a little black book, and he was followed by a wedding procession coming nimbly down after him. There was little chance of stopping him now.

But as he went by, she called softly: "Steve, Steve! The telephone!" But he only shook his head and went solemnly on, marching into the living room with stately movement that was unutterably comical. He was met with much laughter and applause, and though she really tried her best to follow him in and whisper to him to come at once, he went right on playing his part. It was so like Steve to go right on with what he was doing, regardless of anything else.

The act wasn't long of course, and he came rushing back to the stairs, and was about to stride up to get ready for the next act. But this time Rae caught him firmly by his sleeve.

"Steve!" she said urgently, "you simply must come! There's a—a—" she hesitated. She had been going to say "lady" but that didn't seem to fit the occasion, and she finished "girl." "She says her name is Mysie, and she is very much excited to speak to you at once. You'd better come right away. I'll explain to the rest."

Steve's eyes suddenly became blank and then he gave Rae a quick searching look as she uttered the name

"Mysie." A flood of crimson swept over his white sensitive skin. She could see he was wondering what she thought. Then suddenly he frowned.

"To heck with the girl!" he said furiously. "Tell her I'm busy!"

"But she says she is waiting for you somewhere, and she must speak to you at once."

"Well, she can't!" said Steve firmly. "Just tell her I can't come back and I can't speak to her at present!" Then he dashed up the stairs and there was nothing for McRae to do but go back to the telephone and give the message as coolly as was possible.

"I'm sorry!" she said and her voice was a bit haughty. "It is quite impossible for Mr. Grant to come at present. He asked me to tell you that he finds it impossible for him to return tonight. He sent word for you not to wait for him any longer."

"Can you tie that?" said the raucous voice of the infuriated girl. "Well, you can just go back and tell that insufferable boy that he will come, and right away too or I'll make him plenty sorry. Tell him he knows I have ways of making it very unpleasant for him, and I'm counting the minutes. See?"

McRae was quiet for a moment thinking, and then she said in her gentle voice,

"I'm sorry, but I couldn't give Mr. Grant a message like that. You'll have to excuse me. He said that he definitely cannot come at present."

Firmly she hung up the receiver and walked back to the living room.

She was not surprised to hear the telephone ringing furiously again in a minute or two, and it kept on ringing insistently and briskly, till suddenly she saw Link get up and hurry out to answer it.

She slipped through the door after him hoping to get

a chance to explain to him what was going on, but Fran Ferrin came rushing up to her.

"Give me a spoon and a glass, Rae. I need it for the next act," she whispered. "Quick! They're coming down!"

Rae turned and reached the required spoon and glass from the shelf beside her, and Fran rushed away.

As she turned back she heard her brother's voice.

"Yes? Who is this? Oh! You are the young woman who was at the night club this evening, aren't you? But you are mistaken in thinking that Mr. Grant promised to return to you this evening. I was with him and heard what he said. He told you in answer to your request that he would return if he found it was advisable to do so, but he was almost certain that it would not be possible. And now he has found that it is not advisable. You will have to excuse him. No, I do not think it will be possible for you to speak with him now. He is very much engaged at present. A friend of his? I must say you certainly don't sound like a very good friend. I should call that a threat of blackmail. I shouldn't advise you to try any such thing as that if I were you. You will find it might react upon you in a very unpleasant way. You will have to do what you will of course, but I warn you that Mr. Grant has a good many warm friends, and you wouldn't get very far in a thing like that. Oh! You would? Well, that being the case I don't think we care to hear anything more from you tonight. I shall tell Mr. Grant what you have said as soon as he is at liberty. He probably knows where to communicate with you if he has anything further to say. Good night!" Link hung up with a gray determined look around tired eyes, and a firm set of his lips. Poor Link! He was the goat again, thought McRae. First Minnie, and now Mysie. Why was it that Link always seemed to be the dependable one for all unpleasant matters that needed a wise head and a steady hand? And he always succeeded. That girl was not likely to call again. She must have met Link when he went after Steve, and she knew she couldn't very well bully him.

The sister drew a relieved sigh, slipped out through the kitchen to see if her mother needed her help, and found that mother had everything ready to serve as soon as the charade should be over. So she went back to the living room to enjoy the final scene and think over the turn of events.

It was Curlin who stepped up beside her a moment when the last act was over. They were all laughing and shouting the word they had guessed. He bent and said in a low whisper: "Was that somebody calling Steve on the phone?"

McRae lifted troubled eyes to his face and nodded.

"A girl?"

She nodded again.

"Did she give her name?"

"She called herself Mysie!" Her answers were low and troubled.

"That's the girl," said Curlin sadly. "Did you tell Steve?"

She nodded.

"What did he say?"

"He said 'To heck with the girl' and ran off upstairs. He wouldn't talk to her."

Curlin smiled grimly.

"I didn't think he had that much sense! But—after all, it was a cowardly thing to do. He ought to have gone and told her a few things and ended the matter. Now he'll have it to settle again."

Rae nodded somberly and considered the future, sighing softly.

"Has—this been going on for some time?" she asked drearily, "or has it just begun?"

Curlin frowned.

"Well, I'm not exactly sure. It isn't the first time, I'm sure of that, but how he got started on a number like that I can't figure out, with all the fine girls who have been around him all his life."

His glance fell admiringly on McRae's lovely face, bright, capable, intelligent, beautiful, her sweet eyes clouded now with anxiety.

"I suppose it's just the devil getting into girls," she said with a weary little sigh.

"I'm sorry you had to get in on this," said Curlin with a troubled look at her. "It doesn't seem as if anything like this ought ever to come near to you. It was my fault. I shouldn't have told you where he was. I ought to have known better. I was just sore at him or I wouldn't have let on that I knew where he was."

"Why should I be protected?" said McRae with a sad little smile. "I've got to grow up like other people and know things. I've got to be able to understand sin and temptations and help other brothers and sisters in temptation."

"No!" said Curlin sharply. "It doesn't seem right. It seems as if you ought to be having a lovely Eden to walk around in and enjoy, one where sin and sorrow could never enter."

"Well, I would probably listen to the first tempter who came around. Perhaps if Eve had seen somebody else in temptation she would have understood better, and wouldn't have eaten that apple. We have blamed Eve a lot, but wouldn't we likely have done just the same if we'd been in her place?"

"No!" said Curlin earnestly again, "I can't think you

would. You've always seemed like one of the angels to me."

"Thanks, Curly!" said McRae with a quick brightness in her eyes. "I'm not, of course, but I'll remember that you thought so, when I get utterly discouraged with myself. But, Curly, look at me sitting here discussing deep philosophical questions and there's poor mother out in the kitchen getting little trays ready to be brought in. Let's go and help her!" She started up with Curlin following, and soon they were hard at work.

8

THEY ARRIVED in the living room door with tempting trays in their hands, just as Paul Redfern was beginning to sing a solo, and they were all still, listening. Even Steve stopped joking with Fran Ferrin, and as his attention to the general fun relaxed, a troubled uneasy look passed over his face.

Rae and Curlin stood in the doorway with their trays, waiting till the song should be finished, and as they waited they looked around upon the faces of their friends. Rae wondered to herself if any of the rest of them had hidden worries, or temptations, or sins. If she knew as much about some of the others as she did about Steve tonight, would she be carrying them all on her heart? Did everybody need to be prayed for? Were there flaws and weaknesses in every one of them? Was there one anywhere who did not need help? Why, she wasn't even sure whether some of them were saved or not. There was Sue Richards. She had never seen her except for brief visits. Had she left a witness with her, so that if she never heard the truth of salvation from anyone else, she would not be without it? Oh! Life was a great responsibility, with so many unbelievers about on every side! Why, here she had been brought up next door to Steve all her life and it had never occurred to her before tonight that he might need help.

"Is Fran Ferrin a real Christian, do you think?" asked Curlin suddenly in a low voice. He had been watching Steve, and saw the girl turn a quick glance toward his brother. It was a warm, comical glance, as if she admired Steve and enjoyed his company, and there came at once the question of what kind of influence she was.

"I'm not sure," answered Rae. "I was wondering the same thing."

"Well, this song is about over, and I know Carey means to ask Paul to sing again if we give her half a chance. She's been watching him with all her eyes. She confided in me a while ago that she'd like to hear him and Link sing some weird modern thing together, so she'll probably try to bring it about if we let her."

"Let's go!" said Rae to Curlin, and they moved out into the midst of the group with their trays, which most effectually broke up any musical intentions any of them might have had.

Link was on duty at once when he saw his sister with the tray and afterwards she noticed that Link had waited upon Carey and come with his own plate to stand beside her chair, and finally to bring up another chair and sit there talking. And Carey seemed nothing loth.

She had a passing thought that Carey had looked at Paul Redfern, with much the same consideration that she was now giving Link. Or was there a trifle more warmth in her glance now than there had been for Paul? Paul was wealthy, influential, and very handsome. Well, Link was good looking too, of course.

Then she shrank away from all such thoughts. How

much nicer to be just casual and happy and not be digging into deeper feelings.

There was a dreamy sweet look in her eyes as they rested on her brother's earnest face. How he was watching Carey! How keenly he seemed to be studying her. Was Link beginning to care for Carey? What kind of a girl was Carey? A church member, yes. A charming, alert, attractive girl, but was she one who would stand by Link all through the days and be ready to go even to death beside him, if the way of the Lord seemed to call? That was what Link would need. Link wasn't just the ordinary Christian. Link even as a young boy had been deeply spiritual, full of life and joy with all his sincerity. Was it just because he was her brother that she felt he was so wonderful, or was he really rare? He was so quiet with it all, keeping himself so utterly in the background, that people might not recognize the beauty of his Christian faith. Did Carey? When she really stopped to think about it it did not seem as if there was anybody she knew who was good enough for Link. Dear old Link! Link should have a very wonderful girl.

Then they began to sing again.

And now Carey had her way and Link and Paul were singing a duet. Their voices blended beautifully, and it was hard to say which had the finer voice. Another and another was called for, and then someone insisted on a male quartette. But after one number Link suddenly called on Luther.

"Now, Link!" protested Luther. "I have a voice like a crosscut saw. You sing on. I'm just having the time of my life listening. I'm no primmydonner!"

But Link insisted.

"Yes, Lute! You've got to come. I want you to sing that hymn you sang down at the mission the other night.

Then we'll learn the chorus and sing it with you! Come on!"

"Mission? What mission?" asked Carey. "How did they get you to a mission, Lutie?"

"Oh, it's just a little dump where I teach Sundays and other times," answered Luther backwardly. "No, Link, I can't sing here. My voice is only fit for a little back alley mission!"

"Back alley missions are the hardest to reach, Lute, and you reached 'em! I heard you! Come on now, get up, old fellow. You sing the whole thing through first, and then Paul and Steve and Curlin and I will catch on to the chorus and come in on it the next time."

Luther came hesitantly forward and Carey looked dismayed.

"Have you got the music?" she asked. "I can't play just anything out of the blue without music."

"Oh, McRae can play it," said Luther unexpectedly. "I taught it to her one day not long ago."

So Carey slid from the piano bench. McRae took her place, touching a few chords quietly, and suddenly Luther's big sweet voice rang out clearly:

> "I was just a poor lost sinner,
> Till Jesus came my way.
> He smiled into my eyes and said,
> 'Come walk with me to-day!'
> A sinner! A poor lost sinner!
> Not fit to company
> With Jesus Christ, the sinless One,
> Nor walk with royalty.
> Me! A sinner! A poor lost sinner!
> He wore a diadem!
> I was not worthy e'en to touch
> His very garment's hem!

"I looked upon His loving smile,
His gracious hands outspread,
I saw my sinful worthless self
And sadly shook my head.
'I cannot walk with Thee,' I said,
'With sins upon my soul!'
But tenderly He told me then
That He would make me whole.
Me! A sinner! A poor lost sinner!
Condemned eternally!
He died upon the cross Himself
That He might set me free!

"Right joyously I came to Him
And took Him for my Lord.
He took my sin, He washed me white
With His own precious blood!
And some day He'll present me
To the presence of my King,
Without a spot or wrinkle
Or any sinful thing.
Me! A sinner! A poor lost sinner!
I'm telling you it's true!
He died upon the cross for me!
He's done the same for you!"

Luther Waite sang the simple words with such power that there were sudden tears in every eye, and when he finished there was an utter stillness. Till unexpectedly Curlin spoke.

"Waite! That's great!" he said with earnestness. "That's better than any sermon I ever heard. You make it real!"

This from Curlin meant a lot. There was another moment of silence, almost embarrassment on the part of some of the girls, and then Lincoln Silverthorn spoke, in a natural everyday voice:

"Well, fellows, shall we try it? I've scribbled off the words as he was singing. Suppose we come in on the chorus each time. Let Lute lead it. Raise your hand, Lute, when you want us to come in."

Then Luther started again, for all the world as if he were telling a story that was very real to him, and his voice had such power over them all that the others as they tuned in sang in that same telling way, telling a story that was real to them. If any one of the four voices was out of key, or rather out of sympathy with the sentiment of the song, it was Steve's smooth sweet tenor. He sang, and his voice blended with the others exquisitely, but there was somehow an alien touch to it, as if Steve was outside of the experience of which the song told.

Nevertheless, as the rehearsal went on even Steve caught the spirit of it, seemed a real part of the whole, and McRae watched him in wonder.

"Now," said Link when the song was finished, "I think that was fine! And perhaps I'd better tell you right now that you're all going to sing that in church tomorrow morning in my choir. Yes, you are!" he added as the quartette began to protest. "I haven't had time to get up new numbers this week, and you're going to help me out. That's the reason I asked Lute to sing. Now, will you try it again? I'll have some copies made by morning for you, but I guess we can rub along through a practice or two without more than one."

"Why, I'll make some copies for you now," offered Carey. "Isn't your typewriter here in the library? Where shall I find paper and carbon?"

"Right hand middle drawer of the desk," said Link, smiling his thanks. "Carbon in the bottom drawer. It's awfully kind of you, I'm sure!" And he flashed his gratitude in one of his charming smiles.

Then all business he turned back to his quartette and began directing. Link was a real musician, and he did his work well. It was the first time any of them but the Grants had seen this side of Link, and they were filled with wonder. So was Carey when she presently came back with five copies of the song.

They went to work in real earnest, and were all more than a little interested in the service in which the boys were to have a part on the morrow. All but Sue Richards who sighed to her roommate as she prepared for rest.

"Well, I suppose we're all slated for church tomorrow morning," she said dolorously. "I don't see what Link had to do that for! I thought of course he'd have us all out to the country club for golf!"

"Oh, my no!" said Betty Patterson. "Don't you know the Silverthorns better than that? They never play golf on Sunday!"

"They don't? Why? Are they so awfully religious?"

"Well, yes, they are," said Betty. "I've always heard that. Although they're such jolly good company that nobody seems to mind. And after all, you have a good time here, even if you do have to waste a little time Sundays going to church."

"Oh, yes. But how much nicer it would be if these Silverthorns weren't so awfully narrow. If they would just try to adjust their ideas to others' point of view it would be more comfortable all around."

"In other words if they wouldn't carry their religion all the way. If they would just compromise enough to be fashionable and take in the world to a certain extent you would like them better. But you don't have to come here if you don't like it, you know."

"Oh, I like it all right of course," said Sue. "Take

today. It was a real godsend, for I would have had an awfully dull time if I had had to go back and hang around till Monday."

"And yet you kick because you have to go to church for an hour or two! Of course you can always profess to have a sick headache and stay in bed till they get back if you feel that bad about it."

"Well, don't you hate it yourself? Come now! Tell the truth."

"No!" said Betty sharply. "I'm rather intrigued by it. In fact I'm really looking forward to it. I never heard a man sing a song like that. I'm convinced that Lute meant every word he sang. I never knew Luther Waite was like that, and I want to hear it again. If all professed Christians were like that I'm not sure but I'd be a Christian myself. I mean a real out and out one, not just merely a church member such as you and I are."

"Thanks awfully," said Sue, and she turned over on her pillow and closed her eyes. "I shouldn't care to be any out and outer than I am. I wouldn't want to get so narrow I couldn't be like the majority of decent people. I would hate to be peculiar."

"Well, I wouldn't. Not if there were something real behind it!" said Betty, and flouncing over set herself to slumber.

Over in the next room McRae and Carey were lying side by side talking of generalities at first, and then settling down to the surprises the evening had brought them, that is, some of the surprises. Carey didn't know them all of course. She hadn't heard a thing about Steve.

"I didn't know Luther Waite was like that, did you?" said Carey yawning sleepily. "I just thought he was a born comedian, didn't you?"

"Oh, no," said McRae. "He has been that way ever since he was saved. About two years ago or a little more perhaps. But he always was reserved in speaking of his innermost feelings. He doesn't talk about those things unless he feels someone can be helped by it. He shrinks awfully from talking about himself and his personal experiences.

"Well, it's a revelation to me," said Carey. "I thought he was just a nice boy having a good time. I never knew he had a serious thought."

"Oh, he's very serious," said McRae. "We see a good deal of him. Link and he are great friends, and it's wonderful how interested he is in that little mission of his. He's all wrapped up in it."

"Well, it's a new slant on him for me," said Carey. "I don't know that I'd want to go as far as he does. It might be awkward at times when one was in company where they weren't interested in such things. Although of course Luther didn't do much talking tonight, did he? He just sang it, but somehow he sang it as if he were preaching. As if he were telling just what he thought about such things. He really was very impressive. But I was wondering what others would think of his way of singing. Your brother Lincoln, and Paul Redfern are so much more sophisticated in their ways, aren't they? I couldn't quite imagine either of them working in a common mission. To tell you the truth I never like things to get too personal, too emotional, you know. That song was almost too emotional. It didn't seem the style of either your brother or Paul Redfern."

McRae laughed softly.

"You don't know my brother very well if you think that of him," she said happily. "I don't know so much about Paul, but I know Link would rather talk about the things of the Lord than anything else. You know it was he who suggested Luther's singing it."

"Yes, I know," said Carey thoughtfully, "and of

course it was a very lovely song. I'm really eager to hear it in the church. I would like to see the reaction of the people."

"I hope it will bring somebody to know the Lord," said McRae with soft eagerness, and then turned over to go to sleep. But Carey only said "Yes?" politely, as if she felt that the other girl had said something that wasn't exactly respectable.

But McRae, as she drifted off to sleep found herself disappointed in Carey. No, she just wasn't Link's type, well not yet, anyway. And then she was remembering the look in Curlin's eyes, the unusual tenderness of his voice when he told her that he had always felt that *she* should have an Eden to live in because she belonged in one. It gave her a special kind of a thrill to think of that, for Curlin had always been such a quiet practical fellow, and seldom spoke of things romantic. She had never known he felt that way about her. Of course he hadn't meant anything but pleasant brotherly affection, but it was nice to know he liked her, felt she was fitted to walk in an Eden. Then with a sweet smile on her lips and a prayer in her heart she drifted off to sleep.

9

IT WAS a lovely morning. Sue, who had wanted to play golf all Sunday morning, groaned to her friend Betty.

"Think what a day this would have been on the golf links! And I just know Link Silverthorn is a great player. I don't see why he had to have this religious complex. I wonder what made it? It isn't natural for a young man to be religious. It must be that mother of his."

"His father too," said Betty, arranging her topknot of curls engagingly. "Do you know, they have that quaint old-fashioned habit of having family worship? I suppose we'll experience it this morning. It's so embarrassing to kneel down when there are a lot of people around."

"Heavens!" said Sue. "Can't we sleep late and avoid it? I detest getting in on queer things like that. It seems awfully rude to me to have people force their religion on their guests."

"Don't be so silly!" said Betty. "Stay in bed if you like, but you miss a lot of fun. Besides, I'd say that would be fully as rude as having worship. After all they show us a good time, and if that's what they want let 'em have their prayers. I can stand them if they can. But if you expect to get down to breakfast you'd better arise, young woman. They have awfully good breakfasts here Sunday morning. I stayed here one week-end and I know. They had the most delicious cod fish cakes that I've ever tasted, crisp and brown and a cream gravy. They had hot muffins, too, that would melt in your mouth, and great luscious strawberries. I've never forgotten that breakfast. If I ever have a home of my own I'll learn how to make them all."

"Oh, stop! You make me hungry! Now I suppose I'll have to get up and take the day as it comes, prayers and church and all! And I had it all planned that I would coax Link to take me on a long walk and end up at the golf links. I would have done it too, if it hadn't been for that silly music he's planned!"

"Try and do it!" sneered Betty. "You don't know Link if you think you could get him into an act like that on Sunday. Link is heart and soul in that church of his and you couldn't pry him away from it."

"Oh, he's probably under his mother's thumb. But I'll bet I could lure him away if he hadn't fixed it all up to have the boys sing. Say, doesn't it surprise you that Steve Grant falls for that sort of thing?"

"Oh, well, he's got a mother likely, too," said Betty. "But all the same he gets out from under sometimes or I'll miss my guess. He isn't like that hard and fast Curlin. *He* never seems to see a girl."

"Only *one!*" said Sue significantly. "Did you notice how easily he drops into conversation every time McRae comes near him?"

"Oh, they've just lived next door to each other all their lives," said Betty indifferently. "Rae isn't interested in him. She couldn't be, with Paul Redfern around, I should think. Say does he watch her! Did you notice him? He's awfully well-bred of course but he didn't miss a trick Rae did."

"Well, he divided his looks with Carey Carewe. She certainly is a winner if there ever was one. The way she kept Paul Redfern and Link Silverthorn dancing attendance on her. She acted as if she were trying to make up her mind which one she'd take."

"I don't know Carey as well as the rest of the gang," said Betty. "Maybe she has a lad at home somewhere."

"Then why does she stick around here?" said Sue. "You're telling me she isn't out to get one of those two? In my opinion it's Link, the way she looked at him. You can generally tell by the eyes, and hers were simply languishing when she turned them on Link. But then of course I suppose Paul has the most money!"

"I don't think Carey would stop on that account," said Betty thoughtfully. "Carey has slews of money herself. Her grandmother's fortune was left to her."

"What luck!" said Sue. "But then people who have money can always do with a little more. I don't suppose Link has a cent to his name, has he? This place is comfortable and nice, but it's awfully old-fashioned."

"You can't tell anything by that," said Betty loftily. "This house is an ancestral place, over a hundred and fifty years old I think, or maybe more. The identical old farm house Mr. Silverthorn's ancestors lived in three generations or more. But Link is in business, you know. He has a very fine position, good salary and all that."

"Has he really? When I heard him talk last night I supposed at least he was going somewhere as a missionary. Africa or China, or some pestilential isle of the sea where they cook and eat their missionaries. Well, it's a hopeful sign if he can command a salary. I might even take him on myself."

"Try and do it!" laughed Betty. "Come! I hear them

going down to breakfast. Let's go!" and then the two girls in bright array joined the others on the stairs and went down to see what the day had in store for them.

There was nothing dismal in the atmosphere of the house that morning. The sun was shining brightly and there were many wide windows, for old as the house was the Silverthorns had managed to let in sunshine everywhere. More windows had been cut in the massive stone walls, and the sheer organdy curtains disguised none of the light. There was light and a gorgeous view on every hand. There were flowers everywhere, outside and in the house. The garden in full view from the dining room window was gay with daffodils and narcissus, bordered with scylla, blue as the heaven above them. There was a great bed of hyacinths of all colors, filling the air with sweetness, blue and purple and pink and white, and beyond them another bed with myriads of dazzling tulips, crimson and bronze and gold and white.

And in on the white damask of the breakfast table a crystal bowl with slender fluted rim bore white violets, a mass of them, bordered with purple ones. On the sideboard a taller bowl had masses of lilies of the valley, filling the air with their heavenly fragrance.

The house might be plain and old-fashioned, the family might have unpopular religious ideas, but the worldly guests could not but own that it was a sweet holy atmosphere into which they came as they entered that sunny dining room and took their seats. And even the most unsanctified hearts could not but feel the beauty of the thanks that Father Silverthorn gave in his gracious tender tone before they ate.

Some of the guests looked about in wonder, and felt somehow that they had entered a sacred place, only they called it to themselves "Fairyland," which perhaps from childhood had been their nearest idea of Heaven.

The family worship about which they had speculated, was held at the table, where the head of the house read the Bible. They all sang a verse of an old, well-known hymn, and then Mr. Silverthorn looked down the table to where Luther Waite sat beside Fran Ferrin and said:

"Luther, will you lead us in prayer this morning?"

The guests looked up, startled. Could this young man pray, as well as sing hymns? They had been used to hearing him tell funny stories, and give marvelous comedy sketches full of mimicry, but to have him asked to pray before them all was something unheard of, and they were sorry for him. If it had been Curlin, with his quiet ways, they would not have been surprised, or of course Link, for they sometimes spoke of him as "the deacon," half in fun. Or if it had been even Paul with his aristocratic bearing, his well-modulated tones, they would not have felt so sorry for him, for they would have expected any one of those to have carried off the occasion with credit. But Lute! They were almost shocked that Mr. Silverthorn had been rude enough to embarrass him that way. They looked to see him flush, and laugh and hesitate, but there was nothing of that about him as they shoved back their chairs, and knelt following the household's move.

Luther knelt and his voice was steady and clear as he began to pray. Oh, it was no unaccustomed prayer of a new petitioner. It was rather a happy child talking with his Father. And the words tumbled out impetuously, just as Luther talked. They heard themselves prayed for, not exactly by name, but as if each one was introduced to the Father, His attention called to them, for the day's mercies. And then the church service. How it came in for petition! The audience that would be shortly gathering was brought before the throne and entreated for. The two girls who had discussed the service and the proposed song, heard themselves brought to the attention of the Most High God, not by name of course, but they recognized themselves as their innermost thoughts were described, pardon was asked for them. Before that prayer was concluded their tears, astonished tears, were flowing down their faces.

Yet it was not a long prayer. A sentence or two to each thought. The language was very simple, like a child bringing a sheaf of petitions, including all who were dear, and all who were present. Bringing them all, down to the amen, with utter confidence that what was asked would be given. Those who listened looked about upon one another wondering if there were already a change brought about in themselves, and whether others could see it, such assurance he had brought to them that he would have the things for which he had asked.

When they arose from their knees some of the guests kept their glances down, and some drifted over to the window and remarked on the lovely flowers, and there were several minutes when the air was tense with stirred feelings.

Then suddenly Curlin appeared at the side door coming across the side yard from his own home.

"Time to start to Sunday School, boys!" he called. "Who's going? All of you?"

Some of the girls looked surprised. Here was a new consideration. One went to Sunday School! Did one *have* to go to Sunday School? One hadn't gone to Sunday School since he was a child in the primary class. Did one *have* to go?

Still, one went to week-ends with other people, and if so be that their hosts went to the country club for golf or a swim, or tennis, on Sunday morning, one went along of course even if just to be polite. And now if hosts and hostesses proposed Sunday School did one have to go along just to be polite? They looked around aghast, and hastened to find excuses, but suddenly Luther Waite spoke up in his quick humorous gay voice:

"Why, of course we're all going, Curly. Come, gals, go get your bonnets on and don't keep us waiting."

Suddenly, without any consultation with one another, they all hurried to get ready. And somehow they liked it. It was following the gang, and it was pleasant even if it was in the name of religion.

That Sunday School was a strange experience for those girls, and perhaps for Paul Redfern also. He belonged to a rich and modern church in the city, and it was safe to say he hadn't been to Sunday School since his childhood. But he was interested. It was all new to him, this vital joy and interest in things spiritual. Theoretically he approved of it, and it took a hold on him. That Sunday School was different from any he had ever heard of before. It was real Bible study. He and Luther had gone into Link's class of young men, a large class of fine young fellows. They weren't all members of the country club. Some of them were students in the local college, some of them were workers in the mills round about. Some of them were mechanics in automobile plants, some were salesmen, and some were men from filling stations and other local places where they were earning their living, but they were all interested in studying that Bible lesson. And Paul was amazed how much Link got out of just common statements in the chapter they were studying. How he directed them to other chapters and other books of the Word. How much he seemed to know!

The church service that followed that study hour was full of vital meaning. A sermon that was short and went to the hearts of the hearers; music which was tender and appropriate to the theme of the day; and then that song at the close of the sermon, with Luther Waite standing up there in the choir, a little apart from the other four who grouped behind him. It stirred them all as much as they had ever been stirred by music or play or any best seller they had ever read.

They walked home from church in the bright sunlight, more quietly than was their wont, and they went through the rest of the happy day with a kind of awe upon them.

"Well, it's been an awfully queer day," said Sue that night when they were preparing for rest, "but I don't feel sorry I went through with it. I'll never forget it of course. Why, sometimes it almost made me feel as if I would like to be religious myself. I never will of course. But it made me sort of restless inside. I never could be religious. You couldn't yourself, Betty. You know you couldn't."

"I guess I could as well as anybody," snapped Betty. "That is if I wanted to bad enough."

"I doubt it," said Sue. "You'd go off to a dance some night and that would be the end of it."

"What's wrong with dancing?" said Betty.

"Well, they don't do it," said Sue. "I was asking Rae last night if it was very gay here and they had many dances through the winter, and she said she guessed they did. That dances weren't in her line. She didn't say that her religion forbade it or anything, but I gathered that her church was against it or something. I didn't want to call down any more religion than I'd had so I didn't ask her, but she did tell me out and out that she didn't go. That's the Silverthorns for you. They put their religion first, no matter what!"

"Well, I suppose that's the way it should be if religion is worth anything."

"Yes? Well, you never could do that!"

"Yes, I could if I wanted to bad enough!"

"But you never *would* want to, you know. You just *couldn't* want to. You've always had too good a time. You couldn't settle down to a solemn staid life with no fun in it. You couldn't stand it not to have a good time."

"I don't see but the Silverthorns have a pretty good time out of life. I think they seem happier than any people I know. I'm not sure but I'll try it myself."

"Oh, you wouldn't," said Sue yawning sleepily. "I'll bet on you to stay the way you are the rest of your time down here."

"And then what?" asked Betty, after a significant pause. But Sue didn't answer, and Betty lay there thinking the day over and asking herself the question, "And then what?"

10

MINNIE LAZARELLE dropped down in the seat of the Pullman and watched eagerly out of the window as the train slid slowly out of the station, to catch a glimpse of Lincoln Silverthorn, and get the grave courteous bow he gave her in farewell.

The girl pressed closer to the windowpane and strained her eyes for the last glimpse as she smiled a wistful serious smile at him in acknowledgment of the strange part he had played in her life for the last two days. He was actually the first young man who had ever talked with her seriously, or taken her as if she were a human being with possibilities like other girls. The rest of the young men had always treated her as if she were a gaudy toy flung in their way for a brief space. They had seemed to talk to her with only half their minds, just passing the time till they could find somebody more interesting.

So she looked back at him as he replaced his hat on his head and began to walk along with the train toward the stairs that led to the floor above. She wanted to impress him upon her memory as something she must never forget. Every line of his fine straight form, every motion, every turn of his head, the light in his eyes, even the tones of his voice as he had told her ugly truths about herself. He seemed almost like a god to this girl who had been so universally disliked.

Other people, both girls and men, had treated her like an ugly joke. They had half sneered, half laughed. But this young man had come straight to the point and told her what she was. Told her bare truths that she had only dimly suspected were so, truths she had kept well hidden even from herself, lest they should come out in the open some day and prove frightening. Link Silverthorn had torn away the covering and made her see herself. And now this morning he had told her a way to cure all this silly soul-sickness of which he had convinced her.

But there wasn't any foolishness about her feeling for Link. It was all too terrible and real for that! Too sudden and convicting. His face had been like the face of God, as she imagined it would be if God looked at her, his voice like God's voice, condemnatory. Yet she did not want to forget how he looked. For with the condemnation he had also given her a gleam of hope, and she clutched at that in her heart. She must not forget it and let it pass into oblivion, for if she did, the horrible reality of her unloved life would return, and she would be just as she had always been, an unloved child in the midst of a world that did not want her, did not like her. And she could not bear that!

She shuddered as she settled herself in the seat a bit more comfortably. She *could not stand* that!

The train had slid out from the tunnel and was hurrying into the outskirts of the great city now. Morning was on the way and all the busy streets were bathed in sunlight. Towers and steeples, great buildings reaching toward the bright sky, filled with gleaming windows, the sunlight glancing from them blindingly. Now and then there were crowded cross streets with busy people hurrying along. She had a hungry sense of wishing she were one of them out there in the brightness, going along to some real interest in life, and not merely returning to a life she hated. It was what she had tried to run away from when she came up to this wedding that didn't want her. Could she ever be like other people? Beloved, wanted? Link had implied that she could and she clung to that thought, deciding that she would do her utmost to attain that end.

The golden morning-crowned city was slipping past her now, it was almost gone. She gave a fleeting thought to the way it had looked a couple of days ago when she had arrived so hopefully, telling herself that she was going to have a wonderful experience now, all on her own, going about with these wedding people. She had been so eager and anxious lest those cousins of hers would try to frustrate her plans! And they had! *How* they had frustrated her.

Her mind went back to the hour when she had arrived in the Hollis house and found conditions so favorable, all the family away for the moment, giving her a chance to get established before they came back and spoiled her plans.

And then McRae Silverthorn had been in the coveted room she had hoped to get before anybody else came! Always McRae had been the favorite one! She had been frightfully jealous of McRae. Yet she had acknowledged to herself that she would like to be like her. Everybody loved McRae, and she wasn't in the least disagreeable. Only, well, she had been cute, taking her dress and running away! Minnie had thought that dress was wonderful. Not her style exactly, because from babyhood she had been trained to the showy, tawdry style, instead of the dignified and tailored. But that dress had been wonderful. She just knew when she first glimpsed it how she would look in it herself. She had a gripping desire to try that style and see if it would suit her. The dress that Link Silverthorn had selected and bought for his sister! Think of having a brother who would use his own money to buy a lovely dress like that for his sister!

And she couldn't blame McRae for running away with it. Of course, though, she hadn't believed that it was true when McRae told her it was a present from her brother. It sounded fantastic. But she hadn't really known much about Link then. She had only seen him once or twice very briefly, and never to talk to. But now she had talked with him. He had told her she was a sinner, and thinking of him in the light of the things he had said to her, an almost utter stranger, she could see that it was probably true that he had selected such a dress.

Sometime, after she had been trying the new way that Link had suggested for long enough to have it make some difference—if it really did work—she would buy herself a dress something like that one of Rae's and go back to their city, and maybe call on them, and let them see her in a new light. Would that ever be possible?

The conductor came around then for the tickets, and diverted her thought for a little while, but later she went back to it and enshrined it in her heart like a beautiful goal toward which she meant to press for accomplishment. If she could only go back there and surprise them, have them get to know a new girl in her place, a new Minnie Lazarelle!

How she hated that name! How she wished she had a new name!

Well, Minnie wasn't her real name anyway. Why did she use it?

Her own name was like her grandmother's, her

father's mother, Erminie Lazarelle. Why didn't she go back to it?

How did it ever happen that she was called Minnie? Her mind went back over the vague years when she was a child.

Her mother had died when she was only a small mite, but she dimly remembered that she always called her Erminie. It was her stepmother who had started the name Minnie.

The stepmother had entered her life after an interval of drab years in a nursery school, during which she had seen very little of her father, and nothing of any other relatives.

The stepmother had been a showy beauty, with a prettily empty face and lazy ways. She had resented the presence of the child and prolonged the days of boarding schools as much as possible, although the girl had always suspected that the reason for her father's remarriage had been an uneasy mind about the child who was his responsibility.

She remembered her father as a gravely gay man of alternate moods, whose one reverence was for his dead wife. He had made only this one gesture of responsibility toward the child she had left to his care.

She was not quite sure what her father's business was, something connected with oil, perhaps, or gold, and western lands. She never had thought about it seriously. It was spoken of as just "business," and no one ever thought any more about it. There had always been plenty of money, spent in a harum scarum way, never a real need for anything, and no sense of responsibility in connection with finances whatever. The advent of the stepmother had not made any improvement. She was a spender, not for the home and family, but for herself. She collected a handsome wardrobe with no lack of furs and jewels and imported garments.

And one day she had remarked impatiently:

"Heck! I can't be bothered thinking up that queer name of yours every time I want to speak to you. I'm going to call you Minnie after this!" And call she did, often shortening it to Min.

The girl hadn't thought much about it in her younger years until it finally became fixed upon her. She had idly suffered it as she grew up, realizing that it had the ugly carelessness of the smart patter of the day, and she let it go at that.

But now it suddenly stood out before her as something that she loathed, something she would like to get rid of, along with the whole character of her unloved life. Though of course there was no likelihood she could ever get rid of it. People who knew her at all would always call her "Min." It was something one could never get rid of, a name. One was almost born with a name.

Still, Link Silverthorn had made it very plain that people didn't have to stay the way they were born. They might be born again! He had said that those few words she had said, accepting what the great God had done for her, had made her what he called a "born-again" one, and if she was born again why not adopt a new name? Especially when it was a name which was rightfully hers?

She decided that when she got home she would tell her stepmother and everyone else, that her name was now Erminie, and she wouldn't pay any attention to anybody who called her Minnie. They might not like it, but she didn't like the name they had given her and she wouldn't have it any longer.

As the day wore on and she continued to sit and stare out the window, more and more the things that Link had said to her came back to her consciousness, and phrases of the subject became plain to her little by little that she had not taken in when they were spoken. "New creature in Christ Jesus." That was one phrase that he had used. Suppose she just went on that supposition, that she was a new creature? Then she wouldn't have to go on being burdened with a personality that hampered her. A personality that she was ashamed of, that she was continually trying to make smarter and more up to date. Of course this new personality wouldn't be up to date. It was old-fashioned, and she had always despised being old-fashioned. But then it hadn't got her anywhere to be smart. Perhaps it was just as well to be out of date. Anyway people might not notice her so much.

It was well that the new-born child of God had ample opportunity to look herself in the face, and begin to see herself as she really was, begin to count her former behavior as sinful. Perhaps God Himself spoke to her as she rode away back into a life she hated, to begin anew. It was a kind of clearing house time for her soul, as if God were taking stock of her, and showing her what had cluttered up her life, spoiled it, and kept Him out of it. A time when the great God came into her consciousness, as the only One who could possibly care for her, or help her, or make her different.

So, for the best part of two days she went on companying with God, getting to know by a kind of inward experience that there was a God, and that He was willing to become real in her life.

The third morning when she woke it came to her that she was almost at her destination. The fact appeared grimly out of oblivion when she opened her eyes and realized that before night she would be back in the ugly house from which she had fled only last week in a vain attempt to get out on her own and have a good time. And now what was she coming back to?

Nothing pleasant, that was sure. She'd got to discover a new way of life under very unpleasant conditions, and she didn't relish the thought of it. She had thought that the way was to run away from it, but it seemed that hadn't worked. She had to begin at the bottom and work up.

Everything looked just as it had when she went away. The house was ugly and ornate. She would never have picked it out, but her stepmother liked ornate things.

She ran up the steps drawing a deep breath to meet whatever was waiting for her, and as she opened the door she heard a dreary wail. A little stepbrother in some sort of trouble. And then an angry snarling voice from a larger stepsister. It might have been the very day she left, from the sounds. Then there came a resounding slap, and a louder wail increasing into a roar of fury.

"Now you stop that, you old devil-cat you! I'll write a letter and tell my daddy about you! I'll go tell a p'liceman you stole my choc'late candy an' et it up yourse'f. You're a mean old devil-cat you!" That was Billy, aged three.

Erminie had a passing wonder as to what Link would think of a little boy talking about the devil that way. A lovely home to arrive in!

"It wasn't your candy!" burst forth the angry voice of the sister aged four. "It belonged ta Mom an' I'm gonta tell her on you, so I am!"

That was Blossom. Her mouth was still full of the stolen sweetmeat.

"I don't care how much ya tell! Yer a devil-cat too, that's what ya are!" The remark was climaxed with a louder roar.

Then came the voice of the sister aged seven storming down the stairs. "Hey, you kids, shut up! Mom says if ya don't shut up she'll come down here an' skin ya alive."

Erminie drew a sick tired breath and shuddered. It was awful getting back into this again. Mariana the seven year old had left the door open and she could see the three angry children, fighting and snarling and roaring at each other, slapping miscellaneously. Billy was on his feet suddenly, kicking right and left at his sister's shins, and the screams of the girls added to the general melee. It was from continual scenes just such as this that their older sister had fled, and now here she was in the thick of it again!

Weak with fury at it all she stepped quickly to the door and was about to administer some of her old-time vengeful punishment, when suddenly it came to her that she was born again, and it gave her a strange feeling as if she had suddenly died and was no longer under the laws of this earth, as if her body was dead, and it was only her spirit that had come back here to her father's house, and her young stepbrothers and sisters. It gave her pause. What did a born-again one do now? Surely she was meant to do something about these little brats of children. Their mother ought to do it of course, but Erminie knew by experience that she would never lift her finger to the task if there was anyone else by to send after them. Their mother was probably at this minute deep in the mysteries of some murder or love story, a big box of sweets by her side and a cocktail near at hand. That was the woman her misguided father had married to look after her in her youth. How she loathed it all! Could anyone in his senses expect a newly born-again soul to go into a house like that and live herself, let alone trying to bring order out of confusion? Yet, if she was really born again, and was a child of God, as Link had assured her she would be if she accepted what Christ had done for her, then God likely expected her to do something about it. Maybe that was why He had made it so plain to her that there was only one thing she could do, and that was to go back home.

She stood for an instant in the doorway looking at them until they became aware of an alien presence and suddenly ceased their rollings and tumblings and strikings and screamings and stared at her wide-eyed, as if she were a disembodied spirit in their midst.

"Min's here!" Blossom gasped, a new kind of horror in her voice. It was plain they had felt free from interference before they saw her.

Their faces were smeared with chocolate from brow to chin and there was chocolate in their hair and on their dirty hands, to say nothing of the marks of chocolate down the front of their garments.

She took a deep breath and then she went forward and grasped the little boy firmly by one writhing wriggling arm, which instantly became as slippery as an eel. Then she took one step and caught Blossom by her thin little shoulder firmly. "Come into the kitchen!" she said in a low determined voice. "Mariana, get me a wash rag, quick."

"I don't know where thur is any wash rag," said Mariana with a toss of her head. "Find yer own wash rag!" said the seven year old airily, her chin lifted defiantly.

Erminie had her hands full for the moment, because Mariana's reply served to build up the morale of the other two young rebels and they began to pull away from Erminie and then to kick her with all their young might.

Her answer to that was to sweep Billy into the broom closet and snap the catch on the door. Then with Billy imprisoned and howling roundly, battering on the closet door with the dust pan and keeping up a terrible hullabaloo, Erminie addressed herself to Blossom. Still keeping a firm hold on the little girl's arm she seized the doubtful looking roller towel, held it under the cold water spigot, and then suddenly surprised the howling Blossom by dashing it full in her face. As the howl subsided to a frantic splutter, and gurgle, and gasp, she firmly but gently rubbed the hot angry little face till all the chocolate smears disappeared, and finally wiped her face dry and set her up on a chair, quivering and subdued. Then she went to the broom closet to get her other victim.

She opened the door quite unexpectedly to Billy, who was preparing for another onslaught on the door with the dustpan for a weapon. Billy fell forward into her arms, silenced for the moment, and thoroughly frightened.

She gave him no time however, but applied cold water freely to his streaked face. He uttered one terrific scream, got a mouth full of cold water, and emerged choking and spluttering a moment later just as the stepmother opened the kitchen door, and stood there with displeasure written over her face, surveying the scene. Her look gradually changed from the fury of a lazy woman to cold disapproval over a hated stepdaughter that she thought she had got rid of for awhile.

"Oh! So it's you, is it? I wondered! What in the world are you doing here? Making trouble as usual, I see! What did you come back for?"

Erminie shut close her lips on the accustomed angry retort and went on wiping the little red snorting face of the baby for almost a full minute. Then she said:

"I thought perhaps this was the place I ought to be, and it certainly looked that way when I came in."

Mrs. Lazarelle flashed her eyes furiously.

"Well, you can stop hurting the child now, and since you're here you might as well go to work. That lazy girl

I hired has left in a huff, and the house is a mess. Go change your fancy clothes and do something about it, won't you? I've got one of my terrific headaches and I can't be bothered!" and she turned and dragged herself up the stairs and back to her movie magazine and her depleted box of chocolates, where Mariana had been improving the time getting her share.

Thus Erminie Lazarelle entered upon her new life as a child of God, without the faintest idea what to do next.

PAUL REDFERN'S family came home a few weeks after the houseparty at Silverthorns, but by the time they arrived Paul had made himself very much at home in the Silverthorn house. He seemed to be very fond of McRae.

Sometimes the Grant boys were there in the evening, but more and more Curlin had business that either kept him away from their festivities, or brought him late after a busy evening. And Steve was often absent also. McRae wondered about this, wondered if the girl Mysie was still alluring Steve. But she had no opportunity to ask Curlin about it. Paul was almost always on hand when Curlin came over for a few minutes, and she couldn't of course speak about that girl before Paul. Still she was often troubled about the grave seriousness of Curlin's face.

And then one evening she decided to do something about it in spite of everything, so she followed Curlin to the door as he left, calling out, "Wait, Curlin, I want to ask you something!" and hurried out to the porch, where he stood with one foot down on the second step.

"Curlin, listen, I hate to speak about it in a hurry this

way, but is Steve all right? Has that girl made any more trouble?"

Curlin's face had brightened when she called him, but when she spoke the gloom returned.

"Oh, *Steve!*" he said, and drew a deep sigh, looking up at her keenly. "Why—yes, I believe he's snapped out of that now. At least I think he has. He's been pretty busy. He has a job in sight and that seems to steady him a little. I hope he'll get wise to himself and be worth something after a while. It's awfully kind of you to ask."

There was a formality about Curlin's manner that puzzled McRae. They had been intimates so many years that it seemed strange for him suddenly to get dignified with her.

"Kind?" she said, with a worried little frown. "What do you mean, *kind?* That's a queer word for you to use. Steve has always been one of us and I couldn't bear to think he was getting into anything that was going to harm him."

"No, of course not," said Curlin embarrassedly. "But I think you can rest assured he is okay! I'm keeping tab on him pretty closely, and I think he's cut out that girl! But I think he misses you a lot, McRae. He said the other night he didn't see much of this family any more. He's always kind of idolized you, McRae, you know that. And he says you're always busy when he gets home."

"Oh, but I'm never too busy for you folks!" said McRae with a dazzling smile. "You know Link and I would always rather be with you and Steve than anybody else?"

"Oh, *yes?*" said Curlin with a rising inflection and that aloof, diffident expression he had been wearing lately. "Well, that's nice. But you know you've had a lot of guests lately."

"Oh!" said McRae with a puzzled frown. "Why, I thought you liked Paul."

"Oh, sure, I like him fine!" said Curlin. "I think he's great! But somehow it's not just us any more the way it used to be, you know. I think Steve feels that. Oh, of course he likes Paul, too, and Carey. Steve falls for any girl right off the bat. But still, it isn't just the same you know, McRae."

McRae gave him a sudden, startled look.

"Don't you like Carey, Curlin? Is that what's the matter? Or doesn't Steve like her?"

"Oh, sure, we both like her all right. I guess Link likes her a lot too, doesn't he? Only somehow we are sort of out of things. Paul comes along with his limousine, and wants you in the front seat with him, and Link and Carey pile in behind, and if Steve and I go it just breaks up the game. Don't be silly, McRae! It's just life, that's all. We're perfectly good friends of course, and ready to help in any free-for-all where more are required, so don't you worry about us. And as for Steve, I think he's coming around all right, so you don't need to worry about that any more either. But say, McRae, I've got to hurry. I've got a little new calf that needs to be fed. Good night! Don't you think a thing about it all any more. Just go ahead and have a happy time! So long!" And he was gone!

McRae stood for a moment or two on the porch alone watching Curlin's long legs stride across lots toward the old Grant barn, sudden tears smarting to her eyes, her hair blowing wildly about her face, a strange goneness coming over her. Was it in her heart or her stomach? And what made it? Curlin really hadn't said anything disturbing. It was just his attitude, his whole make-up, tone of voice, and aloofness. It wasn't like Curlin.

Was it Steve after all, in spite of what Curlin had said? Was he worried about Steve and didn't want her to know it?

She watched him disappear across the grayness of the pasture lot, his tall figure quickly growing into a dim shadow, and then one with the blackness. She sighed as she turned back toward the lighted door, with trouble in her eyes. It wasn't in the least like Curlin to act this way. Something surely was wrong.

But now she saw that Paul Redfern was coming out, and Carey trailing him.

"Where in the world are you, McRae?" called Paul. "Come on in and play for us. Link and I want to sing that trio Carey brought out, and she can't play it and sing too."

McRae drew a deep breath and snapped back into the picture.

"All right," she said pleasantly, with her mind still on the quality of Curlin's tone when he had said good-bye, "but I think Carey can play as well as I can, and better, for she knows it. However, here goes!" and she sat down at the piano and slid her fingers into the chords.

And out in the dark pasture across the meadow Curlin slackened his steps, and turning stood and watched the house hungrily. He saw Paul come to the door with the bright hall light back of him, saw Rae Silverthorn turn at his call and walk side by side with him into the house. He drew a deep breath of a sigh and went slowly on. What did it all mean anyway, this life? Must one always give up the things that were dear in order that someone who seemed to have everything worth while should have one more? Almost since babyhood he had grown used to having to give up things for Steve. His mother had so ordered it when he was small. She wanted to teach him to be a man and a gentleman, an unselfish one.

But the habit had grown with the years, and he had somehow come to feel that if there was anything that Steve very much desired he, Curlin, must not wish for it himself. Steve must have it if he wanted it.

And now as he plodded slowly across the wetness of the dark pasture toward the little new calf that was not doing so well, he began wondering about Steve.

For long years as they were growing up, it had been Steve who had trailed along with McRae when he and Link went anywhere. He had grown up feeling that McRae was Steve's companion.

Had it been possible that his care in always leaving McRae to his brother's escort had helped to spoil Steve? Had made him feel that everything would always be easy for him? That others would step aside and let him gather all the brightness of life for his own—if he wanted it? Had it made McRae too cheap in Steve's eyes, so that he thought he could stray away and take up with another girl when the fancy seized him? Had he been to blame for his brother's irresponsible behavior?

And now was McRae having to suffer for it? Could it be that McRae was in love with Steve, and that that was the explanation of her anxiety just now over Steve? Was she breaking her heart about Steve's disloyalty to her?

But no, that could not be, for there had never been any direct attention on the part of Steve, more than a playmate and childhood's companion might have given. Of course Steve was good looking. Curlin had always felt that his brother looked like a young god. And all girls fell for him everywhere.

But if she were breaking her heart over Steve that would not explain the way McRae had been in the constant company of Paul Redfern the last few weeks. If she was so much troubled about Steve, why did she go constantly with Paul?

Of course Link had been pretty thick with Paul lately and certainly Paul had acted as if he admired McRae very much. One could see that by the way he looked at her. Curlin could remember Paul watching her at Sydney's wedding supper. And yet, sometimes he had seen Paul look that same way at Carey, just occasionally.

He ground his teeth in the darkness, as he swung into the barnyard, and went toward the quarters of the calf. If anybody dared to play fast and loose with McRae they would have him to reckon with, he vowed to himself. He didn't know what he would do, or what right he would have to do it, but no one should get away with hurting McRae, even if it was his own brother Steve!

Meantime the song was going on over across the road, and Link Silverthorn standing at the right, watching Carey Carewe carefully, studied her as she opened her pretty coral lips and let forth an exquisite volume of sound, blending it perfectly with Paul's rich baritone.

There had been times when Link had admired Carey very much indeed. Times when he felt that she was lovely in every womanly sense, and times also when he felt most certainly that she was deeply interested in himself. In fact he had been pretty sure for some weeks now that if he wanted Carey he could have her, even against all competitors.

But then there had been other times when he hadn't been quite so sure, either of Carey or himself.

There for instance was the evening he had taken her to hear that wonderful Bible teacher from England whose address had thrilled him with a sense of the nearness of his Christ, and whose scholarly, but simple way of stating facts had seemed to lift him nearer to heaven. But Carey had only yawned afterwards and asked him on the way home if he didn't think the poor man was awfully dull. What did people see in him to rave about?

Still, of course, everybody couldn't like the same speakers. He couldn't expect to find a girl whose tastes would be identical with his own, not in every little thing. But he felt he must go cautiously. Carey was attractive. He could easily grow fond of her. She had really lovely eyes, great blue ones, and a smile like a rosebud. She didn't wear too much make-up like some of the other girls. He wished she didn't wear any. He didn't like it. But of course that was a small matter, and in things like that a man could hope to influence a girl, if she really cared for him. And Carey seemed really to like him. She was always ready to go with him in preference to other invitations he had heard her receive.

But she certainly had a charming way with her. Perhaps if she had been brought up differently, more as he and his sister had been, he would not feel so doubtful about her. What for instance had she meant last Saturday night when he had told her he promised Luther Waite to go to his mission with him and sing? She had taken on a contemptuous scornful expression and said: "Oh, do you *have* to? Tell him you've promised to go with me to the Flower Show. Let Lutie cultivate the slums if he wants to. It's more in his line. For Heaven's sake don't you waste your time singing for common people who would much rather hear radio jazz. You're too fine for that sort of thing, Link!"

She had looked straight into his eyes, and her look had said as plainly as words could have done that she liked him and wanted him to stay with her. It also had held contempt for the mission, and Link was too much interested himself in the work that Luther was doing, to let her speak of it in that scornful way. He had tried to argue the matter with her, telling her that the work was

God's work, and that there were souls in those meetings that might be reached by a gospel song who might not be saved any other way. But Carey had smiled with that unbelieving shrug she had, the lifting of her delicate eyebrows, the amused look on her perfect lips, and laughingly answered:

"Don't kid yourself, laddie. You aren't so important as all that. God can get those poor creatures saved if He wants to without your assistance. Besides, if He needs you He certainly has cut you out with a view to a better line of converts than those to be found in Lutie's slum mission. Come on, Link, I really want you to take me to the Flower Show. Some of my friends from New England are going to be there tonight and I promised to introduce you to them."

Link had not gone to the Flower Show. He had shaken his head gravely and told her he had promised to sing, and Carey, chagrined over her inability to persuade him, had pressed Paul into service, and tried to make McRae go too. McRae of course had been firm, having promised Lutie to play for him, so Carey had walked off with Paul, half triumphant, half depressed. She wasn't getting very far in trying to reform Link, and she couldn't understand it. He seemed refined, and yet he was willing to hobnob with those poor unfortunate men, the very riffraff, the off-scouring of the earth!

The next day she talked to him about it.

"I just can't understand you, Link," she said in a pretty petulant tone. "You are so fine yourself, and your family are grand. Your mother is such a lady, and has brought you up so beautifully! Why do you seem to have such low tastes? Why is it you are willing to spend so much time in missions? Why, if you must do a preaching act, don't you go to college students, or even to some of the professors? You have a fine education, and it would take somebody with a fine education to reach students, or professors. That is if there are any of them that need saving."

Link gave her a bewildered look, and then spoke gently as to a child who didn't understand.

"I do try to witness everywhere, Carey, whenever the way opens. But most of the class you mention are too wise in their own conceit to listen, or else they have heard the message over and over again. It is to the poor and needy, the down-and-outers that I feel the gospel should be taken. Some of them are not only ready but eager to accept salvation. They have no other hope. It is wonderful to them that there is a salvation for them."

"Oh, well, I suppose they think they've got to get back to respectability or they never can make a living. But Link, really, what makes you think God wants such people saved? Personally I don't believe He does. I should think He just intends to let them die off and be out of the way. What kind of a place would Heaven be for the rest of us with a lot of such people hanging around, anyway? People who didn't care to make anything of themselves? Really, Link, I think you are making a mistake."

Link looked at her in astonishment.

"Carey! You can't mean that!" he exclaimed. "Why, Carey, aren't you a Christian? I always supposed you were."

"Why certainly, Link. I joined the church when I was fourteen, and I've been more or less active in church work ever since. But I understand this mission of Lutie's isn't even supported or backed by any church. Just a bunch of disreputable men got together, probably to be fed and clothed gratis. I don't think such things ought to be encouraged. It simply makes paupers of those men."

"But Carey, haven't you forgotten that Christ died to save those men?"

"Well, why aren't they saved then? That ought to be enough for them that the Lord died, without having to have every respectable man give up his time babying them. If they don't want to be saved, why bother?"

Link gave her a sad look.

"Because Christ has said we must go out into the highways and byways, and compel them to come in. Because He has said we who accept Him as Saviour are His witnesses, and our one job in life is to witness for Him."

"Well, I can't see it!" said Carey crossly. "I think you are wasting your time, and spoiling your life. You never can have any fun anywhere. You are always having to go out and minister to the off-scouring of the earth, and you miss a whole lot out of life. You're only young once, and you don't want to be an old man before your time. Link, really, it's awful, the way you just go along and let life slip through your fingers! There was that uncle of Sydney's who came down to the wedding. He told me you were a brilliant young man, and he said there was a job he knew of up in New York where you would just shine. He said he had told you about it, and was willing to put your name in. He practically said you could have it if you would speak the word. Have you told him you would take it yet? He spoke as if it wouldn't be going begging long."

Link flashed a look at her that seemed to search her for an instant, and his eyebrows lifted just a trifle.

"No," he answered, almost coldly. "I did not want the job. It involved the lowering of standards which are a part of my life. I am a Christian first, Carey, not a business man. I am not out to get rich quick."

"Oh, nonsense, Link!" said Carey in a vexed tone.

"Just think what a lot of good you could do if you had a lot of money. Don't be a fanatic! It would be a great deal better if you were to spend your time getting rich, and use some of your money to hire some poor theological student to go down in the slums and preach, don't you think so? You know that a young man who hadn't so much culture and education might even reach those low-down men better and quicker than you could. They would understand them better than a young man would who had been brought up to better things. You know, Link, I think you lay yourself open to a lot of unpleasant things when you allow yourself to be called on to work in missions and things like that. Look at the way Syd's father took the liberty of asking you to take that impossible Minnie Lazarelle away from the wedding party. It is just such impositions as that I mean. People will take advantage of you. And besides, look at all the pleasure you miss."

Lincoln Silverthorn looked at her steadily for a moment, and then he said gravely:

"I'm sorry you feel that way, Carey. I'm afraid that means that you and I are 'two people,' as Rae's old Scotch nurse used to say. You see I belong to my Lord first of all, and I'm pledged to His service. These other worldly things are definitely out of the picture with me. And another thing, you speak of missing pleasure. You don't seem to know that there is no joy in the world like the joy of bringing a lost soul to the Lord. There is no glory in the world like it."

Then he turned on her a dazzling smile, that made her remember that word "glory" for a long time afterward.

He did not talk much with her after that, and very soon went away on a business trip, so that Carey saw very little of him from that time forward, and more and more turned her attention to other friends.

Paul's sister invited her and McRae to come in for the symphony concerts now and then, and sometimes both girls went, but more often McRae did not go, as her mother was not well and she wanted to stay with her.

Paul of course accompanied them to the concerts, and there were pleasant evenings together, and more and more Carey became Paul's companion, here and there. The Redferns all seemed to like her, and she was enjoying herself hugely. But still she found her heart turning back to Link now and then, and comparing the two friends.

12

A DAY or two after Link returned home Luther Waite came out to see him, and they had a happy evening together planning the winter's work in the mission.

The talk lasted far into the night, and then, when they had been silent for a brief space, and it seemed they were about to go to sleep, Luther suddenly said:

"By the way, Link, I've often thought I'd like to know about what you did to charm that poor simp of a Minnie Lazarelle? How did you get rid of her so easily? How was it she didn't stick and insist on coming back with you? I'd like to know the charm, in case I ever get stuck with her again. You certainly erased her from the scene in short order. How did you do it?"

Link was so long answering that Luther thought he had fallen asleep and then he suddenly turned facing his guest and talked, slowly, hesitantly.

"I've been thinking about that a lot lately, Lute," he said and his voice had a deep concern. "I don't know whether I did the right thing or not. Lute, I gave her a bawling out!"

"Well, I should say you did do the right thing. If ever

there was a pest needed bawling out, she was it. My only surprise is that she paid any attention to it. I expected to see her return with you, or five minutes after, with a vicious little plausible excuse that almost might have stopped the wedding. You certainly must have made a hit with her or she wouldn't have paid any attention to you. What on earth did you say to her?"

"Well, I didn't say much. I guess I just showed how disgusted I was with her. That's what I mean whether I did the right thing, Lute. We've been told again and again that when we reprove we should do it with grace in our hearts. But I was mad, Lute. I had to be the goat, and I wanted her to know I didn't like it. I guess I wasn't doing it as unto the Lord. It hadn't occurred to me that the Lord cared anything about her."

"H'm!" said Luther thoughtfully. "I suppose He does, doesn't He? I hadn't thought of that!"

"Yes, I suppose He does. Cares just as much for her as He does about any of those drunks down at the mission. Yet I didn't see it then. I just sailed in and bawled her out. I asked her why she wanted to be that way. Didn't she know people wouldn't like her like that? Why didn't she be different? Oh, I don't remember just what I said, but it was words to that effect. And she—she just slumped. Quit smirking and putting on an act and went down into nothing for all the world like a balloon that I had stuck a pin into. She went down so quick and fast that I actually felt sorry for her! Yes, I did, Lute! I felt ashamed of myself. But by that time we had got there, and there wasn't anything else to do but help her out and take her in and introduce her. Oh, I gave her a few words more about what she had to do, like a command you know, so she wouldn't think she could barge back and run the act all over again! I was half afraid she would follow me out when I came away, but she didn't. Just sat down as meek as you please at the table and acknowledged the introductions to the other boarders like anybody. I stayed outside in the shade of some evergreens for a minute or two to make sure I had placed her."

"Well, you sure did a good job," said Luther. "I don't see why you are doubtful about it."

"Why, I was afraid I had been too hard on her, all at once showing her herself that way."

"Say, Link, if she couldn't stand the sight of her real self once in a while how would she think others could stand her?"

"But, Lute, that wasn't all of it. I had to deal with her again the next day. It was then the Lord showed me that she was someone He cared about, and I've worried a little about it ever since."

"You should worry, Link! You couldn't be too harsh on that woman! If she had the nerve to come after you again, I can't see why you care if you did hurt her!"

"But she didn't come after me, Lute! It wasn't her fault at all that I saw her again. She was toiling along on the street all alone, carrying two big heavy suitcases, and looking a good deal like that deflated balloon yet, so I picked her up and took her to the station."

"You did, you poor simp! Well, you *are* a sucker! I'd say it was a good thing if she did a thing as useful as carry her own luggage to the station."

"No, but wait, Lute! Hear the rest. When I drew up alongside of her and told her to get in, her face shone as if a king had asked her to a palace."

"I'll bet it did!" affirmed Luther ardently. "That's her line. I know that shine! Boy! Am I glad I wasn't in your shoes!"

"Wait, Lute. You don't understand. She said she was so glad I had spoken to her because there was something she wanted to ask me and she didn't know how to find me. She said I had told her that she could be different, and she wanted to know if I really meant it, and would I tell her *how* she could be different? She said she had been trying all her life to make people like her, and nobody ever had. She gave me the impression that even her family hadn't much use for her, and she'd never had a good time, and if there was any way she could be different so people would like to have her around, and be pleasant to her, she'd give anything if she could find out how."

Link paused, realized the girl's need as he had when he had met her, expressed something of his realization in his voice, so that his friend felt it also.

"Boy! That was some situation for you to be up against!" murmured Luther thoughtfully. "But I never would have guessed she cared about anything. I always thought she felt she was about *it!*"

"Yes, that's what I thought too, and I certainly was surprised. It was then I began to be afraid I'd been too hard on her."

"What did you say? How could you tell her how to be different?"

"That's what I questioned in my own heart," said Link slowly as if he were analyzing the situation over again. "I certainly had to do some quick praying, calling for help. How was I to know how to tell a girl how to change her line? And yet I saw it was important, not only to her, but maybe to God, and I didn't dare let her go off into the world with a great longing in her eyes and heart like that and no one to tell her what to do. I saw she was in earnest, and maybe I'd be the only one she'd ever ask. So I told her what she needed was to know the Lord Jesus Christ."

Luther Waite was breathless there in the darkness listening.

"Oh boy! What an opportunity!" he breathed. "How did she take that?"

"She took it all right. She said how could she know Him, and asked a lot of hopeless little questions that a child might ask. Lutie, she didn't know a thing! She's never, scarcely, been to church or Sunday School at all. Never read the Bible and wouldn't know what it meant if she did read it. But when I told her the way of salvation, and how knowing Christ could make her all over, she went for it like a drowning person for a rope! It was rather wonderful. I felt when I got done as if some angel had given me a commission to point the way to a lost soul. Don't misunderstand me. I don't *like* her any better than I did, but I know what it is to have the kind of love Christ wants us to have for the souls He died to save. She isn't lovely nor lovable, and she's full of self and sin of course, but it's glory when the Lord helps you to see how someone is going to look after He gets them cleansed and saved."

"Say! That's wonderful, Link! I know what you mean, I've felt it sometimes when I've been talking to old Mike down at the mission. It's when you look at those old bums through the glory of the Lord that you can feel that, and understand. Well, say, Link. I feel condemned! I've run from that girl like poison. I've hated the very sight of her, because she took me for a ride one day, *all day!* I couldn't get rid of her! And to think she would react that way about knowing the Lord! Of course I haven't known the Lord so very long myself, you know, and I didn't know Him at all at the time I met her. Maybe that made the difference. Maybe such contacts would always be bearable if one was traveling with the Lord. I was just traveling by myself in those days. I suppose if one went at a disagreeable thing like meeting somebody you didn't like, as if it were a commission from the Lord, it wouldn't be so hard to manage. I can see it's the way the Lord meant us to do about everyone. It makes life a lot more serious, doesn't it?"

"It sure does, Lutie," said Link solemnly.

It was the very next morning, before Luther left, that Link had a letter from Minnie Lazarelle, thanking him for the Bible.

He read it thoughtfully and then handed it over to Luther to read. And afterward, when they were on their way to town together they talked it over.

The letter was frank, but with none of the old gush that used to typify the old Minnie. It was almost dignified, and Luther read it with wonder in his glance. He felt as if he were reading a part of a miracle.

Dear Mr. Silverthorn:

The day after I reached home the wonderful Bible came. Even if it hadn't been something I needed very much, it would have thrilled me, it is so beautiful. I cannot thank you enough for taking all that trouble for a poor good-for-nothing girl like me. And to think you sent such a gorgeous one! Its beauty alone would make me read it, even if I hadn't promised. I love just to feel the soft leather in my hands. Nobody ever got anything lovely like that for me. I think it must be that God put it into your heart to buy it, and He picked it out Himself. That is if He really cares, the way you said He did.

I haven't had time to write and thank you any sooner because I came into an awful mess here. My stepmother was sick, the maid had left, and the children were running wild. Formerly I would have run away somewhere myself to get out of it. But something, I guess it was the bawling out you gave me, made me stay and see it through. But it's not because I wasn't grateful that I didn't write sooner. I just haven't had time.

But here's thanking you with all my heart for the Bible. I've begun to read it already, and if I never get to see you again on this earth, I'll thank you again in Heaven.

By the way, if you should happen to run across my young brother Timothy, you might tell him how to be made over. He needs it. He's only fourteen. He doesn't know a thing about God. And now he's run away. The children say he didn't like it here and said he was going back there where we used to live. I thought perhaps he would turn up in your city. He'll be trying for a job somewhere. He didn't have much money along.

I thought perhaps I ought to do something about him, as my father sailed for China or somewhere far off, and he'll likely be gone a year or two.

If you should find him, please tell him his mother is very sick and she keeps crying for him. I think she isn't going to live long. The doctor says it's very serious.

I'm sorry to trouble you again, but I don't know who else to ask, and I suppose somebody ought to look after him. If you find a trace of him I'll telegraph some money for him to come back. We've still got plenty of that.

You probably don't know that Minnie isn't my real name. I was christened Erminie after my grandmother. So I thought if I was going to live a new life I'd better have a new name, and I'm signing it here,

Your grateful friend,
Erminie Lazarelle

When Luther finished reading the letter he handed it back to Link.

"We gotta find that kid brother," he said thoughtfully. "Poor kid! I'll get after some of the detectives and see if we can't locate him."

Link's eyes lighted up.

"Good work, Lutie! Hop to it!" he said.

The eyes of the two young men met with a look of utter joy in the work they were trying to do, and afterward when Luther had gone on his way, Link marveled at how soon Luther's whole attitude had changed toward the girl he had so despised.

13

McRAE WAS sitting on the wide pleasant porch of her home one Saturday afternoon, reading. Dimly in the distance she heard the bus stop at the corner. A few minutes later she looked up at the sound of the white gate swinging open down the front path. A stranger, a showily dressed girl marched arrogantly up to the house staring around her. Once she paused an instant to bend over a border of bright flowers that edged the stone flagging, and reaching out her hand grasped a bunch of forget-me-nots, and tore them from their plant, bringing up some of the roots also. A moment later she stooped again and deliberately twisted a lovely half blown rose from its stem, twitching it angrily as it resisted her, mutilating the whole delicate plant.

McRae suddenly rose and laid down her book, calling out to the girl:

"Why, what are you trying to do? Please don't do that. That is one of my mother's rarest roses."

"Oh!" said the girl straightening up with the rose in her hand, lifting a thorn-torn finger to her lips to suck it. "I wasn't doing anything but picking a rose. That won't do the bush any harm. You don't grudge a rose now and then to a visitor, do you?"

"I'm sorry," said McRae politely. "I can get you some flowers from the garden if you need them, but that one there is a specially choice one my mother has been raising. However, as you've picked it, it's too late. Will you come up and have a chair? Did you want to see my mother?"

"No, certainly not. What would I want to see your mother for? What's one little puny rosebud? Take your old rosebud!" and she flung the thorny crisp stem straight into McRae's face. "Such a fuss about a lot of weeds! I came out here to hunt up a friend of mine, Steve Grant. Tell him I'm in a hurry too, won't you? The bus goes back in fifteen minutes and I've got an engagement tonight. Tell him to make it snappy!"

"But Stephen Grant does not live here," said McRae. "You have come to the wrong house." McRae calmly and deliberately went back to her seat on the porch.

"Yes, but you know where he is," said the astonishing visitor rudely. "He told me once he lived practically on your doorstep. This is the Silverthorn house, isn't it? The bus driver said it was. And I suppose you're the high and mighty girl that talked to me on the telephone awhile back. I don't forget voices. I knew who you were the minute you spoke."

"I am afraid you have me at a disadvantage. I don't happen to remember your name."

"I should worry. Just tell Steve an old friend of his is here and he's to come at once."

"I don't happen to know where Stephen is," said McRae indifferently. "You'll have to excuse me. His home is over at the next farm to the right. Why don't you go and find out yourself?"

The girl gave her a startled suspicious look.

"You mean at that big old dump over there?" she said pointing to the fine old Grant homestead with its stately row of elms arching over the front walk that led down to the highway.

McRae gave a grave dignified nod.

"It isn't so much of a house!" said the intruder. "Besides it doesn't look as if anyone was there."

"I think the family are usually at home at this hour in the afternoon," said McRae quietly, her eyes still on her book.

"Whaddaya mean, the family?" asked the girl.

"Why, at least Mr. and Mrs. Grant," said McRae. "I haven't noticed their going out. I think Mr. Grant must have returned from the city by this time."

"Well, say, it looks an awful long way over there up that long walk, and seems kind of spooky up that drive under all those trees. Can't you go to your telephone and call them up and ask Steve to come over here and see me?"

"I don't think I would care to do that," said McRae coldly. "It would be better for you to make your own contacts."

The other girl stared at her.

"Not very accommodating, are you?" she remarked.

"No!" said McRae indifferently.

There was silence for a moment while the other girl alternately studied McRae and the Grant homestead. Then she turned hesitantly and went down the flag stones to the gate.

She was wearing high heeled shoes without socks, and shoes that displayed a full set of healthy bare toes finished with highly polished crimson toenails. Her dress was a sport model, brief in the extreme, made of Roman striped material, with a bare back. The whole costume was topped by an absurd little hat tilted over her right eye, like a gay little colored wheel strapped across the back of her head with a wide black band. She walked with a tilt and a swing, slowly down the walk to the gate, out the gate and across the road, not in the least as if she were in a hurry, in at the Grant gate, and slowly up the walk.

She was halfway up to the house, when suddenly, with a low rumble like distant thunder, and then a sharp bark of enquiry, Bruce, the great yellow mastiff belonging to Curlin, came bounding down from the back of the house and made straight for the intruder.

The girl saw the dog and stopped short, wavering backward.

The dog came on in majesty, like a conqueror who would be obeyed, and the girl began to scream.

"Go away!" she cried, and her voice rang out in sheer terror. "Get *out!* Go away! Ow! Ow!"

She turned and fled blindly, and the dog came bounding on.

Then the girl stubbed her ridiculous little toe and went down flat. The screams that came from her terrified lips were fairly bloodcurdling.

McRae dropped her book on the porch, hurried down the steps, along the walk, running as hard as she could now, to the rescue, for Bruce was no mild foe, and well knew how to utilize his advantages. He understood that he had successfully vanquished this intruder, and he meant to go on to the finish. He bounded on to the fray till he stood above the prostrate girl, barking his utmost disapproval, and Mysie, too frightened even to struggle up, turned her screams into howls, and cried "Help! Murder! Help!"

"Down, Bruce!" called McRae's clear voice, as she ran. But the girl and the dog were making too much noise for her voice to be heard.

McRae ran through the familiar gate toward the girl, and just then a sharp penetrating whistle broke above the tumult. It was Curlin Grant, and the dog recognized the imperative note and stopped short in his tracks.

Another sharp imperative whistle, nearer now and coming on, and Bruce turned obediently, almost shame-facedly, and trotted back to meet his master.

Then there was Curlin, stooping and lifting the fright-ened furious intruder, setting her upon her feet, asking anxiously if she was hurt.

The girl was a wreck! Her funny little hat was all awry, her hair stood seven ways. Angry tears were racing down her painted face, and rouge and mascara had blended gaily in with the tide and were making havoc of what had been a dashingly pretty face. One spike heel had come off, and let its owner down to original height, and the other slipper had escaped in the melee leaving its foot entirely bare.

She stood there an instant, just crying, her lips trembling, her whole face a quiver of indignation. And then she recognized McRae.

"Oh! It's *you,* is it? You sent me over to get scared, did you? You knew they had a dog here and you just did this for meanness! I suppose you're jealous. You probably want Steve for yourself, and you wanted to get it back on me for telephoning your house the night you had the party!" she burst forth. "You're a contemptible snob, that's what you are! Now you tell me where Steve is and I'll see that he understands just how you've treated me. I won't stand for any more nonsense from you!"

Curlin had been holding the girl up courteously, helping her to get her bearings after her fall, but now his eyes flashed fire.

"Stop!" he said, gripping her arm fiercely and giving her a shake. "What do you mean, talking that way to a lady like Miss Silverthorn? She came all the way over here to help you when you were frightened, and you speak that way to her! Don't you *dare* to say another word like that!"

Bruce had been standing near to the house watching the outcome of the affair, but now at the sound of his master's definitely severe voice, he bristled all over and suddenly began stepping quickly, silently down toward the group till he stood close beside Mysie again, uttering a low warning growl, as if adding his voice to what Curlin had said.

The girl had turned, startled, at Curlin's words, her eyes questioningly on the young man, but suddenly she heard the dog, and turning frightened eyes toward him uttered another terrific scream, clutching at Curlin's arm.

"Oh! There's that horrible brute again! Save me! Save me!" she cried.

"The dog won't hurt you," said Curlin in a low almost contemptuous tone. "Bruce, go back to the house and lie down!" he ordered the dog.

Bruce uttered a low menacing growl, that in a man would have sounded like swearing, and slowly took his way back up the hill.

The girl watched the dog fearsomely until he rounded the corner of the house and was out of sight. Then she turned to Curlin, and perceived that he was a personable young man.

"Who are *you?*" she said insolently. "What do you have such a beast as that around for?"

Curlin gave her a steady glance.

"My name is Grant," said Curlin. "I'm sorry my dog frightened you, but at that I don't see that he behaved any worse than you did. We don't often have such insolent guests as you are, insulting one of our best friends."

"Grant!" said the girl, assurance swiftly returning to her voice. "Any relation to Steve?"

Curlin gave her a swift keen look.

"I have a brother Stephen."

"Well, where is he? Just tell him a friend of his is out here! That's what I came for, to find Steve."

Curlin surveyed her with a firm look on his pleasant lips and unfriendly withdrawal in his eyes.

"My brother is not at home!" he answered haughtily.

The girl frowned.

"When will he be home?" she asked.

"I can't say," answered Curlin. "He is away indefinitely on business."

"Well then, give me his *address* and telephone number. I've got to talk to him right away. It's im*por*tant!"

"That's quite impossible!" said Curlin firmly. "He wasn't sure just where he was going first, and I don't have an address at present nor a telephone number. But even if I had one I should *not* give it to you. Now, would you like to go up to the house and wash your face before you leave? It seems to be rather the worse for wear. McRae, would you take her up to the house? Mother is in bed with one of her sick headaches today or I'm sure she would have been down to offer assistance."

"Oh, no!" cried the girl. "I can't go up to that house where that awful dog is. I want to get away from here at once. Where is my other shoe?"

Curlin proffered the heelless slipper.

"I'm afraid it's rather the worse for wear," he said. "Ah! Here is the heel. If you will come into the house I can take it down to the village and have the heel put on."

"No!" said the girl. "I will not go into that house! I'll

manage to get into the bus, somehow——" Her voice trailed off perplexedly.

"Come over to my house," said McRae pleasantly. "You can wash over there, and perhaps we can find a pair of my shoes you can wear."

The ungracious guest finally agreed to that and ended by taking off both shoes and going barefoot.

"Now," she said looking at Curlin as she turned to leave, "I want Steve's address, and I want it mighty quick too!"

"Sorry," said Curlin firmly, "that's something I can't give you."

"Well, you'll be good and sorry if you don't, that's all I've got to say. I can give information that will connect him up with a gangster's crowd and a big holdup, quick as a wink! How would you like that?"

"You don't say!" said Curlin looking at her steadily. "What a very good friend you must be to Stephen!"

"Well, I can do it, and I *will* if there are any more double crossings from Steve. I think you ought to know that I'm a very special friend of your brother's. He's engaged to marry me!"

"Indeed!" said Curlin. "How interesting! But he hasn't mentioned it to his family yet, you see."

"No, I asked him not to, until my divorce went through. But it's all okay now, so I came out to tell him. Now, will you tell me where to find Steve?"

"No," said Curlin, "I will not! Not now, nor at any future time when he lets me know where he has decided to stay. You are definitely out of the picture as far as I am concerned."

"Well, you'll be sorry!"

"Yes? I'm sorry now that you ever met my brother."

"Yes, and you'll be sorrier yet!" warned Mysie.

"I wouldn't be at all surprised!" said Curlin. "From

the little I have seen of you this afternoon I should suppose that you wouldn't be a person who could make anybody very glad as a friend or in any other relation. Now, can you walk or do I need to carry you?"

"I'll walk!" said the girl fiercely. "But I'll see that you get yours pretty suddenly if you don't give me that address. I know one other place where there's somebody who might know it. If I don't get it there you'll begin to understand that you've been monkeying with a buzz saw."

McRae walked silently down to the gate with the girl, and Curlin stood for a moment and watched them, his eyes full of trouble. It was terrible that McRae had had to go through this scene, unfair that she had to come into any sort of contact with a girl like this one. It was all Steve's fault of course. How could he have had anything to do with a girl like this when McRae had been his friend for years? And how sweet McRae had been, offering her shoes. It was not mere politeness that had made McRae so kind, it was Christian grace. After those disgusting things the girl had said to her!

But was it possible that there was anything to that? Did McRae love Steve? It would be a wonderful thing for Steve of course if she did. That is, if he knew enough to appreciate it. But it would be a mistake for McRae. She would have a hard life if she ever married Steve. Fun-loving, spoiled, handsome Steve! His beloved brother, yes. But spoiled. Could God somehow take the spoil away and set Stephen right?

He watched the two girls cross the road together and go up to the Silverthorn house. He waited out of sight until he saw them return to the porch and hurry down the walk just in time to catch the bus returning to the city. He noticed that the alien girl was wearing shoes of some sort, and carrying a neat bundle. McRae had fixed her up.

Then the bus went on its way, and McRae went back into the house. Curlin drew a heavy sigh and turned back to his evening duties in the big old stone barn. Bruce stole near, with a wistful questioning motion of his tail, and drooped along beside him, until at last his cold wet nose touched Curlin's fingers with affectionate pleading. Curlin's hand came lovingly down about the dog's big silky head, and fondled him.

"Hard lines, old fellow!" he murmured tenderly. "You have to be careful about a lady, you know, even when she's *not* a lady. I'm afraid you were a bit rough, even allowing for the circumstances. Next time perhaps you'd better just stand and bark, keep a safe distance back, you know!"

Bruce yearned toward his master with a low breathing sound that seemed to say he understood, and the two walked together in sober understanding up to the barn. Solemnly Bruce went about nosing the calf into place, standing guard over Curlin, sitting alertly, but subdued, near Curlin as he milked the cows. Sliding affectionately up to Curlin's riding horse, and rubbing his nose against her fetlock. All the little gestures that were a loving part of the day's work between his master and himself.

After the work was done at the barn Curlin went in and got ready a nice tray for his mother. Beautifully browned toast and a little old silver pot of scalding hot tea, a tiny pat of butter. He knew just how she liked it. He had done it before. Dear mother! She had had those headaches so many times, especially since Stephen had been growing up and getting out away from home.

Not that mother knew anything definite about Mysie. He had tried to keep that from both mother and father. But somehow mother must have sensed there was something wrong. Mother knew life. She had imagination enough to work out the possibilities whenever Steve stayed out very late. So often she would be in her room quite late in the morning after father had gone to the city, and would come out with her eyes all tired and red around the rims. She had been praying for Steve, he was sure, because one morning he had been hunting her and had softly turned the knob of her door to make sure she wasn't there, and opening the door just the faintest crack, had seen her down upon her knees beside the bed, with her dear face buried in the old brown bedquilt. Curlin had watched and agonized with her after that, and had done everything he could to save Steve. But he wasn't at all sure about Steve yet. Neither was mother. The only difference between them was that mother knew she could absolutely trust God to take care of Steve, even though she shouldn't live to see Steve safe, while he, Curlin, wasn't so sure but a lot of the responsibility belonged to himself.

And in a way it did of course. What did God give boys brothers for, if not to help watch over them? Look at what God said to Cain, "Where is Abel, thy brother?"

Curlin stirred up the fire and put some potatoes in to roast. His father would be coming home on the next bus. There was just time for the potatoes to get done. There were meat balls for supper, too. Mother had prepared them before she went to lie down with her headache. There was a can of tomatoes on the kitchen table, and a nice apple and nut salad in the refrigerator. A rice pudding also, ice cold in the refrigerator, rich and creamy with fat raisins in it. Mother never humored even a sick headache until she had her family's needs all provided for. She knew that Curlin could do all she had left to be done.

And while Curlin worked away, getting out the pan

for the meat balls, the butter, cutting the bread, starting the coffee in the percolator, he kept on with that thought: "Where is Steve, thy brother?" It was as if God was asking that question of him.

It wasn't the first time of course that the idea had come to him. The night McRae had called up for them to come to her party it had taken the greatest hold on him, and he had been ashamed that his own hasty temper had prevented him from insisting that Steve should not go away to a night club instead of coming home with him. Even then he wouldn't perhaps have thought so much about it if that girl hadn't come into the picture, telephoning to Silverthorn's. But from that night on, when he had talked with McRae about it he had felt a definite responsibility laid upon his soul to do something for Steve. Perhaps because McRae had seemed so troubled about him, and the suggestion had come to his mind that perhaps McRae was in love with Steve.

It had wrenched his heart terribly, and had revealed to himself that his own heart was involved there also. But he had definitely put it aside, realizing once more that if Steve had set his heart upon McRae, Steve would probably get her. He always got what he went after from everybody.

So, if for no other reason, he must look after Steve for McRae's sake. He could not see McRae suffer, when a little trouble on his own part might save her peace of mind, and help Steve to be a man worthy of a girl like that.

As the days had gone by Curlin had grown more and more into the feeling that Steve must be saved for his own sake, as well as his mother's and father's, and the girl who might be loving him. Even if it meant a painful sacrifice of his own heart's wishes, there must be no risk that McRae should suffer through a lack of diligence on his part. And so, tenderly, he had come to care for his brother as a sacred trust. And little by little Steve had noticed it and began to realize a stronger bond between himself and Curlin than he had ever felt while they were growing up.

And now, today, with the coming of this extraordinary girl into the picture, Curlin felt that Steve must be protected at all costs.

He could not get the Mysie girl out of his thoughts. How terrible for mother if Steve was really involved in any serious way with a girl like that.

Of course all that talk about gangsters had been only so much baloney. Steve had never been away from home long enough to get involved in anything such as she had hinted. He had kept pretty thorough check on his brother's movements of late, and had planned a number of lures to keep him in safe surroundings. But a girl like the one who had visited them this afternoon was equal to anything. She probably was after money. She could threaten Steve with blackmail. Well, that would be something to think about, to pray about. But the whole thing had left his heart anxious and troubled. What would be the immediate outcome of all that they had tried to do for Steve? Would it do any good, or would Steve just find some new way of going astray in the new venture which he had entered upon that morning?

Curlin heard the bus stop and pass on again, heard his father's steps coming up the flagging, rather slow, elderly steps. Dad wasn't quite so spry as he used to be. A quick anxiety stabbed him with possibilities. Life seemed so awfully full of things one didn't dare look in the face!

Curlin turned the meat balls over again to be sure the other side was just the right brown, lifted the percolator from the grill, gave the coffee a stir with the silver spoon mother had left in readiness, and set it down on the kitchen table.

"Hello, dad! Dinner's all ready!" he called cheerfully. "Mother had a bit of a headache this afternoon and I made her lie down. But she feels better now. I took her a tray. Go up and see her a minute, but hustle for these meat balls are just ready to eat!"

A quick anxiety passed over the older face.

"Oh, I was afraid she wasn't feeling so well," said the father. "She didn't sleep much last night of course, Steve starting so early. Well, I hope it's going to turn out to be the best for Steve."

He hung up his coat and hat and hurried up the stairs.

"Hurry up, dad. I don't want my dinner spoiled. My honor as a cook is at stake."

"Oh, steak for dinner?" grinned the father. "I'll be right down."

"Only Hamburg steak, dad," laughed Curlin, and turned out the stewed tomatoes into the china dish set ready. Then with a silver fork, and a dry dish towel he began taking out the crusty roasted potatoes, giving each one a scientific squeeze to let out the steam and keep them dry and fluffy as his mother had taught him.

He brought the salad, and he dished out two helpings of rice pudding. Then he rang the bell good and loud at the foot of the stairs, and his father came laughing down the stairs.

"Coming!" he shouted. "Your dinner smells good. I told mother she was missing out on it, and she declared she was coming down as soon as she finished her toast, but I forbade it. Told her I'd come up there and read to her all the evening if she would be good and stay in bed, so she promised. I think she feels better tonight, says the pain in her head is all gone, but it's just as well for her to be careful. How have things gone today? All right?"

"Okay!" said Curlin, thinking of the afternoon visitor and thankful that there was such an indiscriminate word as "okay" to use on occasion.

There was silence for a full minute while the two began to eat, and then the father said:

"Well, Steve got off all right this morning. The pilot said the air conditions couldn't be better. I suppose we'll hear from him tomorrow sometime!"

"Yes, probably, although he told me he would give us a call late tonight if there was any opportunity. But I told him he'd better hold off till morning or mother wouldn't sleep all night waiting to hear from him."

"Well, I hope we did the right thing," sighed the older man, "letting him go off that way, so far!"

"I think you did, dad! You know Steve always did do better when he was absolutely on his own."

"Yes, I suppose it'll do the lad good to take a few burdens on himself," sighed the father.

Curlin made short work of washing up the few dishes and putting things to rights, all in readiness for breakfast the next morning, and then he made a hasty toilet, and went in and kissed his mother.

"I'm just running over to Silverthorns a few minutes," he explained as he saw his mother's questioning eyes on his freshly combed hair. "I won't be long. Everything's all ready for breakfast, mother, and you don't need to get up early. Take it easy a few days and get back your pep." He smiled, as he took his departure.

The mother's eyes smiled a benediction upon him as he left. Mother was very fond of the Silverthorns.

But Curlin wasn't so sure he would stay even a few minutes at Silverthorns. It depended on who was there. Paul often came out with Link to spend the evening, or McRae might have some girls overnight. If so there was his new farm magazine that he wanted to read. It would be all right. To tell the truth he didn't just know why he was going, only that he somehow wanted to speak to McRae again, perhaps tell her how sorry and ashamed he was that she had had to have a part in that disgraceful scene of the afternoon. Perhaps he was only going over there like a little boy who wanted to be comforted a bit. And McRae was always good at comforting.

14

BUT THERE were no lights in the great front room of the Silverthorn house where company was usually entertained, just the two reading lamps in the library and the comfortable outlines of Father and Mother Silverthorn sitting around the library table, both of them reading. Then as he drew nearer the house he could see a dim figure in a white dress sitting alone over on the wide comfortable hammock known as a "glider." That was McRae and she was by herself! His heart gave a happy bound. At least he might have a few words with her alone, before anybody else came.

So as he drew nearer the steps he was whistling softly, though there wasn't any definite tune to it at all. He hadn't been coming over here lately as often as in past years and he almost felt shy about it.

"Hello!" he called, as he came up the steps, "is that you, McRae? Link anywhere about?"

It was the old question he had used so much during the years that it hardly seemed strange on his lips, though it was really Link's sister he wanted to see. But he wanted to make McRae feel utterly at her ease, and if McRae had her heart full of Steve, and was worrying about him, he didn't want to obtrude himself into the picture.

"Oh! Curlin!" said the girl springing to her feet, "I'm so glad you came over. I've been wanting to talk to you. Come over here and sit down awhile with me. No, Link isn't home yet. He telephoned at six o'clock that he had a man to see at eight-thirty and would come home as soon as he got free from him. I guess it won't be long now."

There was so much eager welcome in the girl's voice that Curlin's heart lost a beat before he sat down. She really seemed glad to see him. But likely she only wanted to ask something about Steve.

"I've been hoping you would come over. Curlin, did I do wrong to let that girl come over to your house? You see, first she seemed to think Steve was here, lived here, or something. Then she insisted I send for him at once. Of course I recognized her voice at once as the girl who telephoned to him that night over here. And I didn't know just what to do about it. It didn't seem the right thing to send her over there if Steve was there, but I hadn't seen him around all day, and I didn't know what else to do. Has Steve really gone away?"

"Yes," said Curlin, gravely. "He went this morning, and I'm not sure where he finally brought up. You see he's been taking flying lessons for sometime now, and he's off for a job. He thinks he's got a real one. The telegram came late last night. I don't know how it'll turn out, and mother is all jittery about it of course. She feels it is an awful thing to fly."

"Oh, Curlin! Of course she'll feel that! But maybe it will be good for Steve."

"Yes," said Curlin thoughtfully, "I hope so. Of course dad thinks it's all right or mother never would hear to it. And I had got almost to the point where I was willing to see him take up anything, just so he had a job and a little responsibility. You know he's always been babied a lot at home, and maybe this will sort of steady him. He's always loved taking risks and all that too. Anyway it will get him away from this dumb bunny of a girl for the time being. But say, I'm terribly sorry you had to get in on the scene of the afternoon. I'm sorry you saw Bruce go for her. It would have been better for me to have dealt with her. There are a few things I could have told her that might have frightened her."

"Well, I wasn't sure whether anybody was at home over there and I didn't know but Bruce might decide to eat her up, so, as I had sent her over there I thought I was responsible to some extent, and I just flew. I certainly never expected a girl like that to get frightened over a dog. She acted as if she had all kinds of courage beforehand. To hear her talk you'd think she was really tough."

"Well, you know there's something about that dog," grinned the dog's owner, "that puts the fear of death into timid souls, no matter how tough they may appear. I've seen a mean tramp or two just fairly wither up and turn green when Bruce came out and gave 'em a sample of his voice. And that dog has discernment. He knows a mean nature when he sees one, and he gives 'em plenty."

"Yes," said McRae giggling, "he certainly does. If I hadn't been so excited I would have laughed. I wished I had a camera. But Curlin, was there anything to be alarmed about in what that girl said about Steve? *Could* she possibly tell lies enough to get him into trouble? Is she really in with the gangsters, do you think?"

"Well, I don't know much about her except that she's been a hostess or something at one of the night clubs in the city. Can't be much of a night club to have a girl like that working for them of course, but she doesn't look to me like one who would stop at anything if she thought she could make a little money. I have no doubt she'll do all she can if she gets in touch with Steve. I think perhaps she only wants to scare us and win him back. But it may be she is a gold digger and wants to get him into some kind of trouble so she can ask him for money. However, that's something that time will have to show. Just now there's some praying to be done. I'm sure about that, and I hope you'll help. That's what I really came over to ask."

"Of course," said McRae softly, "you knew I would be doing that."

"Yes, I knew it," said Curlin. "You're a wonderful friend!"

Curlin laid his hand for an instant on McRae's with a quick warm pressure, and then as swiftly drew back. If this should turn out to be Steve's girl he must not let his own feelings carry him away.

In the soft darkness he could see dimly the outline of McRae's lovely face. The tender smile that quivered over her sweet lips. If she had been caring for Steve it must have been dreadful for her to hear the coarse taunts of that girl this afternoon. He longed to put his arm about her and draw her head down on his shoulder and comfort her the way he did his mother sometimes. But perhaps McRae wouldn't understand. What was there to say? She was just McRae Silverthorn, the good true friend she had always been. She wouldn't understand why he felt all this so keenly, and he mustn't let her know that his feelings were more than ordinary. She might be Steve's girl, in her heart, and he must just act as if that were true until he knew beyond a doubt whether it was or not.

But it was McRae who broke the sweet silence.

"Curlin," she said gently, laying her hand on his arm, "what's the idea of Steve going off? Do you think he's aiming to get into the war?"

Curlin looked at her startled.

"Why do you ask that?" he said, his voice deeply troubled. "Did Steve ever say anything like that to you?"

"Why yes, several months ago. I thought he was just fooling, at the time, but it came to me how he had always wanted to be a flyer, and how he said he'd like to get into that war and do something real. Do you think he has that in mind, Curlin?"

"I'm afraid he has, Rae," said Curlin with a note of sadness in his voice. "I'm afraid that's just his idea."

"Afraid?" said the girl. "Why do you say afraid? Don't you think perhaps it might be something that would help Steve to grow up? If I were only sure that Steve is a real Christian I would think that it might be good for him."

There was a clear ring to her voice. Not the kind of sound that would come from an anguish of soul if she loved Steve. Or was it?

"Yes," said Curlin thoughtfully. "We had thought that, father and I. Of course mother doesn't know what kind of things Steve has been dipping into lately. Or—at least—does she? I can't be sure. Mother has a lot more insight into things than we sometimes give her credit for. But dad and I have talked a bit, and it was dad who wanted him to go. Thought it might be the making of him. It was dad who took him up to the flying field this morning."

"That's good!" said McRae. "Whatever comes you'll feel glad your father knew about it and was in favor of letting him try. Has he gone to Canada? Don't worry, I'm not scouting for Mysie," and she laughed a sad little trill of a laugh.

"Yes, he's gone up to get a tryout, or whatever they

call it. Some man he met at the flying school told him about it and got him all worked up wanting to go. This man is going to pull some wires to get him in. Of course he has to have a certain amount of training before he gets sent over to the other side, weeks or months or maybe only days, I really don't know, but by that time you know it *might* be all over."

"That's true," said Rae with a cheerful tone, "though of course it doesn't look much like it now. But at least it gives an interval, and changes the course of Steve's thoughts. And it gets him away from Mysie's vicinity. Though she isn't the only one of that kind in the world."

"No," said Curlin sadly, "Satan has his emissaries everywhere. However, I don't think just that form of temptation is so likely to strike my brother again. He has always seemed to have rather decent tendencies."

"Yes, of course," said McRae. "And I ought to know him pretty well. We've practically played together since we were babies. I guess we can trust him with God, can't we? I think I understand him almost as well as if he were my own brother."

"You should," said Curlin, his mind still trying to solve the problem of whether Rae was caring a great deal for his young renegade brother, and he just couldn't tell.

But her voice was almost gay now.

"Well, Curlin, you aren't going to tell anybody just yet where he is, are you?"

"Not if I can help it," said Curlin. "It will be some little time before he knows whether he'll be accepted or not, and it's just as well to keep that piece of dynamite from finding out anything about it, the way she talked this afternoon."

"Yes," said McRae. "Well, of course you know I won't tell anybody. But we'd better have some answer ready for the crowd if they ask where he is. Luther might ask, or Paul, or one of the girls when they're out here. But I should think we could easily put them off. Not that they couldn't be trusted. But of course what a few know gets to be common knowledge without intention. Does Link know?"

"Not yet. That's one thing I came over for tonight, to talk it over with him, that is, if there wasn't a whole raft of people here. He knows about that girl of course, and he'll be able to appreciate why I felt it might be a good thing. There's one thing about Link, anything you tell Link never goes any farther."

"No, of course not!" said Link's sister proudly. "Link never lets you down. Even though I'm his sister, he never let me down."

"No, he wouldn't. He's been a great brother and a great friend."

There was a sweet silence for a moment and then McRae spoke.

"You've all been great, you and Steve too. It's been like having three wonderful brothers! You've all looked after me so carefully, made me have such a nice time growing up. If one of you wasn't there when I needed you, there were always the other two! I shall never forget that! Do you remember the time the bees were swarming and I got into them and ran screaming away, and you came and helped me to get out of them, and put mud on the stings, and wiped my tears away? I'll never forget that!"

"Yes, I remember!" said Curlin gently, "and you were so brave, holding up your little frightened stinging face, and your poor little hands. I remember feeling that I was crying inside with you. I wouldn't have let anybody know I felt like crying of course, not for the world, but my heart was crying for you, because I knew those stings hurt."

Curlin's hand stole over in the darkness and found hers, and gave it a warm pleasant pressure, holding it close.

And then they heard Link driving in the gate, and Curlin drew away, more moved than he wanted her to know. It had been hard to say all these things and make them just casual, because his heart was suddenly overflowing with a warmer deeper feeling than he had ever experienced, although for sometime he had known that she was the only girl in the world for him.

Link came out and sat down with them for a little while. Their mother had made frozen custard for dinner that night, and there was some left in the freezer. McRae excused herself and went after it, and they sat there eating ice cream and sponge cake, and telling Link about the girl and what a time they had had with her.

Then Curlin told more in detail of Steve's going to Canada, and the possibilities for him, and how Mysie was threatening all sorts of things. Then McRae said good night and went to talk with her mother about some things they were going to do on the morrow, and Link and Curlin sat some time on the porch and talked it all over again.

"What do you think I ought to do about the girl, Link? About that threat of hers? Report it to the police? I'd hate to have it get back to mother, and dad. They wouldn't understand it, and it would give them great pain and humiliation."

"I wouldn't yet, Curl," advised Link. "You let me make some enquiries about that girl first. I've got a few contacts down there in the mission where I go with Lute sometimes that might throw some light on her companions and habits, and my enquiries could never connect the matter with you. There's a Christian policeman down there that we trust a lot. I'll see what I can find out and let you know as soon as possible. I believe that girl is only a silly fool with a nice line of baloney that she thinks will get her somewhere. I hope that's what it turns out to be. But it's just as well to be sure before we make any rash starts."

"Thanks a lot, Link. That eases my mind mightily. There's nobody on earth I would as soon trust with my perplexities. And I know Steve means something to you too."

"I should say he does! But I think it's fortunate that he was away already when that girl turned up. Sorry to lose his company, and I know how your mother must feel about the flying, but it may turn out to be a great thing for Steve, especially now since this girl is in the picture. Cheer up, Curl! I think Steve is saved, don't you? And you know the Lord is caring for His own, even though He may not always do it in the way we think it should be done!"

"Yes, I know," said Curlin. "I hope he is saved. You know you can't always tell those things about your own brother. He certainly isn't as fully surrendered as some I know. You wouldn't have a question like that about your sister, or Luther Waite, for instance!"

"No," said Link thoughtfully, "nor some of the others of course. Curlin, had you been noticing Paul Redfern lately?"

"No, I hadn't," said Curlin, and there was a sudden coolness in his voice.

"Well, you ought to have a talk with him. He's really out and out for the Lord. He was down at the mission last night, and had Carey with him. I was surprised about that for she isn't keen on missions, but she seemed really interested."

"Yes?" said Curlin with a rising inflection. And then with sudden interest, "Did McRae go too? She didn't say anything about it."

"No, she wasn't there. Fran Ferrin came down to stay over night with her. I called up to see if she'd like to come down on the train and let me meet her, but she and Fran had some plan. By the way, there's another who seems to be asking questions. She and Rae spent the evening studying the Bible. Rae says she had a lot of questions to ask, and she started the subject herself. We must remember to pray for her, brother. Say, did it ever occur to you that Steve seemed interested in her at the time of the wedding?"

"Why, no, Link. I never thought of that," said Curlin in surprise. "He always enjoys her. She's very bright, and Steve likes a good laugh."

"Well, perhaps I was mistaken," said Link. "I thought they were together a lot at the time of the wedding. And again that evening here afterwards, charades and so forth, you know. But it occurred to me that if Fran was a Christian she would be a big influence the right way for Steve. However, he's gone, and the Lord must be working out something right for him. We've got a lot to pray about, Curlin."

"We sure have!" said Curlin getting up. "Well, I guess I'd better be getting home and snatch a little sleep. We didn't get much last night at our house, and I'm expecting Steve to call in the morning sometime. You won't forget to make those enquiries about that girl, Link?"

"No, I'll not forget, and if I learn anything important I'll call you up and let you in on it. By the way, if Steve calls in the morning keep me informed. You know I'm as interested as you are."

And so the two parted for the night with a warm handclasp.

Out in the clear moonlit night Steve Grant was sailing a silver sea, and thinking more serious thoughts than he had ever thought before. Alone in a silver sky with a wide stretch of space about him, going into an unknown country, and taking a chance to be accepted as a volunteer.

It had not been so planned that he was to drive himself alone to the Canadian airport where he was supposed to arrange for his training. His friend and instructor who had instigated this whole plan had expected to be with him, and be the pilot. But his friend had answered a hurry call from his home at the last minute and Steve, nothing daunted, agreed to go alone. With inward trepidation though outward calm he had started on his way.

But now as he wended his way skyward into an untried heaven and saw the wideness of it, and the nearness of the stars, and the greatness of the moon, his thoughts were filled with awe. In spite of himself he began to feel as if God were quite near, and he was suddenly conscious that he hadn't been treating God very well. Oh, he had known Him of course through his parents, through the Silverthorns, and the church services he had been expected to attend whether he liked or not, but somehow he had never considered himself in any personal relation to God. He had always felt that he was a pretty nice Steve, and that God of course loved him much. It hadn't seemed strange to him that God loved him.

But now as he considered the far empty reaches below him and the unknown sky through which he was passing, he suddenly remembered a great many things in his life that must not seem nice to God, and a kind of shyness came over him. Perhaps God didn't find his life so altogether satisfactory as he had thought.

He remembered some of his actions of late, during college years, and just recently since he was through college. He remembered that girl Mysie who wasn't at all the kind of girl a child of God should take for an intimate friend. He remembered times when he had deliberately turned away from God, and gone to places that he knew were not good for him. He knew his father and mother would be bowed with shame and sorrow if they knew he had allowed himself to visit them. And then perhaps for the first time in his life he began to realize what sin meant when it came into a life that was supposed to belong to God.

He didn't care for the Mysie girl. She had come after him, and it had intrigued him to have a girl so eager for him, so filled with admiration for him. He knew he was good looking, and he liked her to tell him so. He knew it was she who had coaxed him to drink. Not much. Only a few times. The habit of the years of abstinence was still upon him. But she had taught him to think of things that shamed him now. In a way he was glad to get away from her and from all the temptations that she represented. He had plenty of nice girl friends. He thought of some of them now. There were a few he would have liked to have here riding with him now. Yet up there in the silver he was so conscious of God, that other people of earth did not seem to count. It was almost as if he was on his way to God, to be judged to see if he were fit for this job he was going to seek.

And so he sailed his silver sea in awe, while three to whom he was dear knelt at home and prayed for him, and his mother and father slept soundly, serene in the trust they had in the God to whom they had committed the care of their beloved son.

And out along the horizon of that wild expanse of sky

there began to be etched a panorama of the young man Steve's life and doings before he had started on this temeritous expedition alone with God. Till almost, the intrepid Steve Grant was frightened. It had never occurred to him before that he would ever be alone with God.

15

LUTHER WAITE was sitting one night at the back of the mission room while a meeting was going on. He let his eyes travel over the throng that had gathered. The weather was getting cold, and a shrill wind had blown up. This alone would bring forlorn ones into a warm lighted room, ones who would not otherwise have been attracted to a religious meeting. They drifted in by ones and twos. Many of them Luther recognized as men who had been there the year before. Some the hardened criminal type, and some merely lazy paupers who went wherever there was hope of getting anything for nothing.

Luther's mind, as often during these days, went to Timothy Lazarelle, wondering what had become of him. Wondering if by any chance he could have come to himself and gone back west to his family. It was a matter that was more and more on Luther's heart. It somehow seemed to him that he owed something to that girl he had so despised. As if the only way he could possibly make up to her for his lack of interest, nay, his intense aversion to a soul who was hungry, was to find that brother of hers.

He had hired a detective, wise in finding lost people, but there was as yet no trace of Timothy. He had half a mind to write to the girl, or get Link to write, and find out if she had heard any word from him. It was foolish of course to go on in a hopeless search if he was already at home, living a normal life. He really ought to have done this before.

Just then the door into the street opened half hesitantly, and a pair of hunted eyes looked in.

Luther had trained himself never to look around directly at newcomers. Experience had taught him that it sometimes frightened them away. Therefore he had chosen a seat where he could see, and not be noticed himself. He had taken his tactics from a bird man who had taught him to get a good sight of birds and their habits by apparently paying no attention to them.

Luther watched the boy's glance go hungrily around the room and something in those eyes seemed familiar. He had never of course to his knowledge seen the Lazarelle boy, but his memory of the sister's eyes was still with him, and perhaps he imagined it, but there was something in this boy's look that reminded him of the girl.

A hymn was being announced now, and the assembly arose to sing it. The boy at the door suddenly slid inside and slumped into the corner of a back seat. He had the attitude of one who was accustomed to slipping in places without being noticed. Luther's heart went out to him. One of the ushers by the door stepped over and smilingly handed the boy a book, and he turned with a start and looked up at the smile, with a strange, half-fearful, half-yearning look. Frightened at a hymn book. Poor kid! He must have had hard experiences. And yet there was nothing soft about his face. Those wild brown eyes that still held yearning were almost fierce in their defiance.

Luther changed his seat while they were standing to sing, and went nearer to the lad, sitting where he might watch him more closely.

There were lines around the young mouth, dejected weary lines that a much older man might have had. There was a weary look, like an animal that had been hunted. Whenever the door opened and closed he started and looked around furtively as if he expected someone were after him, and there was a pallor upon him. He looked hungry. Perhaps he had come in here to the mission knowing that they gave out coffee and buns sometimes after special meetings. Though this wasn't one of the nights for buns and coffee. Poor kid! He needed something to eat! Was there any way he could manage it for him? But he'd have to go carefully. This wasn't a kid who would jump at a chance. He was suspicious, fearful, self-assured. He might be starving but he wasn't one who would beg.

Luther felt strangely interested in the lad. Of course this wasn't the Lazarelle boy. He likely only imagined the likeness to the girl of course. He must go warily. But whether he belonged to the girl or not he knew he was going to scrape acquaintance and get him fed.

Once the boy stirred restlessly and then slumped sideways letting his head fall dejectedly against the wall. His hair was too long, and his face and hands looked as if they hadn't been washed recently. His fingers were grimy. He wore a torn pair of cheap trousers, and an old sweater with a hole in each elbow over a dark blue flannel shirt. He looked like a young outcast, and yet there was about him that fragileness of feature that reminded him of the delicate features of the girl he had shunned so long. Could it be possible that he was the boy for whom he had been searching?

The boy's eyelids drooped, and when prayer-time came and the audience closed their eyes, the long lashes fell on his thin tanned cheeks, and his breath came intermittently as if he were asleep.

The closing hymn, with everybody standing, roused the young sleeper and he darted a quick glance around.

Luther had come over to sit on the end of the boy's seat, and he spread his arm comfortably out across the back. The boy could not get out without passing him.

The quick glance came to search his face, and Luther turned and gave him a blinding smile. Luther was like that. He could always summon a smile that won people.

"Hello, buddie," he said pleasantly, "have a pleasant nap? Wanta sing a little now? I made free to open your book. Come on, let's sing together."

The boy shook his head.

"I can't sing," he murmured.

"Okay!" said Luther. "Just look over with me for friendliness then," he said, and smiled again.

The boy shuffled his feet, and reached an unaccustomed reluctant hand out to the book, his head turned quite away from the page. But Luther sang on contentedly, and before a minute had passed he had voiced the words so clearly that the boy turned furtive eyes to the book. Luther was past master at getting words down into a human soul by song, and this melody had a lilt and was most intriguing:

"To Jesus every day I find my heart is closer drawn;
He's fairer than the glory of the gold and purple dawn";

sang Luther, and the boy drank in the song. He had witnessed more than one gold and purple dawn of late, from a chilly burrow in a sparse haystack, or from a park bench. It hadn't spoken of glory to him. It had seemed sinister, menacing. Another dreary hopeless day of searching for something that wasn't there.

> "He's all my fancy pictures in its fairest dreams, and
> more;
> Each day He grows still sweeter than He was the day
> before."

The song went on, and the big sweet voice beside the boy went on:

> "The half cannot be fancied this side the golden shore;
> O there He'll be still sweeter than He ever was before."

The boy stole a furtive glance again at the big pleasant man singing there beside him and wondered as he heard the words:

> "He fills and satisfies my longing spirit o'er and o'er";

sang the man, and a feeling like sudden tears crept into the boy's eyes. Was this Someone about whom the song was written the thing that made this man look so happy and satisfied? Oh, but he wasn't a bum and an outcast. One could see by a glance that he wasn't. He had clean hands, well-cared-for hands, clean fingernails, close cut hair, a look of well being about him. He probably never was hungry nor cold. He didn't look as if he drank. What was he doing in this dump then? What was it all about? The boy shivered with the memory of the cold and suffering he had borne since he started out on his own, with no one to care.

Well, whoever this guy was he certainly never knew real suffering.

> *"My heart is sometimes heavy, but He comes with*
> *sweet relief;*
> *He folds me to His bosom when I droop with blighting*
> *grief,*
> *I love the Christ who all my burdens in His body bore;*
> *Each day He grows still sweeter than He was the day*
> *before,"*

sang the man, and somehow the way he sang the words carried conviction to the weary young soul that this was all real to the man. He knew what trouble was and would understand all about it if one told him. Or was it only the guy in the song that knew?

He stole another good look then at the man beside him, and was met at those closing words by another blinding smile that seemed to be genuine and personal, meant for him, a boy who had stolen into a mission to get warm, and maybe a bite to eat.

They stood up for the final prayer, and the boy shuffled to his tired feet. He had walked miles that day over rough roads. His money was gone and he was desperately hungry. The sole was half off one shoe, and just getting to his feet brought back the weariness and sharp pain, the darting soreness where the blister on his foot had broken.

Then gently, pleasantly there came a big arm around his slight shoulders, a comforting, friendly arm, that not only encircled his shoulders with friendliness, but seemed to offer a restful support, and was good to feel. For an instant the boy yielded himself to its comfortable nearness, and then suddenly suspicion, fear, caused his body to stiffen away from the friendliness. But the strong arm did not force itself. It just stayed there pleasantly, quiet, just resting during that closing prayer. And then before the boy had a chance to writhe away from it and try to escape, the big hand patted the gaunt young shoulder.

"Say, Bud, how about a cup of coffee and some hot soup? Seems as if I'm kind of hungry. Wanta come over to the diner and share a bite of supper with me?"

The hungriness came out and sat in the boy's eyes now, and pleaded, yearning, eager, for the food that was suggested. But all the boy said was, "Sure, I don't care if I do!"

Luther had sense enough not to linger.

"Okay!" he said quickly. "Let's go! I know a nice place right across the corner there, that diner. Ever go there? They have swell food."

With his arm linked in the boy's ragged arm Luther propelled his charge across the street and entered the diner, selecting seats at the counter.

"Hi, Harry!" he called smiling to the man in charge. "Give us a feed, the best you've got. Some soup first, I guess. How about soup, kid, you like soup?" He smiled down at the lad beside him, and the boy turned bashful.

"It's awwright!" he answered indifferently with a shrug, but Luther had sense enough to see the wan eagerness behind the shrug, and the soup was soon steaming before them. The boy ate hungrily, and fairly bloomed under the stimulus of the hot broth.

"What have you got there in the way of meat, Harry?" asked Luther. "Is that a pot roast? Give us each a good slice. And mashed potatoes with gravy? Got gravy? Okay. Any vegetables? Tomatoes and corn. That sounds good to me. How about you, kid?"

The boy nodded his head. His mouth was too full for language.

"Okay, Harry. Got pie? What kind? Cherry? That'll do. And another cup of coffee, or would you like a glass of milk? How you making out, kid? Anything else you want?"

It was not until they neared the end of the meal that Luther began to talk.

"Where do you live, kid?"

"Out west," said the boy briefly.

"Yeah? How'd you come to be in these parts?"

"I ben traveling, hunting a job," said the boy drinking deeply from the foaming glass of milk.

"So?" said Luther. "Get one?"

The boy shook his head, a despairing shadow in his eyes.

"Not yet."

"So?" said Luther again thoughtfully. "I understand it's right hard to get jobs nowadays. Got a line on anything?"

"Not yet!" The tone was most dejected.

"How long have you been in town?"

"Since night before last," said the boy with a heavy sigh.

"Mmmm!" said Luther with a ruminating sound to his voice. "You and I'll have to get together and see if we can't do something about that. What's your idea what you'll do?"

"Oh, anything!" said the boy. "I suppose it'll have ta be labor or laborer's helper. I don't know how ta do much but play ball."

Luther laughed.

"I suppose you didn't try the big leagues, did you, yet?"

The first shadow of a smile that there had been on the lad's face hovered over his lips.

"Well," said Luther, "where you living? Got a boarding house yet?"

The boy shook his head.

"Where'd you stay last night?"

"Oh, around!" The boy's eyes shifted uncomfortably, showing he still had some pride left.

"Well, where'd you leave your baggage? Around?"

The lad laughed miserably.

"I see," said Luther. "Well, we won't say any more about that."

"There isn't any baggage left. I sold it all."

"Yeah? Broke?"

The boy owned he was.

"Well, never you mind. You're coming home with me tonight and have a good hot bath and a sleep. How's that?"

The boy stared at Luther. Swallowed hard, blinked, and then said with the most casual tone he could muster;

"Sounds awwright ta me!" and a faint grin flickered at one corner of his tired drooping mouth.

"Okay!" said Luther in a businesslike tone. "Well, now as soon as you finish your pie we'll get going. But first let's get this thing clear. What's your name, kid?"

The lad's startled eyes studied him keenly, with a glint of fear before he answered almost sullenly:

"Tim!"

"Yes?" said Luther. "That's a good name. Well, are you through? Don't want any more to eat? No more coffee or milk?"

The boy shook his head and sidled down from the high stool.

"All set?"

"Sure thing!"

They started out into the night. Luther signaled a bus and they climbed in.

There was little talk on the way. Tim was on the lookout at the window taking in the sights. Luther watched him without seeming to do so, studied him, the while he seemed to be half dozing on the aisle end of the seat.

When they reached the big apartment hotel where Luther had his comfortable small suite of rooms, a bedroom, a bath and a living room, Luther touched the boy on the arm.

"Here we are," he announced calmly. The boy, wondering, got out and looked around him.

"Ever in this city before?" asked Luther casually.

"Yeah. Coupla times," said Tim. "We useta live up this way."

"Then you know your way around?" asked Luther.

"A little." The boy was not telling any more than he had to tell.

But when Luther walked into the lobby, and started over toward the desk to get his mail, Tim hung back.

"I'll wait here," he said looking down at his ragged garments. "I'm not fit for this place."

But Luther was on the alert at once. He hadn't hunted for this boy all these weeks to let him slip through his fingers now.

"Oh, you're all right, Tim," he said. "Come on. We take the elevator here."

Tim drew back distrustfully. It had come to him that perhaps he was being arrested for something.

"Where 're you takin' me?" he said sullenly. "I think I better go somewhere and find a place to stay. I don't belong in any place like this."

"Why, Tim!" said Luther, "I thought you and I were friends. I was just going to take you up to my room. Didn't you agree to stay with me tonight, and then tomorrow we were going to see about getting you fixed up comfortably."

Tim fixed bright eyes of unbelief on his face.

"I didn't know it was a place like this. What d'you want with me, mister? I haven't done anything wrong."

"Why, son, what do you mean?" asked Luther. "I just want to help you. Come on upstairs and I'll explain it all to you. Then if you don't want to stay you can go of course. But I thought you were my friend. You're not afraid of me, are you?"

That was a challenge, and his code required him to accept it.

With eyes full of anxiety he edged around, shot furtive glances up and down the hall, and then half defiantly he said:

"No! I'm not afraid of anybody, nor anything!"

And just at that crucial moment the elevator door slid open in answer to Luther's summons. Luther put a kindly hand on the boy's shoulder and pushed him gently in, the door slammed shut, and they were on their way up, the boy watching warily all the way up, casting quick glances each side when they were landed in an upper hall. He walked along with Luther to his door, and waited while Luther got out his key and unlocked the room, turning on bright lights. Even when he stepped inside the room and the door was shut Tim still cast suspicious glances around. He had heard all sorts of stories in his young life, had met with many experiences. Even a man you found in a Christian mission, a man who looked honest and had fed you with good food might turn out to be a fraud. Maybe he wanted to frame him. He'd got to be on his guard, even against his own desires.

"I don't think I better stay here," he said firmly turning from his investigations. "I don't look right to be in a place like this. I gotta get out." He walked firmly over to the door which Luther had taken the precaution to bolt with the little brass knob.

Luther smiled at him.

"Sit down, kid! We'll have a talk before you go, anyway. Here. Put your cap on that brass hook on the wall and come in here and sit down. Take this chair. I want to have a good look at you."

"Are you a detective?" asked Tim boldly, and there was a frightened determination in his voice.

"Why no," said Luther. "What gave you that idea?"

"Then I don't see what you want of me."

"Well, now I'm going to tell you, Tim. You see you have a little look of someone I know. Your other name's Lazarelle, isn't it?"

Tim started, and a look of fear came into his eyes. He faced Luther with a trembling lip, and then his face hardened and defiance took the lead.

"What's it ta *you?*" he asked.

"Why, it means a lot to me. I'm not a detective but I've been looking for you for several weeks. I didn't know where to look because I didn't know you at all, but it was important to find you, so I've been on the lookout."

"Who wants me?" said the boy with almost the sound of an incipient sob in his fierce young voice.

A gentle look came into Luther's eyes, and a tenderness into his voice.

"Why, it's your mother wants you, son!"

A hard unbelieving look came into the lad's eyes.

"My mother!" said the boy in a hard tone. "She never wanted me before! You're kidding me, mister. What are ya doin' it for?"

"No," said Luther, "I'm not kidding you. Your mother wants you. She's sick and is crying for you all the time!"

"How could you find out a thing like that? Who are you mister, anyway?" There was a sneer on his young face.

"Oh," said Luther, "your sister Minnie wrote some friends of mine about it. Lincoln Silverthorn. Did you ever hear about the Silverthorns, Lincoln and his sister McRae? They were friends of some cousin of yours, Sydney Hollis, who got married a few weeks ago. Do you know them?"

The boy listened in amazement.

"Sure! I know them. But they never had anything to do with me! They wouldn't know about us."

"Yes," said Luther. "The Silverthorns know about you. Your sister wrote to the Silverthorns to see if they knew anything about where you were, because your mother was very sick. She said the doctor said she couldn't live long. She's got some disease that goes very fast, and the doctor said if they couldn't stop her crying she'd go even faster, and the doctor said they should get in touch with you. She wants you to come back before she dies."

The boy was watching Luther with large-eyed unbelief still.

"If all that was true, why'n't my father come and get me? My father always looked after us kids."

"Your father sailed for China just after you left home, I understand. He doesn't know about your mother either. He doesn't know you are not at home."

And now the boy's eyes were half believing.

"I know!" he said thoughtfully. "I didn't go till after he'd left home. But I didn't know he had gone off for a long time. I didn't know where he went. He talked as if he might come back the next week. I just snuck off in the night. But my sister was gone too. She said she had ta go up ta that wedding. She said Sydney would want her."

Luther looked at him thoughtfully.

"Yes, she did come up to the wedding. I saw her myself there in the church, though I didn't speak to her. But she went right back home the next day."

The boy didn't believe that. He shook his head decisively.

"No, she never would. She told mom she never was coming back. She said she was sick of that old town, and wanted to go back where we came from. I don't believe she came back."

"Yes, she did. I saw the letter myself that she had written to the Silverthorns."

"But I don't believe Min ever wrote to them," said the boy scornfully. "She thought they were a stuck-up lot."

"Well, when you were missing and she didn't know how to get hold of you and couldn't leave your mother and the children while your mother was so sick, she wrote to them to help her. She must have trusted them, even if she didn't like them. She had to have somebody find you because your mother cries all the time after you. Certainly son, your mother must love you."

The boy was still a long time.

"Mebbe she does," he said reluctantly. "She never would let me do anything I wanted."

"Well, perhaps they weren't the right things to do. What was it you wanted to do?"

"Oh, everything. She wouldn't let me come back up here ta our old town where I had my friends. I was captain of the baseball team in my school, and I had a lotta friends, and she said I hadta stay there with them and I hated it."

"Well, of course that was hard lines, son, to have to

give up your school and your team, and your friends, and the things you liked best, but didn't you ever realize it was the right thing to do?"

"*Right!* What's right?" said the young rebel. "Who gave yer parents a right ta boss ya?"

"Well, I guess God did that. But, son, that's a big subject and it's late and you're tired, perhaps we better not go into that tonight. You've got a lot of things to consider now. You don't want your mother to die crying for you, do you?"

Luther was sitting now beside the boy, his big kindly arm around the slender shoulders.

The boy was looking down, picking at the torn sleeve of his old sweater, suddenly sniffing. All at once he ducked his head around and hid his face on his elbow slung over the chair back. Big silent sobs racked the thin young body.

Luther's big hand went tenderly up to the boy's head, smoothing back the rough hair, comfortably nestling the sad young brow in his gentle hand.

"What's the matter of my mother?" he asked, suddenly lifting his head, his eyes fierce even through the tears that streamed down the dirty face.

"They didn't tell me," said Luther. "I got the impression it was something like ulcers of the stomach, or maybe cancer, or diabetes. Something that was pretty hopeless, and it was making her worse to cry so much. It was making her suffer a lot more pain than she needed to have."

The thin frame of the boy was racked again with silent sobs. It went on for some minutes, Luther's hands still comfortingly on the boy's shoulder, sometimes on his head.

"You know, son," he said at last, "your place is down with them now while this trouble is going on. You're sort of the man of the house, with your father so far away they can't reach him. I gathered from what I've heard that they don't know how to reach him yet."

"That's the way he does!" broke forth the errant son angrily. "He never lets 'em know where he is, not for months, sometimes a year or two."

"That's all the more reason they need you, son. They need a man of the house."

"Not with that half-sister of mine there!" burst forth the boy furiously. "She just hates me!"

"No, I don't think she does now. She wants you back. She needs you. I think you'll find she'll welcome you!"

There was a long silence except for the sniffing of the lad trying to suppress those heart-racking sobs.

"What didya mean telling me you would help me get a job then, if you were goin' ta work this off on me?" he said lifting desperate eyes toward Luther. The young man's heart went out to him with yearning.

"Why I meant all that, kid. I'll do my best when this is all over and things straighten out, and you can come back honorably and get to work. But I thought you'd never forgive yourself if you didn't do the right thing now, would you?"

"I dunno," said the boy in smothered tones, with his bowed head on his arm again.

When he raised his head his face was full of perplexity.

"How'm I gonta go back there? I haven't got a cent of money. I'm *broke,* I tell ya! And how'm I gonta go back in these cloes? I'm not fit ta be seen. My mother and sister would give me heck if I went back there and shamed them. I can't go till after I get a job and earn a little money and get some decent cloes."

"Well, now, son, that's all right. We'll find a way to fix that up for you. You know life and death won't wait on things like that, kid. Those aren't so important as they seem. The thing is for you to get to see your mother now while she wants you and needs you!"

The tears came again and flowed freely.

"I hadn't oughtta have gone away that way, I know," he owned at last. "But now I gotta take what's comin' ta me. I can't let you do any more for me. You fed me, and you've been good ta me. An' you're the first person that's spoken kind to me since I can remember. If you hadn't taken me ta supper with ya I think I'd 'a' died tanight and ben outta all this. It would of ben a lot less trouble fer everybody too. I was about ta starve. I hadn't had a bit ta eat except half a rotten apple since day before yesterday, an' I found that in the gutter an' washed it off at the fire plug. You ben good ta me, but I mustn't let ya bother any more for me. If ya'll just give me a reference so I can work a week I'll take the money and go back as soon as I get enough."

"Say, look here, son. No more talk like this! I'm looking after you now, and I say you need to go to bed. You'll get a nice hot bath and then you'll climb into a pair of my big clean pajamas and have a real old sleep, and then we'll see tomorrow morning just how we can make things come out. Here's some towels and a wash rag. Get your togs off and get to work. I've got to make some phone calls while you're scrubbing."

Luther pulled open a closet door, and handed out big soft towels, a cake of new soap, a bottle of shampoo soap.

"There! Get to work, kid. You'll feel a lot better when you get done."

Luther called up Link as soon as the water was running strong enough to cover his voice on the telephone.

"Well, I've found the boy, Link!" he said. "What's the situation now? I'm thinking of taking him back tomorrow. He seems to be at the place where he's willing to start."

"Good work, Lute! The mother isn't long for this world. My sister had a letter from the girl just today. The mother still keeps crying for the boy. I guess the sooner he gets there the better. Anything I can do to help, Lute?"

"No, thanks, Link. I'll manage it myself. If I need any help I'll call on you. I might ask you to go down to the mission pretty often while I'm away and look after some of my special cases."

"Sure, Lute, but—you don't mean you're going *yourself!* Surely the fellow is old enough to look out for himself!"

"Well, yes, I guess he could, but I think this is the better way. I can get acquainted with him. We might drive. I'll see how the trains are. It seems to be an out-of-the-way town. Might be good to have my car there. I'll see."

"But say, that's great of you, Lutie, the way you feel about the sister."

"But I don't any more. I guess everybody is interesting when you think about it. This is something I want to do. I think I should. So long, Link. I'll be keeping in touch with you!"

Luther made several other phone calls, arranged a few matters of business with the man who looked after his affairs, and wrote a couple of letters. Then he heard the light click off in the bathroom, and Tim came out grinning and shamefaced, looking fairly lost in Luther's big garments.

"Well, how do you feel, fella?" he asked grinning back at the boy genially.

"Feel like a four-year-old," said Tim shyly.

"Fine! I thought you would. Now, fold yourself into that bed and sleep as hard as you can. We've got a lot to do tomorrow."

Luther had opened up the wall bed which was always ready for any chance guest of his, and the boy crept in gratefully and was asleep almost as soon as his head touched the pillow, his little pitiful bundle of tattered garments folded neatly in a heap on the chair beside him.

Luther finished his last letter by a shaded light and then came over and looked down at the boy. Poor little fragment of humanity, unloved, uncared for, save by a hysterical mother who had neglected him all her life till now! Luther's heart went out to him again, and quietly he knelt down beside the boy and prayed for him, asking that he might be shown how to guide him aright.

16

LUTHER WAS awake early, going quietly around the room gathering together such things as he would need to take with him on a journey, placing them in his suitcase, and arraying himself for the day. Then he made a few telephone calls, guardedly, to the shops in the building, and presently some packages arrived at the door.

Luther opened the packages, and laid some of the articles out on the chair in place of the soiled belongings of the lad, which he wrapped in a neat bundle.

Then he turned to the bed.

"Hey, fella!" he said. "About time you woke up, isn't it? This is another day."

Tim came awake with a start, rubbed his eyes, looked about him bewildered, and then concentrated on the man beside him. He blinked a moment and said:

"Okay! I didn't know where I was."

Luther grinned at him.

"Sorry to waken you, lad, but it's almost breakfast time and we've got a lot to do. First off there's some things to try on and see if they fit. I had 'em sent up from the shop downstairs. What size do you wear, anyway?"

The boy murmured that he didn't know, and turned his attention to the pile of garments on the chair. Undergarments, socks, a brown flannel shirt, brown corduroy trousers, and a brown sweater.

"O boy!" said Tim, and arose promptly. "Are these for me? I can pay you, you know, when I get that job, if you don't mind waiting."

"That's all right, kid. Don't worry about that. Hop into those things and see if they fit."

Tim obeyed with alacrity, and was soon arrayed and smiling in front of the long mirror on the closet door.

"They're swell!" said Tim turning after a survey of himself.

Luther came and inspected him.

"Well, I judged your size pretty well at first shot, didn't I? Those trousers are not so hot, but they'll do for the time being anyway. I told the barber to come up and give you a haircut. He ought to be here any minute now. Is that all right with you?"

"Swell!" said Tim shyly. "I sure do need one!"

"Okay!" said Luther. "Now, young fella, put your foot down on this piece of paper and let's see what we can do about a pair of shoes for you. One of yours isn't very seaworthy, you know."

"I know," said Tim in a mortified tone, as he set his foot down on the paper and watched Luther draw a firm line around it.

A little later the barber arrived, and while Tim was getting his hair cut a young man came from the shoe store, and took away with him Tim's old worn-out shoes and the drawing on paper. It wasn't long before he was back again with three or four boxes of shoes for the boy to select from. Oh, Luther knew how to go about getting the things he wanted in a hurry. And when the barber was gone and Tim stood in awe before the glass surveying himself, Luther brought forward the shining new shoes.

"Oh, gee, mister!" said Tim. "You didn't needta do that. I coulda made out with the old ones."

"Yes? Well, I didn't think you could. It's a bit dangerous to try to navigate with the sole off your shoe. But say, kid, suppose you quit saying 'mister' to me and call me Luther. That's my name. I like it a lot better, don't you, than 'mister'?"

"Sure! If you don't mind!" said the boy with deep admiration in his eyes.

"No, I don't mind," said Luther smiling. "We're friends, aren't we? Then why go around saying 'mister'? Well, now that's settled let's get to work. Suppose we have our breakfast sent up here and then we can talk without interruption. What do you want? Orange juice, hot cereal with cream, hot cakes and sausage, hot rolls, milk and coffee? How's that?"

"Swell," said Tim with shining eyes.

Luther telephoned down the order, and then turned to his young guest.

"You look fine, Timothy. Now, we've got to decide just how to make this journey."

Tim caught his breath and looked troubled.

"Say mister—I mean Luther—!" and then he grinned sheepishly. "Suppose my mother happens to be better now, and doesn't need me any more. Wouldn't it be better for me to stay here and earn some money to pay for all these grand togs than to go out there now?"

"No," said Luther, "positively not! Besides she isn't better. The Silverthorns just had a letter yesterday begging them to find you and send you home. The doctor said it was the only thing that could help her. And you're the man of the house, you know. It's up to you to take care of them. Aren't there some younger ones you could look after while your sister is busy at the hospital with your mother?"

"Sure!"

"Well, Tim, I've been thinking. How would you like to telephone your sister and tell her you've got her message and you're coming just as soon as you can arrange it? Then she can tell your mother they've found you and you're coming soon. That will ease things up a bit for them."

"Wouldn't it be all right for me to wait till I got there? I don't like ta talk ta my sister. She never had any use for me."

"Oh, that's no way to do!" said Luther in a business-like way. "You're almost a man. Just talk up to her pleasantly the way a man would. You needn't say much."

Tim looked dejected over the idea but yielded.

"Okay!" he said in a low dismal voice.

"Well, then let's get it over with!" Luther got up and went to the phone, a person to person call, long distance, and Tim stood in awe and listened. All this was being done for him. He didn't like it but he couldn't help being a bit awed by it.

Fortunately they got Erminie at once, and Luther signaled for the boy to come to the phone.

Tim cleared his throat and tried to talk like a man.

"Hello! This you, Min? This is Tim."

"Oh, Timmie! I'm so glad!" came back the answer, and strangely the sister seemed to be crying in her voice. It sprung the tears into Tim's eyes, even while he tried to be a man.

"Oh, Tim, where are you? Can't you come back?

Mother wants you terribly. She cries all the time for you."

"Yes, sure I'll come!" assured Tim huskily. "I'll come as soon as I can arrange it." His voice sounded important, as if he were a man of a great many important affairs.

"When will that be, Tim?" asked Erminie. "The doctor isn't sure how long mother will last!"

"Oh gee!" said the boy. "I didn't know it was that bad! Sure I'll get started right away, taday, mebbe. It's a long way, ya know, Min. But I'll get there. Tell mom I send my love. Gub-by!" He hung up the receiver and turned away, rubbing his eyes with the back of his hand.

"That's all right, kid," said Luther with a comforting arm thrown briefly about his shoulders. "Now, here comes our breakfast, and while we eat we'll settle plans for starting. Tell me about train service out there. Is there through-service, or a lot of way trains and missing connections, and waiting and all that?"

"That's right," said Tim with a long dreary sigh. "It's ten miles from our town to the railroad, and the train service is awful. Just an old dinkey worn-out train that's always breaking down."

"Think we'd stand more chance of getting there soon by automobile?"

"Sure thing!" said the boy sadly. "But I haven't got any automobile, and if I had I haven't got any license."

"Oh, but I have," said Luther. "Got both!"

The boy's face lighted as with sunshine.

"Are you going, Luther?"

"Why of course!" said Luther. "You didn't think I was sending you off alone on an errand like this? Certainly I'm going along. Come, let's get busy and eat a good breakfast, so we won't have to waste too much time stopping for food."

He picked up the phone and called his garage.

"Get ready my car," he ordered, "gas, oil, and a thorough checking over. Make it snappy. I want to be ready to start on a long journey by noon if possible. Bring it here to the usual place, and tell the man to wait at the front entrance till I come down. No, I don't want a driver."

He slammed the receiver up and attacked the hot cakes and sausage, and Tim sat there in a daze. Just like that this amazing man gave his orders as if he were used to being obeyed. A man he had found in a slum mission! What could it mean? Tim almost wondered if possibly there wasn't a God after all, although he had never really believed there was.

"We've got a little shopping to do," said Luther. "We'd better go as soon as we're through eating. I want to get back to make a couple of phone calls on business before I leave, and we should start by twelve if possible."

Then he snatched the phone again and called a number.

"Oh, Joe! Got that itinerary ready for me I was talking to you about last night? Can you send it over to my apartment by eleven-thirty so I'll be sure to get it? I'm leaving around that time. Thanks awfully. I'll be seeing you when I get back. So long!"

What a man he was!

They started out shopping, first getting Tim a suitcase which they carried with them. Tim all unconscious that it was for himself admired it greatly.

Then a haberdashery, where Luther made short work of ordering more underclothes, shirts, handkerchiefs, socks. Not too many. An easy load for the suitcase, and then they went to the tailor's and got a new suit for Tim.

"I don't need a suit," said Tim. "I can get home in these things."

"Timothy, you've got to look right when you go to

the hospital to see your sick mother or it will worry her," said Luther.

Timothy subsided and watched the process of getting fitted with shining eyes.

"Gee! Nobody ever took such a lotta pains for me before!" he stated thoughtfully. "I wonder what ya do it for?"

Luther smiled. "Tell you by and by when we have more time," he promised.

Timothy Lazarelle looked like a different lad when he was finally arrayed in his new suit, brown, his own choice, and his new hat, and overcoat. He looked at himself with a new respect and decided that he ought to act a little more in keeping with his garments. He himself elected to wear the corduroys for traveling.

"Cause I might havta change a tire for ya or something," he explained with a grin. "I know how ta do that."

"Well, say, that'll be great!" said Luther, feeling that this kid was going to turn out to be worth while even if he was a Lazarelle. Maybe the sister wouldn't be so bad after all, now that she'd got a Bible!

So Luther bought him a suede jacket for cold nights driving and added a pair of gloves, though Tim rather scorned those, saying he'd never worn any. He had felt it was only sissies who wore gloves until he saw Luther draw on his big fine ones. Then he decided he'd put them on sometime, just for the experience.

They took their purchases upstairs and finished packing, Timothy proudly, for he had never before been privileged to pack his things. Indeed he had seldom had very much to pack. He was going home in state, just as he would have chosen to go had he planned it all, only it wasn't quite fair, because he wasn't doing it himself. He had thought some day to go home after he had a good job and was doing well, and let them all see what he had done by himself. But now instead he was finding out that there was such a thing as grace, favor. It was by the favor of this man Luther that he was going home proudly, like any young fellow who had a regular father and a family that cared. Well, anyway, perhaps they wouldn't bawl him out so much for going. Gee! He wished there wasn't a prospect of a funeral at the other end of this journey. It didn't seem like mom to stage a funeral. A box of chocolates was much more typical of her than a funeral. However, maybe she'd get well after she stopped crying.

They ate a brief lunch in the restaurant downstairs, and then went up for their things. Timothy gave a quick glance about the pleasant room where he had spent such a happy night, wondering if he would ever see it again. Anyway, he meant to have one like it some day if all went well with him.

Then they went down and found the car waiting for them, and stowing their luggage and themselves in started away into what was to Timothy the most notable day of his life so far.

The last thing that Luther did before he left his room was to call up the Silverthorn house, taking a chance that Link might be at home.

Link wasn't there but McRae was, and he talked to her a minute or two.

"Rae, this is Lute. Link there? No, I was afraid he wouldn't be. I'll tell you. You won't mind passing on a message. Tell Link we're starting now, as soon as I hang up. Tell him we're taking my car so we can make better time. The railroad is a dinkey affair, and no connections. The boy is okay. We're going to be good friends. Tell Link to be praying, and you too, McRae! We'll be needing a lot of it, I suspect. Good-by. Tell Link I'll be keeping in touch with him. Say, McRae, what about you writing Minnie a letter. Wouldn't that be a good idea?"

"Yes, I will, Luther," came McRae's answer, "but don't forget that she has a new name now. That might be important, too."

"Yes, I'll remember. Erminie, isn't it? Yes, I won't forget!" Luther hung up the phone, and hurried away with Timothy.

Carey Carewe was spending the day with McRae Silverthorn, hoping to get a little line on what Link was doing now, and she was most curious about that phone call.

"Who on earth was that, McRae? Not Luther Waite? Didn't I hear you call him 'Lutie'? Where is he going now, and who is this Erminie person you were talking about? A new girl? Don't tell me Luther Waite has a girl at last! Who is she?"

"Oh, nothing like that, Carey!" laughed McRae. "Luther is just starting out on a wonderful expedition. I think it is a very remarkable thing he is doing, a triumph of grace over human nature, considering what a dislike he's always had for her."

"What is it, McRae? You know I've been out of the world for the last three weeks and don't know a thing about people."

"Well, you remember Minnie Lazarelle?"

"Sure I remember her. Can anybody forget her? My goodness, she hasn't turned up again, has she? I declare if I were the Hollises I'd do something about her. I wouldn't be pestered that way any longer."

McRae's face grew a little grave, but she went quietly on with what she was saying.

"No, she hasn't turned up here, but word came back to us that when she got home she found her stepmother very ill and that her fourteen year old stepbrother had run away in this direction, supposedly coming back to their old home, and the mother was grieving for him. They couldn't get any trace of him anywhere, so she asked us if we should see him would we tell him how sick his mother was, and how he ought to come home at once, for the doctor said she wasn't going to get well."

"For pity's sake! That's just like her to go and put herself and all her family troubles on the Silverthorns. I don't see how you stand for so much I declare. I should think you would just have told her you couldn't bother. She's the most presumptuous person I ever saw. Why didn't she just put it into the hands of the police? They have people to look up lost numbers don't they. I'm sure I don't see why you should be hampered with a thing like that. A little untrained animal that has run away. But at that I don't see how Luther Waite got into it."

"Why, Luther heard about it and he has been very much interested to find that boy. He has employed a detective, and they have hunted everywhere for several weeks, with no sign of the boy, until last night when he came into that mission that Luther is so much interested in. And Luther discovered who he was and is taking him home to his mother. They are just starting. Lutie wanted Link to know they were on their way. He wanted us to pray for them."

"Of all things! *Taking* him home! A great boy like that! Couldn't he be trusted to go by himself? I think that is carrying things much too far, even for Lutie. You say he doesn't like that girl? Well, I certainly doubt it if he is willing to go down there for her. But where in the world does he get the time, and the money to do things like that? Is he expecting you folks to pay for it all? He probably won't get even thanks from the Lazarelles. What in the world is the matter with Lutie anyway?

Why doesn't he get himself a job and get to work and earn some real money himself. He's lots of fun of course at a party, but nobody would ever take him seriously, not till he gets down to work to make a name and a place in the world for himself."

McRae looked at her friend in astonishment.

"Why, what in the world do you mean, Carey? A job! Don't you know who Luther is? Didn't you know he was the real head of the great Wendling Power Plant that is one of the richest and best known firms in the city? Didn't you know that his Uncle George Wendling has been training him all these years to take his place and that George Wendling just died about a year ago and Luther came into a big fortune? It goes into the millions, I don't know just how many. I think Luther would be rather amused at your idea of his lack of industry."

"McRae! What do you mean? Where did you get a tale like that, McRae? You must have been dreaming dreams. I'm quite sure you are mistaken. A young man with millions would never waste his time going down to the slums singing in prayer meetings. If that is true why do you think he does such silly things as that? Why doesn't he buy himself a yacht and go around the world, or have a string of polo ponies and have himself a time? I think you are all a crazy lot anyway. But even if that were all true what you have told me, it doesn't answer why Lutie goes off with a little blackguard of a runaway, whose sister is a pest if there ever was one. Why do you think he would do a thing like that, McRae?"

"He does it for the glory of God, Carey," said McRae with a quiet look of radiance. "Luther loves to win souls for Christ, and he sees a chance to help that boy."

"Well, who is paying for it? Answer me that?"

"I wouldn't really know," said McRae, "but knowing

Luther as well as I do I suppose he is paying for it, at least for the present."

"Wasting his money on a thankless job like that! It is piteous!" said Carey. "That's what I told Link not long ago. It would be a great deal better for Lutie and Link, too, to make more money and pay some poor impecunious theological student to go down in the slums and preach."

McRae looked up quickly.

"Did you tell my brother that?" she said.

"Yes, I did!" said Carey. "I thought it was time someone made him see straight."

"Oh," said McRae, "that explains!"

"Explains what, McRae?"

"Oh, several things that I haven't understood lately."

Carey studied her friend for a minute or two and then she said:

"About me and Link?"

"Yes, some of them."

"Well," said Carey haughtily, "I'm not a fanatic, and I always like my friends to understand that."

"Yes?" said McRae. "Perhaps it's just as well."

Just then Link arrived and after pleasant greetings they all settled down again to talk, and Carey said:

"Say, look here, Link, McRae has just been telling me something extraordinary about Luther Waite. She says he's wealthy. Is that true?"

"Why yes, Carey. Didn't you know that?"

"No, I didn't. You never one of you said anything about it, and Luther himself never acted as if he had a thing. I don't see why I never heard it."

"Was it so important?" laughed Link. "I don't think Lutie feels that it is."

"Well, I think it's very important. It ranks him in a

very common class with common people when you don't know that."

"How so, Carey?" asked Link. "I never felt that way about him. I like Lutie for himself, not his money, and I supposed all our crowd did. I think it's a grand thing to be a rich man and rise above his riches the way Lutie has."

"Well, I don't!" said Carey vexedly. "What does he do with his money? A man with riches has a right to make the world better for them, to show a good time to all his friends, and do wonderful different things that other people can't afford to do."

"Well, that's exactly what Lute is doing," said Link. "Do you know how many missions he is supporting? Do you know how many hundreds of Bibles he is sending out? Do you know how many missionaries he is supporting?"

"Oh, *missionaries!*" said Carey contemptuously. "What are missionaries?"

"They are the messengers of the Lord Jesus Christ," said Link gravely. "They are about the most important thing in the world. They are Christ's witnesses to the ends of the earth."

"Oh, well, I'm not a fanatic like you, thank goodness!" said Carey with a laugh. "Come on! Let's go out and play tennis! It's gorgeous weather."

McRae looked up thoughtfully at her brother, deciding that she knew now why Link didn't go to see Carey Carewe any more, and in her heart she was glad. Not Carey Carewe! She wasn't the one for her dear brother. She was glad she understood.

17

STEVE GRANT sent word home at last that he had got the commission he had gone after, and a few weeks training would probably see him on his way abroad to enter the army.

His mother shed quiet tears as she went about her daily tasks, and his father and Curlin went gravely through their days, waiting for the outcome, wondering what Steve was doing in his spare time. Curlin was hoping he was not keeping up a correspondence with Mysie, or anyone like her.

Then one day there came a special delivery air mail letter from him.

Dear folks:

I am sailing next week for foreign shores. This is just to tell you that I have been married, and am bringing my wife to greet you before we go. You'll like her, I know. Mother will love her. I guess you all will.

I didn't think she ought to go with me, but she is pure gold and has wangled it to go as a Red Cross nurse or something like that.

Here's hoping you will all be happy over this, I am,

> Your bad boy with love,
> Steve

They read the letter aloud, and then looked at each other with stricken eyes. The one thought was in all their minds. Who was this wife that Steve had married? Poor Steve! Had he spoiled his life already? For they all knew the danger he had been in before he left home. Oh, of course his father and mother did not know Mysie by name, had never seen her, but they knew that there was someone who was exceedingly questionable, and they were frantic with fear.

About the middle of the morning Curlin took the letter over to McRae. He hated to do it. If McRae cared for Steve in the way he was afraid she did it would seem to him almost like stabbing her. But she would have to see Steve when he came, and it was much better that she should be prepared.

So he went over with a face like a death's head, and sat with her as she worked at some sewing.

"We've had a letter from Steve!" he said in a sorrowful tone.

McRae looked up fearfully.

"Oh! Is it that girl again?" she said as she took the letter he handed her.

"I—don't—know—" he answered lamely. "He's married, McRae!"

"Married?" she said giving Curlin a startled glance.

Then she read the letter, and considered it carefully

before she looked up, a faint little hopeful smile in her eyes.

"Don't look that way, Curlin dear," she said earnestly. "It may not be so bad. Of course she's been divorced, and you couldn't like that part, but I guess we've nothing to do with it now it's done. That's Steve's business, and God's. But if he's married he's married, and you've got to accept it in a right way. Cheer up, Curlin. We don't even *know* it's Mysie!"

"Who else could it be?" said Curlin in a doleful voice. "She isn't the kind of girl who lets go easily, I could see that. She's probably been up there with him making hay while the sun shines. That's her method."

McRae was still for an instant, her eyes thoughtful.

"Listen, Curlin. You remember we've been praying about this, all of us together, bringing that promise that where two of you agree it shall be done, and we've all been saying 'Nevertheless, Thy will be done.' So if this is our answer it must be God's will. It must somehow work out to His glory."

"How could that Mysie thing work out for God's glory?" asked Curlin indignantly.

"I don't know, Curlin. But you know in the Bible God did use people that weren't His own. Perhaps God can use Mysie in a wonderful way for Steve's good, and God's glory. It may be Steve had to learn some lesson that could only be learned through this very experience. Some lesson that is going to get Steve ready for the Lord's return, that is going to polish him, and make him conform to the image of God's Son. After all that's what we want for Steve. And we meant it when we prayed 'Thy will be done,' didn't we?"

"Yes, I suppose so," said Curlin dejectedly. "But it does seem so awful for mother to have to go through this, to say nothing of the rest of us. You and Link and all the rest of his friends." He cast a quick searching look at McRae. Was this breaking her heart?

"Yes, but God loves your mother as much as you do. More, you know. And if He wants her to go through a thing like this we mustn't grudge it for her. As for the rest of us, well, we need plenty of lessons of course," and she laughed a pleasant little ripple. "It will be all right somehow, Curlin. Don't let's grieve. Especially not before we actually know just what has happened."

"Yes," said Curlin, a tiny bit of relief in his voice. McRae was really a wonderful girl. How brave and strong she was! "But I guess we know pretty well what to expect."

"Well," said the girl, smiling now, "I think we ought to get our wills handed over to the Lord thoroughly, and then we'll be able to appreciate any pleasant surprises the Lord may have for us in the future."

"Surprises!" said Curlin, with unbelief in his voice, almost contempt as he got up to leave. "I guess almost anything that could happen would be a pleasant surprise after this!" He sighed deeply and dropped down on a chair by the door, covering his face for an instant with his hands, and sighing heavily. "Oh, McRae! I feel as if this was all my fault. I ought to have watched over that young brother of mine instead of getting angry at him and going off and leaving him. I knew how easily he was led. I knew what his temptations would be."

McRae got up and went over to stand beside him, laying her hand on his hair with a gentle touch.

"Don't, Curlin!" she said. "Can't you trust God?"

Curlin with a deep breath raised his head and looked at her, apology in his eyes, and a hint of a brave smile on his lips.

"Yes," he breathed. "Of course!" and the look in his eyes was a promise.

Then suddenly McRae with a look in her eyes such as an angel might have worn stooped and kissed him on the forehead, a kiss like the breath of a whisper, and it brought a glory light into Curlin's face. Glory with a touch of great humility.

Then suddenly they heard Mrs. Silverthorn calling:

"Rae! Rae dear! Where are you? I wish you'd come here and help me a minute. I can't seem to manage this alone!" and they both sprang to answer her call.

A little later as Curlin was hurrying home to see if his mother's reception preparations needed any of his help, he was thinking of McRae. Here he had gone over there to help her bear a heartache, and she had been the one to help him bear his.

And that precious kiss she had given him, would he ever forget it? Like a blessing to his whole life, a benediction.

Of course it wasn't a sentimental kiss. She had trusted him to understand that. It was just a dear precious bit of comfort handed him in a sisterly way. But he was rejoiced that Steve's marriage hadn't hit her the way he had feared it would. That was something to be truly thankful about. It wasn't anything he could speak about at home, or to any of his closest friends. It was just a matter between himself and God.

So, if Steve was no longer a consideration, was it conceivable that he might allow his own heart to try and win her? That was something to think about later. He mustn't go too fast, mustn't even allow himself to *think* of it now.

Then, later in the afternoon, he happened to look up and saw Paul Redfern arriving across the way. Ah! Perhaps that was the way of it. That was why she was not feeling Steve's marriage. She was probably deeply interested in Paul. Well, Paul was the better man. Paul was rich and influential. His wife would have a fine position anywhere, and he, Curlin, was just going to be a plain farmer. He had definitely chosen that as his profession, and perhaps he shouldn't even dream of asking a wonderful girl like McRae to share in a life like that. Well he would trust in God and learn to be content as McRae had suggested.

So he put it all aside and plunged into the preparations his mother was making for the bride, praying continually that the coming days might not be too sorrowful for his mother.

The house was in charming order, and a festive dinner well on its way to perfection, when the taxi drew up to the side door of the Grant home, bearing the recalcitrant Steve and his anxiously awaited bride.

There was a breathless moment after the taxi was sighted turning into the drive, when the family collected itself and gave one wild look at each other, exhorting one another to keep calm and not get excited, whatever was about to come. Then they could hear Steve's beloved voice, gay with happiness as ever, paying off the taxi driver, his familiar footsteps timing with other lighter footsteps coming up on the porch. Then the family stiffened and braced its soul to meet whatever was coming, and Steve burst into the door of the sitting room with his arm around Frances Ferrin.

He rushed her right over to his mother who stood bewildered, tense, and said: "Mother, here's your new daughter! Love her a lot! She hasn't any mother of her own, you know," and he handed her over to loving arms raised with great joy to embrace the bride.

"Frannie, *dear!*" said the trembling lips, while tears of joy sprang to her eyes. "Frannie! To think it should be *you!*" said the mother.

"Now, who else should it be, mother?" said the

groom indignantly. "It's always been Frannie with me, except when I thought I couldn't get her, and then whatever I did was to get it back on her for not seeing it right away!"

Afterwards Steve's family cherished that explanation, which was the only one of Mysie they ever did get. But it rolled away a lot of burdens from all their hearts, and especially from the heart of Curlin, the big brother.

Then presently they were seated around the big dining table. The father and mother at the head and foot of the table, Steve and Frannie sitting together at one side holding hands, partly concealed by the shining damask of the table cloth, and Curlin on the other side alone. Could he be blamed that the unbidden thought came to him what if McRae were there beside him, her hand in his?

The color crept slowly up in his quiet cheeks and he had much ado to keep the thought from showing in his expressive eyes.

"And to think it was Frannie all the time!" said the father looking at his new daughter with calm content.

"Yes, to think it was our own Frannie," echoed Curlin with a sudden streak of impishness. "And mother here had been conjuring up some foreign creature he had found in Canada, who would be the undoing of her Steve!"

Then how they laughed. And Steve returned a loving glance from Curlin as if he would taunt him. "See how foolish was your worrying when all the time I had such a girl in my thoughts!"

So Mysie faded from the family annals like mist before the morning sunshine, and if she had appeared in their midst with a large packet of blackmail in her intentions they would have only looked at her amusedly and laughed her away. There was no room in that house that night for ghosts of the past, even ghosts of wrong doing, because true love had come in, and driven away the foolishness till there was only shame left to contemplate where it had been. A good wholesome shame that would be a reminder in any future time of temptation.

When dinner was over, and all the lovely exciting news told of how and what Steve was to be in the venture that was ahead for himself and his bride; and of how Frannie had come to herself and they had got together after the misunderstandings of the past two years, and been quickly and quietly married; and after the whole family had helped to clear away the table and wash the dishes and put everything to rights for breakfast the next morning, Steve looked up with his blue eyes alight with eagerness and said in his old gay voice that hadn't sounded that way for almost two years:

"Now, come on folks! Let's go over and call on the Silverthorns and spring our surprise!"

There wasn't a dissenting voice, and even Mother Grant though she must have been weary with all the work and anxiety of the day, went eagerly off after her woolly white sweater and started out as spryly as if she were only a girl.

But the bride and groom, holding hands, were speeding ahead of them and arrived by way of the familiar Silverthorn kitchen that had been such an intimate part of their early lives, entering softly and waiting till the rest of the Grants had entered the front door and were being ushered into the living room by Link, with a gracious welcome on his lips. Then waiting in the offing till the greetings were exchanged, and before there was a chance for a word to be said beyond that, Steve drew his bride's arm within his own and they advanced into the room with a low bow.

"Friends," said Steve with a lilting voice, "meet my wife, Mrs. Stephen Whitney Grant!"

They all turned toward the newcomers with instant sharp attention, noted the gay look on Steve's handsome face, the contented joy on his mother's, and then looked at the bride, half afraid to face her as she lifted laughing eyes from the low bow she had been making. Then they all simply whooped with joy.

"Frannie! Frannie! O Frannie!" they cried in chorus.

Steve stood there grinning.

"Put something over on you, didn't I?" he derided joyously.

"Well, Steve, old man, you did yourself proud!" said Paul clapping his shoulder cheerfully. "I didn't think you had that much sense. I honestly didn't!"

"Thanks for the compliment, Fernie," said Steve. "I accept them kind words with reservations. She's a grand girl, and I knew it all the time, only I didn't know I could get her."

And then they all cheered and howled uproariously, so that they didn't even hear the taxi that brought Carey Carewe unheralded and left her at the door.

"Well, really!" said Carey when she could make her voice heard, as she stood in the doorway and surveyed them all in astonishment. "Is this a party? And why wasn't I invited?"

"You've said it," said Curlin arising to the occasion and taking her hand, "only it isn't merely a party. It's a wedding reception. Allow me to introduce the bride and groom, Mr. and Mrs. Stephen Grant, Miss Carewe!"

Carey went over and stood before the two and surveyed them, grinned and then turned to Curlin.

"What is it, a game? Or a charade?"

"Oh, not at all," said Curlin, very formally. "I trust it's going to last longer than that!"

But it was some minutes before they actually made Carey understand, and even then she was bewildered.

"Why, and we're almost all of us here again!" she exclaimed. "Who is missing? Lutie! Lutie Waite. Why don't we call him up? Have you tried? What's his number, Link?"

"Sorry," said Link dryly, "I'm afraid I can't favor you tonight. Lutie is a good many miles away just now, and couldn't very well get back. You see, this party is quite impromptu. Otherwise of course you would have been invited. Steve just sprung this on us a few minutes ago. He's sailing next week for service abroad and taking Fran with him, so we had to adjust ourselves to circumstances. But I'm sure Lutie would have been here if he could have arranged it that way. He doesn't know about Fran and Steve, however."

"Oh, for heaven's sake!" said Carey, utterly dumbfounded. "Do you mean to tell me that Lutie is still trailing around with that crazy Lazarelle kid?"

There was instant attention on the part of everybody as Link answered.

"He found that the mother was very low, dying, and that there were ways in which he could be of help, so he is staying a little longer!"

"He would!" said Carey indignantly. "The big dumb fool! Hang around there until he gets that silly Lazarelle girl going again. She'll have her claws in him yet, and she won't let go this time either. Link, I should suppose you would try to protect him. He's such a close friend of yours."

"What's all this about Lutie?" asked Steve, instantly interested.

Link with an annoyed look at Carey started to explain.

"Why, we had word that the fourteen-year-old Lazarelle kid had run away, and was here in the city.

Then his mother got seriously ill and began to cry for him so we were trying to find him. Lute happened on him one night in the mission, and he buddied up to him and got him to go home. *Took* him home, you know! He was afraid the kid might lose his nerve and not go!"

"What a lovely thing to do!" cried Frannie. "I always knew Lutie was rather great!"

"Such an utterly silly thing to do!" cried Carey. "If the kid hadn't sense enough to go to his dying mother what good would he do her when he got there? I think it was utterly silly, and somebody ought to have stopped him. He just hates that Minnie! Now I suppose she'll hang on to him, and come back here, and we'll all have her to deal with!"

"I think you'll have no trouble, Carey. Lutie writes me that she is very different. She has given herself to the Lord, and her whole attitude is changed. She is deeply interested in Bible study!"

"Bible study!" sneered Carey. "As if Bible study could make over a girl like that. Bible study can't change a rotten nature. Lute will find that out soon enough. I think you ought to stop him. Paul, you ought to have a lot of influence over Lutie, why don't you telephone him and make him come back home?"

Paul looked at Carey with a troubled glance.

"I'm afraid I wouldn't care to, Carey," he said in his quietest tone. "I agree with you that Bible study can't change a rotten nature but I know the Lord Jesus Christ can give a new one, and from all I hear about Minnie, He has. And I think what Luther has done is beautiful! He's out on the Lord's errand and I wouldn't dare attempt to stop him. It's just like him to do it, and I honor him for it!"

"You *do?*" gasped Carey weakly, and subsided.

Then Steve spoke, thoughtfully, more seriously than Steve was wont to speak.

"So do I!" he said with fervor. "That's what Frannie and I are going to do when we get a chance, take up serious Bible study. Frannie doesn't need it so much, I guess, but I do, a lot!"

They all laughed a pleasant little laughter that was almost near to tears, for there were so many terrible possibilities in the mission on which Steve was about to set sail.

It developed that Carey had come down to the city expecting to spend the night with Paul Redfern's sister, but when she got there she found that the sister had gone up in the country to visit a friend, and the maid didn't know when she would be back. She said Paul was at Silverthorns. So Carey had taken a taxi and come out. That was the way Carey did. It was impossible to tell whether she came because of Link, or Paul. But if she was after Link she must have been disappointed, for Link definitely did not give her any special attention any more. Still, Carey was satisfied to be in the crowd and watch the two. She had a feeling that she could have either of them, whichever she chose to go after.

It was a gay evening, and rather an amazing thing to watch the difference in Steve, his devotion to his bride. Fancy Frannie, who had always seemed so full of mischief, so taken up with Steve that she had no time for flirtations! Carey studied her between whiles. Had this been going on between the two for a long time, or was it something quite new? Carey just couldn't tell.

And Steve seemed older somehow, as if responsibility had sat upon him heavily during the last few weeks. How they all studied him, and how his mother and father rejoiced in him! But it wasn't going to be easy to let him go away again, into a new world, a world at war, and all enveloped in mystery. How were they going to stand it?

Later they spoke of Luther Waite again. It was Steve who spoke into one of those intervals between talk, when there were so many unspoken thoughts filling the atmosphere that the audible words had died for the instant. Steve said:

"But Link, if I were you I'd keep in close touch with Lutie. You know it would be kind of dreadful if Lutie got in the toils of a girl that wasn't just right. You know the wrong girl can do an awful lot to spoil a man's life."

McRae and Curlin lifted startled eyes and gave one significant glance at one another before they lowered their gaze to the floor. It was strange. But of course Steve didn't know what they knew of that afternoon caller, and probably never would now. After a little they both looked up and smiled. But nobody else noticed their smiles.

That night after they had all gone home, both Curlin and McRae spent time upon their knees, thanking God for what had come to Steve. Pleading that Steve and Frannie would be drawn nearer to the Lord, and never have reason to be sorry that they belonged to one another.

18

ERMINIE LAZARELLE had gone into a very stormy way when she obeyed the new prompting in her heart and went back to her unloved home. That first day had been only the beginning. Her record in the past was not an asset in her favor.

The children resented her presence. She was a restraint from doing the lawless things they desired to do. The apathy of their mother during the last few weeks, especially since the departure of their father and sister and elder brother, had been all to their wishes. The mother let them do what they would because it was the easiest way, and they were quick to learn the fact.

Added to all this was the lack of a maid.

Erminie had never had to work. She could not remember the time when there had not been plenty of money, and sometimes two or three servants. Now there wasn't even one. Erminie knew very little about the best ways of working. She knew how she liked things to be, how food should taste, how things should be kept in order for the sake of mere comfort and pleasantness, but she had never had to do it herself.

So now here she was with the whole family on her hands, and a strong desire to pick up her still packed suitcase and run away again.

But she couldn't do that. She was a "new creature in Christ Jesus." That was what Link had told her. She had to stay and see this thing through.

Besides the three youngest children whom she had encountered at the start there were two others: Emmy Lou, aged ten, and Timothy, aged fourteen. Emmy Lou came in slowly, speculatively, around six that first evening, enquired where dinner was, and started to go out again till Erminie corralled her, and demanded help. Timothy did not come at all.

Enquiry elicited the information that Tim had "gone back home," meaning their home in the east before they had moved.

"He said he didn't like it here," said Emmy Lou loftily. She said he had gone a couple of days ago, but seemed very hazy about just when that was. The mother didn't even know that, it appeared. When questioned she only answered "Oh, don't bother me! Can't you see I'm reading?"

It had been several days before she further ventured a question about her father, for her mother seemed very irritable, and seemed to consider everything that happened was Erminie's fault.

But after a few days it became apparent that the stepmother was really ill. She waked them all in the night groaning and moaning, and then demanded a doctor.

The doctor did not get there till morning, and the woman was frantic, screaming and crying out till the children were frightened.

The doctor told Erminie that Mrs. Lazarelle was a very sick woman, and should have a nurse. He asked after her husband and was told he had gone to China on business. But after the doctor had left and Erminie persisted in questioning, the stepmother admitted that she didn't know to what port he had sailed, nor when he was coming back.

"I think he's sick of us all and wants to get away!" she moaned. "He said so more than once! He told me we all knew where to get our money every month, and he guessed that was all we any of us cared anyway." And then she burst into soul-shattering tears and demanded that Erminie go to a certain drug store and get a prescription filled.

"But you've got a doctor now," Erminie urged. "Hadn't you better ask him about the prescription before you take anything else?"

"Shut up and do as you're told!" said the sick woman. "Where's Timmie? Send Timmie up here. He'll get what I tell him. Send him here this minute!"

But Timothy could not be found. And it was then the sick woman began the wailing which seldom let up for long, and was interspersed by demands to have her prescription filled, until Erminie in desperation took the prescription and started. But on the way she read some of the scarcely decipherable words in it, and found morphine and laudanum in it. Knowing just enough to be afraid of such things she stopped off at the doctor's and showed it to him. From him she received orders not to get any prescriptions filled except the ones he gave her, and he promptly substituted another prescription for the one she had brought.

But the doctor's medicine didn't work the way the other had done, and the sick woman complained, and wept and demanded Timothy until it came to be a regular obsession with her.

Then at last the doctor told Erminie how serious was

the stepmother's condition, and ordered her to be sent to the hospital.

It was then that Erminie had written to Link asking him to try to find her brother. The doctor said it was important that the woman's son should be found and that weeping and hysteria stopped. So Erminie wrote the letter, and then, relieved somewhat since the nurse and invalid were out of the way, she set about trying to make living a little more possible.

The maids she secured, a succession of them, would not stand the impudent children, and Erminie perceived that to conquer the home she must first conquer those children. And how could that be done?

It didn't take long to discover that in herself she was utterly inadequate to the task, till she remembered Link's last words that she could take all her cares and perplexities to her new Lord. So she began to pray for the children and hand them over to the Lord asking Him to dominate them. Then she would rise from her knees and one by one call them and set them some interesting task.

"Emmy Lou, how would you like to cook some cereal for breakfast?"

"I don't like cereal," said Emmy Lou. "I'd rather make scravveled eggs."

"All right," said Erminie pleasantly, "then we'll let Mariana make the cereal, because some of us like cereal, you know. Mariana, you may go down to the closet and choose what cereal we shall eat this morning. Would you like that?"

"I choose dry cereal. You don't havta cook that and I like it best anyway."

"All right, Mariana, you can do everything about the cereal," said the big sister, wondering whether the novelty would last long enough for one meal. "You can put on the cereal dishes and spoons, and pour the cream from the tops of two bottles into the cream pitchers, and put the sugar bowl on, and just get everything ready for that part of the breakfast."

"And can I wash the bowls and spoons afterwards?" asked the little girl eagerly.

"Why yes," said the sister with surprise. "That's a nice idea."

"And can I wash my dishes too?" asked Emmy Lou. "I'd like to wash a real frying pan. I never did that. You have to use a steel sponge to wash that, you know."

"Of course!" said Erminie. Things were really getting organized.

"Vat can I do?" asked Billy. "I gotta do somping!"

"Why, surely. You can put on the napkins!"

"Don't vanta put on napkins. I vanta put on glasses and vash 'em atterwuds."

"No, you shan't wash glasses," cried Blossom. "I'm gonta do that."

"Yes, I vill vash glasses," asserted the young man.

"Now look here, Blossom and Billy, you stop that fighting immediately or I won't let either of you in the kitchen. I'm hiring new servants, you see, and if you are good servants and do what I tell you, then you can work and get a penny a day for your work, but I won't have bad servants that fight. Billy, you put on napkins or go out of the room."

Billy considered his sister.

"Could I clean the napkin rings?" he asked with the air of an important laborer, making a bargain.

Erminie was beginning to learn. She smiled at the stubborn little boy.

"Why yes, you could do that while we are getting the dishes washed," she said. So the whole atmosphere was changed, for the time being at least, and they all went to work with a vim. It might not last long of course, but

Erminie at least had learned a valuable lesson in how to manage children.

She instituted regular hours, and naps, and two good playtimes each day, so planned that she could get away to go to the hospital to see the irritable invalid. Not that her stepmother enjoyed her visits. She fretted at her continually, assailed her with bitter sarcasm, and unpleasant tales from her own past.

But Erminie was reading her Bible every day, even if only a few verses at a time. And while she was so ignorant in Bible lore that it was pitiful how little she got out of it sometimes, still she brought to it an absolute faith through what Link had told her, and a simple desperate childlikeness that was able to receive a plain truth and make use of it because of her desperate need. For it would seem that Lincoln Silverthorn's message had reached Erminie at the crucial time of her life, when she had risked all to try to get somewhere out of her loneliness, and having lost was ready to accept any help offered.

So, as she went along through the stormy difficult days she was becoming more and more Spirit-taught.

Also, the occasional booklets and truth-filled magazines that Link and sometimes of late Luther, had sent to her were devoured eagerly, for they made her understanding of the Bible so much clearer.

Often after a hard day of unaccustomed work, when there had been no maid available, or when one she had tried had failed, and she was dog-weary, she would dash cold water in her face to wake her up, and then drink strong coffee to make her keep awake, and would read and study her Bible for a couple of hours, until sometimes she fell asleep in her chair.

And it was making a difference in her. She couldn't see it herself, but the children were noticing it.

"You're nice, Erminie!" said Blossom one day when Erminie had been washing the child's face, and combing her pretty gold curls, and finished up by plumping a little pink gum drop in her mouth.

"Wes," said Billy, standing awaiting his turn. "You is nice, Erminie! I wike you!"

It brought a strange tired thrill to have this tribute to her care. She hadn't loved these little mortals when she began. She called them brats. She wasn't altogether sure she loved them yet, but she had a sense of responsibility toward them that she had never felt before, and there was satisfaction to see them blossoming in response to her care.

But then, as she grew herself, and began to see from her brief reading of the scripture, how much each soul meant to her new Lord and Master, she began to think about Timothy. She had been fonder of him than of any of the others, because he had been the first baby in her life, while she was still young enough to enjoy watching a little child and seeing him grow. So now as she heard her stepmother's continual plaints about Timothy, she began to have a curious amazed interest in him herself, and to wonder where he was and what he was doing? Had he gone straight? Probably not. Why should he? He had never been taught to go straight. She certainly hadn't helped him herself. There hadn't been anything in their home life to give him any ideals. And more and more it was borne in upon her that if she had been sooner born again it would have been expected of her that she should have done something about the salvation of not only Timothy, but the other little souls who had come into the home.

A year ago she would have curled her lip at any such idea. She would have shrugged her shoulders and gone her own way without a thought of the others. She would have said that they did nothing for her and why should she think of them? But now it was all different. She was "a new creature in Christ Jesus." Again and again that phrase from the brief teaching of Lincoln Silverthorn rang its changes over in her soul. She was a new creature, and must live a new life. She must forget the things that were behind her, and live in Christ now, not herself.

But it was a hard weary way she had to go, and there was so little time for rest, or meditation! There seemed no end to it ahead, no looking forward to anything brighter. Oh, the children would perhaps grow up some day and go off and live their own lives, but she would be left alone then, and her time for happiness would be over. Well it didn't matter. If she only could get rested.

Then she left the children with a pleasant elderly kindergarten teacher who was out of a job, and glad to get the few extra dollars for a bit of educational play with them, and hurried off to the hospital in answer to a special call from the nurse.

The patient was worse. Very much worse, and was in a piteous state. She cried continually for Timothy, but Erminie found out definitely that day that what she wanted of Tim was to get her prescription filled. She was continually harking back to the oblivion it had given her. The strange unnatural deceptive exaltation of death. She wanted the glamour of rosy clouds and joy and music that came to her soul when she took that dope. It hadn't been her love for her oldest neglected child that had sent her weeping all these days. She wanted dope.

And suddenly it came sharply to Erminie that her stepmother had been all her life doing just what *she* had been doing when Lincoln Silverthorn had startled her by telling her the truth. When he asked her why she went on as she was when it could bring her nothing? This poor woman had been chasing pleasure of some form all her life. Erminie could remember back in her childhood when the children had all been neglected, and herself left desolate because the stepmother had wanted to go out to her pleasures: theatres, movies, dances, bridge, it mattered not what. She had given very little time or thought to her children. Even when her husband was at home she was off continually. It had been the cause of a great deal of wrangling. That wrangling had been one of the earliest memories the girl Erminie had.

She saw the minute she entered the hospital room that there had been a change. The sick woman's face was ghastly, her eyes were anguished.

The doctor arrived soon after and gave her something that put her to sleep, and then he took Erminie into the reception room and told her very plainly that Mrs. Lazarelle had come to the end. It might now be only a matter of hours, and if there was any possible way to get in touch with her husband or son it ought to be done at once.

She sent a telegram to a man in the east who had charge of her father's affairs telling him Mrs. Lazarelle's condition, and asking that he try to get in touch with her father immediately. Her soul was tormented. It was not that she felt her father would feel so badly to know that his wife had but a few hours to live, for she could not but know that they had not been very close to one another for years. But it seemed such a dreadful ending for a useless misspent life, and it came to her with her new enlightenment that the poor woman was going out of the world without any knowledge of a Saviour, and she had been there for several weeks now and hadn't done a thing about it. Also the outcry for Timothy had been ringing in her ears daily and she hadn't been able to do a thing about that either. She had done all she knew. Should she go to the police and set them to hunting for her young brother? How she shrank from that, for back in her mind she knew there was a fear hiding that perhaps Timmie had been doing something wrong and might get arrested if she started a search for him by officers of the law.

She went back to the house in great distress, marshaled her young forces for their supper and to bed, and then sat down and buried her face in her hands and wept. Erminie wasn't the weeping kind. She had been through enough in her young life to make her weep floods of tears, but that hadn't been her way. She had always laughed and whistled; she had grown hard and blasé and bitter, forcing her way into places where she was not meant to be, and laughing it off gaily as if she enjoyed disappointment.

But now she seemed to have reached the limit. If she only could find Timmie, and not have it to remember after her stepmother died that she hadn't even been able to relieve her by producing the boy.

"Oh God," she said at last, still sitting with bowed head. "Isn't there some way You could help me? You helped people in the Bible when they cried to You. Couldn't You help me just a little? Couldn't You somehow find Timmie and send him home? I'll try to teach him about You if You'll send him."

It was just the next morning that the telephone rang.

Erminie sprang to answer it. It would likely be from the hospital, perhaps summoning her again. Perhaps the end had come, and she would have a lot of sad details to settle, and she didn't know how! And what was to come after? How could she go through the rest of life! She was so mortally tired!

And then there was Timmie's own voice, calling her! Timmie himself saying he was coming, he was on the way!

Something in her heart leaped to greet that voice, glad, glad! And all at once she realized that she loved Timmie! Her little brother! She hadn't ever realized that before. Not, at least, since he had been a mere baby!

If Timmie himself had walked into that room right that minute she knew she would have sprung to meet him, would have clasped him in her arms, and pressed warm loving kisses upon his hard young face. Timmie! Why, he was hers to love and be glad about! Oh, what a relief! And he was coming home! He would be there as soon as he could make arrangements.

Afterwards she wondered why she hadn't learned more from him. Where he was, how long it would take to get there. Was there any place she could get in touch with him on the way, in case she needed to? There were many things she should have found out, and she had been just too dumb with relief to remember to ask them!

But the ringing glad fact was there that she had heard his voice and he was coming. Oh, if it only wouldn't be too late! Oh, if she'd only thought to tell him to take an airplane, and she would telegraph him money for his passage. Then she remembered that there was no airport anywhere near them, and that wouldn't have helped her anyway, for she wouldn't know when to expect him.

But after a few minutes her good sense returned and she telephoned the nurse in the hospital.

"She's sleeping quietly," said the nurse. "No worse, no better for all I can see. The doctor will be in again in a little while."

"Well, you can tell him I have heard from my brother at last. He is on his way. He is in the east and will get here as soon as possible!"

"That's good," said the nurse. "That'll be something to tell her if she goes to crying again!"

There was something kind in the nurse's tone. That

nurse had been kind. Perhaps she too was born again. How else could she bear all the unpleasantness with which a nurse had to put up? Oh, if she knew the Lord perhaps she would be able to tell that poor dying mother about Him. Maybe tomorrow she would summon courage to ask her.

Erminie crept to her bed that night with a prayer on her lips and more peace in her heart than she had had since she came back to her home. She awoke with a rested look on her face, and smiled at Blossom who woke early and had formed the habit of creeping over into her sister's bed and cuddling in her arms for a few minutes before they got up.

"Timmie is coming home!" she announced happily to the children.

"Timmie?" They studied her tentatively. They hadn't such pleasant memories of Timmie themselves, but maybe somehow it would be all right.

"He won't stop us washing the dishes and getting the breakfast, will he, Erminie?" asked Emmy Lou anxiously. It was the first evidence Erminie had had that the children really liked the program she had established with them.

"Oh, no, Timmie won't stop you. I think maybe Timmie may want to do some grown-up help himself after a while when he gets used to being here."

"Oh, I don't know!" said wise Emmy Lou. "I don't think he'll wanta be bothered."

"We'll see!" said Erminie with a hope in her heart that Timmie might not be another problem for her already overfull hands to deal with. And then she began to plan about getting Timmie's room fixed up to surprise him, so he would want to stay and help them all. That interested the children immensely. They eagerly went to work, washing paint, hunting attractive old pieces of furniture stuck away in the attic. Nothing had ever been done, apparently, to make Timothy's room pleasant. But Erminie was determined that it should be done now.

It was wonderful how much three delighted determined children could do towards getting a room ready for a prodigal to return to. Billy puffed and snorted and scrubbed away at a base board and fairly polished all the paint off of it in some places, and was so determined to make his work the best that was done that he was quite worn out by lunch time.

And it was remarkable how as they worked a new interest in and love for the absent Timothy developed. Erminie wondered if you always loved somebody more when you were doing something for them.

The woman who came in for their lessons in the afternoon while Erminie went to the hospital was told eagerly about their brother who was coming home again, and when the older sister went away she could hear the children planning to write a note of welcome with their colored crayons to tack up on Timothy's door. She was quite sure as she thought it over that that must be the suggestion of the teacher, for none of them had ever had any training in doing things for one another, but they had taken to it with a vim, and were happily working away with crayons, each drawing some letter, or word, or a bird or flower wherewith to decorate the lovely white card that the teacher was providing for them. What a lot Erminie was learning about taking care of children. And what would their mother think of it all in case she were going to come back and go on living instead of dying with a dread disease and going away from them forever? Oh, life and death! How near they were to each other, and what a serious thing life was, with death just around the corner. Would she ever be able to teach those children all about it?

When she got to the hospital the nurse was waiting for her in the hall.

"I told her," she said in a whisper, "but I don't think she took it in. She's just wakened. Perhaps you'd better speak of it yourself."

So Erminie went in and stood beside the bed, and her stepmother looked at her with unseeing eyes.

"Oh! It's only you," she said disappointedly. "I hoped it was Tim. Why is it always you?"

"But Tim is coming pretty soon, mother. We've found him, you know, and he's telephoned me that he is coming just as soon as he can arrange it to get here."

"Arrange it to get here? What do you mean?"

"Why, I suppose he must have a job somewhere, and he had to fix it up with his employers to let him off to come and see you because you were sick."

She tried to speak in a most comforting tone.

"A job!" said the woman's querulous tone. "Why, he's too young to have a job. Don't ever let him go back to it, Minnie. He's a mere baby. He ought to be in school of course, only he never gets on with the teacher. We'll have to find a teacher who can get along with him somehow."

"Yes, mother," soothed Erminie gently. "We'll find a good place for Timothy. We'll look after him. I'm glad he's coming back. And see, I've brought you some pretty roses. Don't you like those? I thought they would make you feel a little more cheerful."

"No!" said the sick woman sharply. "Take them away! I don't like roses! They make me think of funerals. I don't like hospitals nor funerals. I don't see why there have to be such things in the world. I should think in this age of wisdom and knowledge there might have been found some way to stop dying, and not have to have hospitals and funerals. I always did hate them, and I never understood why people put up with it. Why they didn't do something to put a stop to it."

"Well, you know Someone did do just that, mother," said Erminie, wondering if she was saying it right. It seemed almost childish to herself, but she must make some answer to that pitiful cry.

The sick woman turned wondering eyes toward her.

"Someone did that? Why, I never heard of it. Who was it? What did they do about it?"

"Why it was Jesus Christ, you know. He died on the cross and then rose again from the dead. He conquered death forever. Surely you have heard about Him."

"Stop!" said the sick woman. "I won't hear such talk as that! I don't want any religion talked at me. I never held with things like that. Take her away!" she cried to the nurse who came in just then. "She's trying to preach to me, and I won't listen!"

"Oh, but Mrs. Lazarelle, I should think you would be very happy with your son coming back," said the nurse gently.

"Yes, I am!" snapped Mrs. Lazarelle, "but this is a pretty way to meet him, lying sick in the hospital. I never was sick in the hospital in my life before, and I don't like it. I think I'd better get up and go home, don't you? Bring me my clothes and help me get dressed. I'm going home!"

"Well," said the nurse quietly, "I think we'd better wait till your doctor gets here, don't you? You know we have to get his permission before you could be allowed to leave the hospital. That's the rule, you know, and you couldn't get out until he says so. He's got to sign the release."

"I don't see what business it is of his, if I choose to go home. This is a free country, isn't it?"

"Why, yes, but it isn't a free hospital, and you were

very sick indeed when you entered the hospital. They took you in with the understanding that you would abide by the rules of the hospital, so of course you want to be polite and do what they ask. Now, you take this medicine, and then we'll have a few spoonfuls of orange juice and then you'll take a little nap till your doctor gets here. Say good-by to her, Miss Erminie, and we'll get calm and rest a little."

Erminie, with tears, unbidden tears, upon her cheek went back to the children again, marveling at the nurse and her wise loving ways, and shuddering at the thought of the woman who was going out of this life so soon, hand in hand with death, without any hope to comfort her.

19

TIMOTHY, AS he rode along in the shining beautiful car beside Luther Waite, rested his head back against the soft cushions and marveled. Was it really Timothy Lazarelle who was riding in such state, with this wonderful man beside him, making friendship with him so genially?

It was a long way ahead, but somehow the hours were slipping by with wonderful rapidity. He almost grudged the brevity as he looked forward to it, and knew that soon, too soon it would be over, and he would be back in a life he hated. This was the first man who had ever acted as if he cared for him in the least, and he hadn't fathomed yet why he was treating him in this wonderful way, like a prince.

Of the sad reason for his return he thought very little. He didn't want to think. He knew little or nothing about death. It was a gruesome horrid necessity, this going back. He couldn't make it seem real that his mother could die. He had little love for her. She had always been extremely selfish. Yet she had yielded to his desires many times just because it was easier to do so than to contend.

Of course he knew this, and it had made him feel that it was up to him to get the best for himself that he could out of any situation. His mother had always been so hard on him, so indifferent to his wishes.

And now this was one more situation in which she was taking advantage of him by her tears. He couldn't really believe that she cared enough about him to shed genuine tears.

He didn't reason that out in words even to himself. He didn't want to get that near to the facts of the case.

They talked much of little every day matters as they rode along, and the boy without realizing that he was doing so told the young man a great deal of his family and early life. It was a pitifully empty tale, and more and more Luther Waite thought of the girl he had so disliked, and felt pity for her.

He began to wonder how he should meet her, what he would say to her. Would she recognize him as an old acquaintance? Of course she would. But after all it didn't matter. He would go in the strength of the Lord, and let a higher power than his own direct him. But just on general principles, if the choice came to himself he would keep away from her as much as seemed right. He would take a room at a hotel of course, and only appear on the scene when necessary. Then the girl could not possibly misunderstand him. But even in that way he must set down no hard and fast rules. He must be ready for service should the Lord require.

When they arrived in the town that was their destination Luther had gone a far way into the heart of the boy, and a word, a smile from him, was almost a command. Timothy was willing to follow this man's lead wherever it went.

"Now," said Luther as they began to enter the town, "you'll have to direct me. Where is your home?"

Tim slumped down in the seat and a gray shadow passed over his face.

"Down this street, four blocks, then right three," he murmured. Luther could see he was pretty badly sunk.

"Now, look here, son, you've got to brace up. You're the man of the family, you know, and you must remember they're probably feeling pretty badly themselves. Don't look so down."

"Well say, what've I gotta do? Go to a hospital? I don't like hospitals."

"No. Of course not. Nobody does. They're wonderful places if you're sick and need them, but we're all afraid of them unless we are. Now you brace up, son. If your mother's been crying for you you'll have to go of course. Wait till you see your sister and see what she says."

"Will you go with me?" Timothy asked shyly.

"Why, yes, I'll go as far as they'll let me. However, I don't belong to the family, and I wouldn't insist on anything like that if I were you. Remember you're a man. Act your age. But I'll be around to help out whenever I'm needed. Now, is this the house? You'd better go ahead, hadn't you?"

Timothy swallowed hard and blinked.

"I think I better take you in an' interduce ya," he said with downcast glance.

"Okay, kid! Let's go!"

They got out and walked gravely up to the door.

Mariana heard their steps and opened the door a crack, then flung it shut and went tearing back to an inner room.

"Erminie!" she called. "Oh, Erminie! Timmie's come back! You better come quick, Erminie, or he might go away again!"

Luther looked down and grinned at the disconcerted boy.

"That's your little sister, Tim? Which one?"

"Sure! That's Mariana."

"Well, come on! Let's go in. You lead the way!"

Timidly Timothy pushed the door open and entered, looking wildly around to see if aught was changed since he left.

It was. There were no longer rolls of dust on the floors. The chairs were set about in an orderly manner as if people used them for comfort. The furniture was dusted, and the few little ornaments that no one had bothered yet to unpack when he came away were nicely placed on table and mantel.

Of course Timothy didn't name all these changes, didn't really notice them separately. If he had been asked to describe what was different he probably would have merely said it looked pleasant or comfortable. But he drew a deep breath and relaxed a little from his tensity. There was another thing! There was a delicious smell in the air, a smell of broiling steak, and coffee, and possibly something like cinnamon buns or apple pie. He drew a deep breath and decided it wasn't going to be so bad as he had feared.

And then Erminie came from the kitchen, untying a big apron as she came. She was dressed in a simple blue-checked gingham and there was a pretty flush on her cheeks from being over the stove. When she opened the kitchen door the delightful savory odors came in strongly on the air. The door was open into the dining room, and they could see the table neatly set. The little girls had done that. There was a low bowl of flowers brightly nodding there. It seemed a real home coming after all. Timothy just didn't know what it could mean.

But the thing of all others that Luther noticed was the

beautiful blue leather Bible lying on the living room table, with a book mark in it as if it were used often. Lying *open* too, with a marked verse distinctly showing. He looked at it with a growing smile and turned to meet the girl he had shunned so long.

But Erminie was not seeing him just then. She had eyes only for her brother. The long wait and the anxiety had nourished a genuine love for him, and she came toward him with her arms outstretched and a real welcome in her voice and eyes.

"Oh, Timmie, Timmie, I'm so glad you're here!" she said tenderly, a little tremble of joy in her voice, and her arms thrown eagerly around the astonished brother's neck.

"Aw, gee! Min! I didn't know you cared!" he said shamefacedly.

"Her's not *Minnie* any more!" shouted young Billy. "Her's *Er*-min-ie!" He pronounced each syllable slowly and distinctly. "You mayn't call her Min enny more! Not enny more 'tall!"

Billy had come up quite near to Timothy, and was shaking a small index finger in his face.

Ordinarily Timothy might have smitten his young brother indignantly, but Timothy was overwhelmed with the loving interest that his family were manifesting, and he only grinned. Then suddenly he came to himself, as Erminie released him from the unexpected embrace.

"Oh, I forgot!" he exclaimed, and turned toward Luther, having privately rehearsed this scene in his mind many times that morning. "Lemme interduce Mr. Luther Waite, an awfully good friend of mine, that brought me over here in his car."

Then the family turned silently and stared at Luther, and Erminie opened large eyes of wonder as she came forward.

"That's wonderful of you, Mr. Waite!" she said shyly. "I can't begin to thank you. I was so worried about my brother. He isn't used to traveling by himself, and I didn't think he had much money with him. I was so troubled after I hung up the telephone that I hadn't asked him if I should telegraph some money to him."

Luther looked down at her, seeing her for the first time without exaggerated make-up, and his heart went out to her in sympathy. She seemed so young and troubled, and so frail, so entirely different from the way she used to be. He put out his big nice hand and took her little one in his with a warm grasp.

"I'm sorry you had to worry any about us," he said in his pleasant hearty voice. "I should suppose you had trouble enough without taking that too. But we were all right. We looked up trains and found that on account of poor connections we could make better time by car, so we came by car. I hope we got here in time. How is Mrs. Lazarelle? Timothy has been very anxious."

Timothy flashed Luther a duly grateful smile for paving the way for him back into ease from his embarrassment.

Erminie answered with a troubled look in her eyes.

"She's very low," she said sadly. "The doctor says it may be only a few hours now."

"Oh!" said Luther alertly, "and does she know she is going?"

Erminie's eyes suddenly grew very troubled.

"I'm not sure," she said. "She won't let me talk to her about it, and of course no one else has tried. It seems so awful to have her go this way, all alone."

Something of understanding flashed between the two in a glance.

"You think she's not saved?" asked Luther in a low tone. "Has her pastor been to see her?"

"She hasn't any pastor," said Erminie. "I don't remember her ever going to church since I've known her. I'm sure she never went anywhere in this place. I didn't know what to do about it. Someone ought to pray with her, oughtn't they?"

"Can't you?" said Luther, quietly, watching her reaction.

"No. I wouldn't know how. I'm just new at praying myself. And anyway she never would stand for it. She doesn't think anything I do is right in any way. She never has. She's always hated me because I was a stepchild. I'm afraid it would just make her angry if I were to try."

There was distress in Erminie's eyes.

Luther was watching her, and thinking how very different her eyes were now from the time when he had last seen her. How very sweet and wholesome and earnest they seemed.

Then Erminie looked up wistfully.

"Couldn't you do it?" she asked shyly, in a low tone, almost as if she were afraid to suggest it.

"Sure, he can pray swell," said Timothy unexpectedly. "He's prayed with me."

"Oh!" said Erminie. "*Would* you? It doesn't seem right to let her just go out this way."

Luther turned gravely to her.

"What reaction would she have to that? Me, a stranger?"

"I don't know. I think maybe that would be best. She's more apt to be nice to strangers, and she likes men better than women. At least she might hear enough to help her to understand *something*. But anyway God would understand. It would be sort of introducing her to Him, wouldn't it? Or isn't that right?"

Luther smiled. "Yes, that's right. I'll be glad to do it if you feel there is an opportunity."

"Oh, thank you! That is a great burden off my heart!" said Erminie. "And it is so wonderful that you have brought Timothy back."

"Well, he and I have been growing very close during this journey, and I really enjoyed it a lot. We've got sort of a permanent crush on each other. How about it, kid? Isn't that so?"

Timothy's eyes shone proudly.

"Sure!" said Timothy flushing with pleasure. "He's a swell guy. You'll all like him!"

Erminie's eyes were bright with sudden delight.

"Of course we will!" she said earnestly. "That's wonderful. If I had known you had a friend like that I wouldn't have worried so much about you."

"Gee!" said Timothy, "I didn't know you ever worried about me!" and he looked at Erminie as if he had never known her before.

Then suddenly Billy and Blossom approached him from opposite sides.

"Wes," said Billy, "and ve vill be your fwiends too!" Blossom lifted up pretty red lips and eager little face and said,

"Sure, I be your friend, too!"

And suddenly Luther reached down and caught them up in his arms, one on either side.

"That's a compact!" he said. "We'll seal that with a kiss each," and solemnly kissed each rosy lifted pair of lips, and then set them gently down. "Now don't forget that," he said as if it were a matter of grave import. "That's a life contract!"

"Awwight!" they said in chorus.

Then approached Mariana, who put out an important young hand and shook Luther's hand.

"You too?" said Luther. "That's great! And say, isn't there one more sister? Emmy Lou, where is she?"

Emmy Lou came into the doorway, having been just out of sight in the offing, and lifting her abbreviated skirts, made a formal little curtsy. Luther saluted her in a most military manner.

"Your meat's about to burn," said Emmy Lou cryptically, and Erminie fled in haste.

When she returned she said with a glance that included Luther, "The lunch is about ready. Timmie, will you take Mr. Waite up to your room? He may want to wash his hands."

"Oh, but I didn't intend to intrude upon you now," said Luther. "Timothy was going to show me where the hotel was. Then you can send him over, or telephone if there is anything I can do."

Erminie regarded him gravely.

"It's all right of course, if you prefer. We mustn't keep you, but we hoped you'd stay at least to lunch."

Blossom sidled up to him and took hold of his big warm hand.

"It's a nice lunch," she offered, looking up wistfully with her big beautiful eyes. "I peeled the beets my own self!"

"You *did!*" said Luther. "Why I'd love to stay of course if you are sure I won't be in the way!"

"Course we want ya, Luther," said Timothy earnestly. "Come on if ya wantta wash yer hands. Only—my room isn't sa hot. I kinda left things in a mess when I went away in a hurry. If ya'll wait a minute down here I'll run up an' put a few things away."

"Your room is all right, Timmie," called Erminie from the dining room. "We cleared it up."

"I vashed the baseboards my own se'f," said Billy, plodding up the steps beside his brother. And Timmie unwontedly took hold of the small hand comfortably and said, "Okay, kid! *Did* ya? That was swell!"

The children trailed upstairs to see what Timothy would say to his fine room, the new curtains they had helped to put up, the set of brushes Erminie had contributed.

"There's p'fumery in the soap!" announced Blossom. "Just smell it!"

But Timothy stood in the doorway of his new-old room and stared about him.

"Gee! Luther! It never looked like this before!" he ejaculated wonderingly.

Luther looked around approvingly.

"Nice, isn't it! And you thought they didn't care anything about you, kid! See how wrong you were!"

Billy was presently heard ringing the lunch bell. Luther and Tim came down promptly, Luther coming out in the kitchen and offering to carry in the hot platter with the sizzling steak.

They had a pleasant meal, with Emmy Lou and Mariana serving importantly, and doing very well at obeying the high signs that Erminie gave. Before they were done they all felt better acquainted, and Timothy was beaming at the way his family had accepted Luther as a part of themselves. He felt more at home with all of them than he had ever felt before.

The teacher came while the children were hurrying through the work of clearing the table and washing their special dishes, and it wasn't long before Luther was taking Erminie and Tim over to the hospital.

The nurse reported that the patient was very low, but she was rousing now and then and asking if her son had come.

They went in to see her, Luther standing in a corner out of sight of the patient; in the offing if he should be needed.

Erminie went forward to the bed and Mrs. Lazarelle looked up.

"Here's Timmie, mother!" she said, and laid the boy's hand in the sick woman's grasp.

The mother looked up with dull eyes.

"Timmie!" she said, "You've—come—at last!"

Her breath was coming in short gasps.

"I'm *glad*." She looked at him bewildered, trying to focus her gaze. "You look nice, Timmie!" She spoke slowly. "All fixed up real pretty!" Then her eyes dropped shut again, and her breath was shorter.

Timothy stood looking down at her in great distress. This didn't seem like his mother who had been so cross and exacting.

"I'm glad I came, mom!" he murmured awkwardly and slipped down on his knees beside the bed, stooping over and laying his lips in an unaccustomed kiss upon hers.

She opened her eyes again, eyes that were already looking into a world that she had not known.

Erminie slipped over to the door and met the doctor as he was coming in, whispered a word or two to him. He nodded, stepped over to the bed, touched the fluttering pulse, and looked at Erminie again with another nod. Then she motioned to Luther.

Luther took a step nearer to the bed, and bowing his head, prayed:

"Our loving Father, we want to speak to Thee about this dear soul who is coming over there. We don't know whether she has ever taken Thy Son Jesus Christ for her Saviour, but we are asking Thee now to speak to her and make her understand that it is not too late even yet. Help her to know that Thou dost love her with an everlasting love, that Thou didst put all her sin upon Thine own beloved Son, and judged it there. We, her friends, and her children are here together pleading Thy precious promises of salvation for her, and asking Thee to make it plain for her to understand. Show her that Thou are waiting to welcome her into loving arms if she will now just let her heart call upon Thee. Help her to take the precious gift of salvation Thou dost offer, right now, and be safe and happy with Thee forever!"

The dying woman stirred, opened wild astonished eyes for an instant, with a look around for the voice that was praying. They searched and came to rest on Luther's face, with a startled wonder. She held her gaze upon his face an instant more, with hunger in her eyes.

"Help her to say yes to the Lord Jesus," went on Luther tenderly, "and to find Thy great peace and rest in trusting Thee. May she just put her hand in Thine and go with Thee into her everlasting Home, not to be afraid any more. We ask it, claiming Thy word that 'God so loved the world that He gave His only begotten Son, that whosoever believeth in Him should not perish but have everlasting life.'"

The eyes closed, and a soft breath of a sigh that sounded like assent came. She was gone!

Timmie was weeping now. It was the first time he had ever seen anyone die. It was also the first real gospel he had ever heard, and his young heart was deeply stirred. Tears on his face, and on his sister's face, even for an unbeloved mother!

Luther led them away, back to the house, and to the little children who seemed to sense the tenseness of the atmosphere.

There were arrangements to be made, and Luther made them, taking Timothy with him, after they had talked things over with Erminie.

It was that same afternoon that the message came from the ship on its way to China.

"Mr. Lazarelle died of pneumonia two days ago. Was buried at sea. Details follow in letter."

And now how they all leaned on Luther, Timmie most of all! Though he seemed to have grown older and more dependable in the last two days. He went about gravely and wisely consulting with his sister, being gentle with his younger sisters and brother, but depending on Luther. More than the death of their mother, they seemed to sense the changes that would come with the death of their father, in spite of the fact that they had seen him so seldom, and then only for brief intervals.

Luther and Timmie had browsed around and discovered a minister to conduct a Christian service for the forlorn family. And when it was all over and they sat down together for a quiet meal, the excitement past, a new order of things begun, all of them, even the younger children began to wonder what they would do now if Luther went away from them.

It was after the supper was out of the way, and the younger children put to bed that Luther sat down for a talk with Erminie.

"Now," he said gently, "had you thought at all what you are going to do? Were you planning to stay here?"

"Oh, no!" said Erminie with a shudder. "Not if we can help it. Of course we'll have to wait to hear what arrangement father left, whether he had any directions that I would feel obliged to carry out. Of course he was my own father, though he never acted much like a father. But as far as I am concerned I think we should get away as soon as possible. You wouldn't want to live in a forlorn town like this, would you, after what has happened here?"

"Well, I should scarcely choose it," said Luther. "But what is your idea? Have the children other near relatives who would want them? Or what were you thinking of doing with them?"

"Why, we would all be together, of course. No, there are no relatives on either side who would want any of them, but I wouldn't think of letting them go anywhere anyway. We have grown to be very near to each other during these awful days since I came back home, and they are my responsibility. Father would have expected it, even if I hadn't wanted it, which I certainly do!"

Luther's eyes lighted. Then she wasn't the selfish creature he used to think her.

"That's right of course," he said. "It wouldn't be right to leave them stranded, or put them with strangers."

"Certainly not!" There was a quiet dignity about her bearing as she said it that made her seem rare. "Of course you don't understand, but our home life was rather a mess. Nobody made a real home for any of us, and I'd rather like to plan to have one for the children before they get too old to be influenced by it!"

"Grand! I hoped you'd feel that way!" said Luther. "Had you thought where you'd like to be?"

"Oh, we would all choose the east, I am sure. I think Timothy must have made you understand that. About the place I'm not sure. Tim would love to go back to the old home, I suspect. He has a lot of boy friends there. Personally if I had my choice I'd like a house out in that suburb where the Silverthorns live, only I know they'd all hate my coming there now. Nobody likes me in that crowd now because of the way I acted when I was among them the last time, and I don't blame them," she said sadly. "But I thought perhaps it might be best to go somewhere else for a while till they forgot about me the way I used to be. I suppose some house in the village where we used to live. For I'm quite sure that's where Tim would like to be, and I'd like to make him happy."

"You got another guess coming," said Tim suddenly emerging from the dark dining room door. "I useta wanta go back there, but I'd rather be in the city somewhere near Luther. He's gonta get me a job there somewhere, and I'd like that better than anything else."

"Come here, son," said Luther, making a place beside him on the couch and putting a brotherly arm about Tim's shoulder. "Let's talk this thing over and find out just what is the best thing to do."

So Tim nestled up to his new friend with his head against Luther's arm, and utter confidence in his expression as he watched Luther's face.

"It's wonderful for him to have a friend like you," said Erminie. "I can't thank God enough for that. I'd be willing to live anywhere for Timmie to be near you where he could see you sometimes. Perhaps there's some other suburb that would be all right for the children, and near enough to the city for Tim to be able to come in and see you sometimes if you wouldn't mind."

"Wouldn't mind?" said Luther, drawing the boy closer to him. "Erminie, don't you know how much you all are to me? Don't you know that it seems to me that you have grown to be my own? Just in these few short days the tie has become strong. There's nothing like going through trouble together to bring hearts together, especially hearts of those who belong to the Lord. Now just put such an idea out of your head, please. Don't you know I haven't any family left of my own, and didn't I make a compact with your young sisters and brothers? Please understand that I belong!"

Suddenly the tears came smarting into Erminie's eyes.

"Thank you!" she sobbed softly. "I never expected to hear you say that."

"Well, it's true!" said Luther vehemently.

But suddenly Erminie put her face in her hands and cried, her slender shoulders shaking.

"It's beautiful!" she gasped. "And we needed a friend so much! It's been just like Heaven having you here to help us and care for us—"

Luther's voice was suddenly very husky.

"Timmie," he said, his hand on the boy's shoulder, "would you run up to my suitcase and get me a clean handkerchief. Get me two, in fact. You'll find them in the little pocket under the tray. And then would you please look around and find that bunch of timetables I have? They're somewhere in the room. And would you stop up there and look up the trains home? I want to talk to your sister a minute."

Timothy was all alert.

"Sure!" he said, and flew up the stairs. He didn't care for sob-scenes much and was glad to get away.

"Listen, Erminie," said Luther as the boy's footsteps were heard on the floor above, "I'm a queer fellow and I don't do things the way other men do. When I want something I go for it right off. Maybe I ought not to say anything about this yet, not at a time like this when you've been through all sorts of trouble, and you don't know me very well, but, it's just this, Erminie. I love you, and—if you don't mind, that is, if you think you could learn to love me, why don't we get married? That would solve the whole problem."

Erminie sat up and brushed a torrent of tears away with the backs of her hands.

"Don't, please, Luther," she said, between the catches of sobs in her breath. "You're just saying that because you pity me."

"Erminie!" said Luther. "Indeed I'm not. I've known for two whole days that I loved you with all my heart and meant to marry you if you were willing. And of course I don't want you to say yes to me just because I've asked you unless you think you could love me too, but I'm sure there'll never be anybody else for me but you. Come, Erminie, come over here and sit beside me on the couch and let's talk about it. Could you ever love me enough to stand me all your life, do you think?"

He brought her over with his arm about her and seated her beside him with his arm still about her shoulders.

"Could you?"

"Yes," said Erminie, "I could love you. I do love you. But I couldn't marry you, because I can never leave my sisters and brothers. They are my responsibility. God gave them to me."

"Oh, that's no reason!" said Luther drawing her closer. "Because they are my responsibility too. Didn't I make a life contract with them the other day? And I love them too. They'd be my brothers and sisters then, too, and of course I'd look after them and support them, and do everything for them as if they were my own. Why we'd have fun, Erminie, bringing them up."

"Oh, Luther! You're wonderful! I shall love you forever for saying that. But Luther, all your crowd at home would despise you. Do you know what I heard Carey Carewe say two years ago? I heard her telling one of the other girls that I was setting my cap for you, and I would drag you off, no matter what you did. She said Paul Redfern or Lincoln Silverthorn ought to do something to get me away from you. That I was a cormorant and a lot of other terrible things! Luther, I couldn't marry you and have them all pitying you for having me on your hands. They'd say I had burdened you with my family, and it was dragging you down to be old before your time. Oh, I know what they'd say, and I couldn't bear it to do that to you!"

Luther's answer to that was to throw his head back and laugh with all his might.

"You think I care about that?" he said. "Just let the poor things talk! Let 'em say all the fool things they want to, and then I'll take them out in a ten acre lot and thrash every one of them. Yes, girls and all. And we'll show 'em. I'd have you to know that *I'm* marrying who I want to, and I'm not asking one of them. But I'll just tell you there are a few of my friends who won't say a word like that, nor even look it, not after I've told them that I love you and all your family, and that if they can't see it that way I'm done with 'em. But Erminie, you and I love each other. Or do we? Perhaps there's someone else you love. If there is, say so now, and clear the atmosphere." He held her off at arm's length and looked at her steadily.

"No! No!" she laughed between her tears. "There's nobody else. It's you I've loved ever since we went to that picnic two years ago, but you can't say you loved me then, for I know you didn't. I saw how you looked once when I came back after you thought I was gone, and I heard what you said about me once. But it doesn't matter if you really love me now. I know what I used to be, and while I don't know that I've had much chance to change, still I do love your Lord, and that ought to make some difference after a while."

"That has made a difference, Erminie. It has made all the difference."

Then suddenly he caught her close and smothered her face with tender kisses, and Erminie sank down in his arms faint with the joy of it.

Till all at once they heard Timothy's footsteps pounding down the stairs, and Erminie tried to straighten up and be decorous. But Luther held her fast, and drew her close.

"Come in, brother!" he cried joyously, "and it's really

brother, this time. How will you like that? Your sister and I are going to be married! What do you say to that?"

"Swell!" said Timothy. "No kidding?"

"No kidding, boy! Now, get to bed and to sleep, and tomorrow we'll make plans."

Timothy flung himself upon them in happy demonstration, and then suddenly he came to his feet and looked down at Luther.

"But say, Luther, what becomes of us? Are you both going away to leave us?"

"Not on yer life, boy! We're going back home and buy a house, and all live together! Now, beat it, boy!"

Timothy went whooping up the stairs and collected his sleeping brothers and sisters to tell them the grand news.

When they were left alone again Luther held his dear girl close.

"You're sweeter than I ever dreamed you were," he said softly, and kissed her very thoroughly. "Now, when can we get married? Tomorrow?"

"Oh, no!" said Erminie quickly, "not yet. I think I'd better go back and buy that house out at Birchwood, just beyond Silverthorns, that long old white one with the avenue of maples, and the evergreens all around the terrace. I've always wanted it. Then I will take the children and go there and live for a little while till everything quiets down, and you can come and see us now and then. Then after people have forgotten all about the way I used to be we can get married."

"Not on your life, sweetheart," said Luther. "We're going to get married before I go home, and I'm taking my family along! Hear that?"

They talked a long time, but Luther had his way.

"You know, Luther, you said you were going to support the children, but you won't have to do that.

They each have an income that comes in regularly. It isn't millions, but it's enough to take care of their necessities. So they won't be a financial burden on you."

"Well, that's okay with me, but I rather liked the idea of supporting them, so we won't worry about that."

The next morning Luther called up and secured an option on the house that Erminie had always wanted, and when that was settled he called Lincoln Silverthorn.

"I'm going to be married, Link, now in a day or two. I thought you'd like to wish me well. And I want you to know that you certainly preached a message to one soul, for she's the most different girl you ever saw. She's really come to know the Lord. What? Yes, she's the girl. Now you needn't throw any fits. You'll like her, and I know what I'm talking about! But anyway I'm marrying her, and taking over the family of children. You know her mother has just died, and her father had pneumonia going across the ocean to China. He was buried at sea. No, I'm not marrying her out of pity, old man. I love her, and if you don't believe me come down to the wedding."

Then Link's voice boomed over the wire.

"Make it two days later, Lutie, and we'll be with you. McRae and Curlin and I. No, not Carey. She's gone down to the shore with the Redferns for the summer. Sure I mean it. I was just being sent on a business errand out to your neighborhood, so it's quite possible. Mc-Rae'll be crazy about it and so will Curlin. Anything I can do for you? Okay. We'll be seeing you!"

"Okay!" said Luther as he turned grinning away from the telephone at last. "We're all set to go! Wedding reception and all. I guess that minister will do for the ceremony, won't he? We'll have the wedding supper at the nearest hotel on our way. Now, hadn't we better be seeing about a mover and arrange with him to get here just as we're ready to leave? I'll get a regular mover from home. They always have vans going back and forth. They're probably coming over this way with a load pretty soon, and can take ours back with them. So, we'd better be looking over things to see if anything is to be sold or given away. Don't throw away anything you really want to keep, you know. There's always plenty of room in a van. But when we get home you can buy all the new furniture your little heart fancies."

They had a wonderful time getting to work right away, and in spite of the shadow of memories that still hung over them they were all cheerful and excited over the fact that they were going back east and that Luther was to be their own brother and stay with them all the time.

And back at the Silverthorn home there was great excitement.

"You don't mean it, Link! Not really? Lutie is really marrying Erminie? Oh, what will Carey say? She'll be horrified. I think she had her mind half set on Lutie herself, ever since she found out he'd inherited a fortune!" laughed McRae.

"Well, don't tell her, McRae. I'm sure Lutie is level-headed about this and he had been praying about it. I think it's great!" said Link gravely.

"Well, so do I," said McRae. "I'm sure she must be different. But anyway it'll be great to go to the wedding. Maybe she won't like it, but I think we can make her glad we came."

"Of course!" said Link. "You're a great little sister! It's a curious thing. This whole story began with a wedding. Another in the middle of things, and another at the end!"

"And still another in the offing!" whispered Curlin to McRae with a sly twinkle in his eye. "Hadn't we better announce ours? And all by way of the Silverthorns."

About the Author

Grace Livingston Hill is well known as one of the most prolific writers of romantic fiction. Her personal life was fraught with joys and sorrows not unlike those experienced by many of her fictional heroines.

Born in Wellsville, New York, Grace nearly died during the first hours of life. But her loving parents and friends turned to God in prayer. She survived miraculously, thus her thankful father named her Grace.

Grace was always close to her father, a Presbyterian minister, and her mother, a published writer. It was from them that she learned the art of storytelling. When Grace was twelve, a close aunt surprised her with a hardbound, illustrated copy of one of Grace's stories. This was the beginning of Grace's journey into being a published author.

In 1892 Grace married Fred Hill, a young minister, and they soon had two lovely young daughters. Then came 1901, a difficult year for Grace—the year when, within months of each other, both her father and husband died. Suddenly Grace had to find a new place to live (her home was owned by the church where her husband had been pastor). It was a struggle for Grace to raise her young daughters alone, but through everything she kept writing. In 1902 she produced *The Angel of His Presence, The Story of a Whim,* and *An Unwilling Guest.* In 1903 her two books *According to the Pattern* and *Because of Stephen* were published.

It wasn't long before Grace was a well-known author, but she wanted to go beyond just entertaining her readers. She soon included the message of God's salvation through Jesus Christ in each of her books. For Grace, the most important thing she did was not write books but share the message of salvation, a message she felt God wanted her to share through the abilities he had given her.

In all, Grace Livingston Hill wrote more than one hundred books, all of which have sold thousands of copies and have touched the lives of readers around the world with their message of "enduring love" and the true way to lasting happiness: a relationship with God through his Son, Jesus Christ.

In an interview shortly before her death, Grace's devotion to her Lord still shone clear. She commented that whatever she had accomplished had been God's doing. She was only his servant, one who had tried to follow his teaching in all her thoughts and writing.

Don't miss these Grace Livingston Hill romance novels!

VOL.	TITLE	ORDER NUM.	PRICE
1	Where Two Ways Met	07-8203-8-HILC	3.95
2	Bright Arrows	07-0380-4-HILC	3.95
3	A Girl to Come Home To	07-1017-7-HILC	3.95
4	Amorelle	07-0310-3-HILC	3.95
5	Kerry	07-2044-X-HILC	4.95
6	All Through the Night	07-0018-X-HILC	4.95
7	The Best Man	07-0371-5-HILC	3.95
8	Ariel Custer	07-1686-8-HILC	3.95
9	The Girl of the Woods	07-1016-9-HILC	3.95
11	More Than Conqueror	07-4559-0-HILC	3.95
12	Head of the House	07-1309-5-HILC	4.95
14	Stranger within the Gates	07-6441-2-HILC	3.95
15	Marigold	07-4037-6-HILC	3.95
16	Rainbow Cottage	07-5731-9-HILC	4.95
17	Maris	07-4042-4-HILC	4.95
18	Brentwood	07-0364-2-HILC	4.95
19	Daphne Deane	07-0529-7-HILC	3.95
20	The Substitute Guest	07-6447-1-HILC	3.95
21	The War Romance of the Salvation Army	07-7911-8-HILC	4.95
22	Rose Galbraith	07-5726-2-HILC	3.95
23	Time of the Singing of Birds	07-7209-1-HILC	3.95
24	By Way of the Silverthorns	07-0341-3-HILC	3.95
28	White Orchids	07-8150-3-HILC	4.95
60	Miranda	07-4298-2-HILC	4.95
61	Mystery Flowers	07-4613-9-HILC	4.95
63	The Man of the Desert	07-3955-8-HILC	3.95
64	Miss Lavinia's Call	07-4360-1-HILC	3.95
77	The Ransom	07-5143-4-HILC	3.95
78	Found Treasure	07-0911-X-HILC	3.95
79	The Big Blue Soldier	07-0374-X-HILC	3.50
80	The Challengers	07-0362-6-HILC	3.95
81	Duskin	07-0574-2-HILC	4.95
82	The White Flower	07-8149-X-HILC	4.95
83	Marcia Schuyler	07-4036-X-HILC	4.95
84	Cloudy Jewel	07-0474-6-HILC	4.95
85	Crimson Mountain	07-0472-X-HILC	4.95
86	The Mystery of Mary	07-4632-5-HILC	3.95
87	Out of the Storm	07-4778-X-HILC	3.95
88	Phoebe Deane	07-5033-0-HILC	4.95
89	Re-Creations	07-5334-8-HILC	4.95
90	Sound of the Trumpet	07-6107-3-HILC	4.95
91	A Voice in the Wilderness	07-7908-8-HILC	4.95

Mail your order with check or money order for the price of the book plus $2.00 for postage and handling to: **Tyndale Family Products, P.O. Box 448, Wheaton, IL 60189-0448.** Allow 4-6 weeks for delivery. Prices subject to change.

The Grace Livingston Hill romance novels are available at your local bookstore, or you may order by mail (U.S. and territories only). For your convenience, use this page to place your order or write the information on a separate sheet of paper, including the order number for each book.